A Stranger in Corfu

Also by Alex Preston

This Bleeding City
The Revelations
In Love and War
As Kingfishers Catch Fire (non-fiction)
Winchelsea

A STRANGER IN CORFU

ALEX PRESTON

CANONGATE

First published in Great Britain in 2026
by Canongate Books Ltd, 14 High Street, Edinburgh EH1 1TE

canongate.co.uk

2

Copyright © Alex Preston, 2026

The right of Alex Preston to be identified as the
author of this work has been asserted by him in accordance
with the Copyright, Designs and Patents Act 1988

This is a work of fiction. Names, characters, places, and incidents either are the
product of the author's imagination or are used fictitiously. Any resemblance
to actual persons, living or dead, events or locales, is entirely coincidental.

No part of this book may be used or reproduced in any manner for the
purpose of training artificial intelligence technologies or systems. This work is
reserved from text and data mining (Article 4(3) Directive (EU) 2019/790)

British Library Cataloguing-in-Publication Data
A catalogue record for this book is available on
request from the British Library

ISBN 978 1 83726 393 6

Typeset in Bembo MT Pro by Palimpsest Book Production Ltd,
Falkirk, Stirlingshire

Printed and bound by CPI Group (UK) Ltd, Croydon CR0 4YY

The manufacturer's authorised representative in the EU for product
safety is Authorised Rep Compliance Ltd, 71 Lower Baggot
Street, Dublin D02 P593 Ireland (arccompliance.com)

To Ary, Al and Ray
And in loving memory of Nikos Louvros

PROLOGUE

Sarandë, Albania, May 1952

THE PRIEST WALKED along Rruga Onhezmi, a dark figure in a city of light and shadows. He was dressed in navy-blue coveralls a size too small for him that pinched at the underarm. Long grey hair spilled from beneath a white *plis* cap. He'd attempted to disguise himself, Benedict thought, but even a glance would mark him out: the thick beard, the gold cross escaping at the neck, the air of a deposed king hurrying through the ruins of his kingdom.

He was breathing heavily. He stopped for a moment, leant against the pillar of a portico for support, and looked down at his briefcase. Benedict hung back and stooped to tie his shoelace, watching for anyone else who might be following.

The priest resumed his progress down the street, which was busy with locals out to shop and walk in the cooler evening air, farmers from the surrounding countryside with their paniers of softly glowing vegetables, and fishermen up from the harbour displaying glistening octopus, sardines and mullet on slabs of ice.

Sarandë was beautiful as ever, Benedict thought. The

jostling white buildings, the castle crumbling on the hill. A sense of southern lassitude so different to the paranoid grandiosity of Tirana. The priest, a stranger here, brought down from the hills only the previous night, checked the street signs and then turned down towards the port.

Humphrey made a convincing farmer. Benedict watched him shuffle his cart alongside the priest, matching his pace in the road. Humphrey had furnished himself with a barrow of aubergines, an ornate *xhamadan* vest over a white smock. From somewhere he'd procured a dog – a scrawny, defeated animal – whose leash he'd looped over the handle of the cart. Humphrey caught Benedict's eye for a moment, the briefest hint of a wink. Benedict thought just then of all they had lived together, of the vast distances travelled side-by-side in the world and in the mind, and it took an effort to stop himself rushing to take this burly farmer in his arms.

The priest came out onto the long, palm-fringed promenade that ran from the garrison to the harbour. The sun was very low over the sea, still, as if painted in the sky above Corfu. Benedict fought another urge: to rush back to the island he had come to call home.

He turned his mind back to the priest, to the ugly necessity of what lay ahead. He could see, at the end of the esplanade, the awning of the Café Lëkurësi, and there, at one of the outer tables, the figures of Harris and Violet, waiting. Benedict positioned himself behind a tobacconist's shack and watched the priest, watched Humphrey, watched the Sigurimi man who had, just then, turned the corner onto the promenade.

The Sigurimi were Hoxha's secret police force: omniscient, inescapable, and answerable to no one but him.

Benedict had developed an eye for them. They wore no uniform, only an air of certainty about their business, men who bent the world to their purpose.

This one wore a gabardine suit despite the heat. He had neat hair brushed severely to the side, a pencil moustache. His eyes were set on the priest, who was by now approaching the table at which Harris and Violet – the travelling businessman and his wife – sat.

The Sigurimi man quickened his pace and Benedict hurried to keep up, moving from the cover of one palm tree to the next, feeling in his pocket for the Beretta Bobcat, a silencer fitted to its snub nose.

Humphrey turned then and Benedict could see that he, too, had clocked the presence of the Sigurimi agent. The priest had almost reached the café, the last of the sun's rays touching his beard, staining it gold. All the shop-fronts and government buildings that sat along the esplanade seemed to release the sun in one golden breath, and it sank behind Corfu, leaving only its memory and a breeze from the mountains.

The Sigurimi man was running now; he'd abandoned any pretence of secrecy and taken a revolver from his jacket. He was twenty yards from the priest who, perhaps seeing something dark in the faces of Harris and Violet, turned to look.

At that moment, Humphrey upended the cart of aubergines, sending them spilling into the street, a slow, dark cascade in the golden dusk. The dog, sensing some climax to its pitiful life, ran barking into the road. The Sigurimi man saw the tumbling fruit and the hurtling dog too late: both dog and leash wound themselves about his ankles.

He made an effort to stay vertical, but teetered and

went down hard in a twist of limbs and burst aubergines. Benedict arrived just as he was sitting up, trying furiously to untangle the dog from his legs, lashing out at the creature with the butt of his pistol.

Benedict bent down. *'Jeni mirë?'* he asked. *'Mund t'ju ndihmoj?'* The man looked up at him with a snarl, just as Benedict pulled the trigger of the pistol he'd placed under his chin.

Benedict turned and disappeared into the crowd that had gathered to watch, with no small enjoyment, the humiliation of the secret policeman. He moved with such swiftness that no one could say, once he had gone, that the small, bespectacled, scholarly-looking man had been the one to fire the weapon, nor that any weapon had even been fired, such was the din of the evening, the silence of the pistol.

But the evidence lay there: the Sigurimi man, one hand pressed to his throat, blood squirting in bright pulses between his fingers.

The priest's face was very still beneath the beard, the weight of his survival setting in. He followed Violet and Harris down to the dock. The fishing boat had a small outboard engine, a jaunty pattern in red paint around its gunwales. Harris placed the priest's briefcase into a strongbox below the wheel. The priest sat down in the boat, murmured a little prayer, and reached into his pocket for a flask and a few gulps of *rakia*.

Benedict and Humphrey climbed aboard. Violet, standing at the wheel beneath a small canvas awning, started the motor. They pulled out into the stillness of the channel, slicing through the streaked reflections of the day's last light.

The priest was in a convivial mood, offering around his flask, jabbering away to Benedict – who was the only one who understood him – about the circuitous manner by which he'd come to possess the documents in the briefcase. A member of his congregation had appeared on his doorstep in Tirana in the early hours of the morning. The Sigurimi were coming for him, he'd said, he had a few hours to escape. Could he leave some papers with the priest, papers written in the hand of Hoxha himself?

Benedict barely listened: he knew all this already. He was scanning the shore for signs of pursuit, looking in particular at the half-dozen military vessels moored by the garrison to the south of the town.

They were in open water now, heading south in the straits that separated Corfu from the mainland. It was quite dark but Violet steered the boat with certainty. It was not the first such voyage they'd made.

Benedict thought about how he'd write up the mission for his superiors in the Office in London. Operation Valuable had been a catastrophe from start to finish, and here was another disaster.

Agent safely conveyed to the boat. Attempts by Sigurimi operatives to intercept the agent anticipated and neutralised. Agent did not possess the papers. Under interrogation, divulged that he had fabricated the story of papers revealing Hoxha's plans to shift allegiances from the Soviet Union to Yugoslavia. Agent in poor health following his escape from Tirana. Suffered infarction or aneurysm on boat back to Corfu HQ. Efforts made to resuscitate him unsuccessful. Body disposed of.

That would probably do, Benedict thought. Detail was, itself, suspicious.

The lights of Kassiopi glimmered to the west, the long north-eastern coast of Corfu bulging towards them and then retreating. The priest was by now quite drunk on his *rakia*, looking out into the darkness, at the stars emerging in the great cathedral of the sky, the beacon of Corfu Town glowing to the south.

It was Humphrey who did it. Asking the priest to move a little so that he might reach a cleat on the gunwale behind him, he pulled a lead cosh from his pocket and brought it down hard on the old man's head. The back of the skull caved in with a sound like a melon dropped from height. Humphrey pressed his handkerchief to the wound, then, gesturing for Harris to help him, he filled the priest's pockets with fishing weights and heaved him over the side. The body was visible, floating for a moment in the dark water, then he was gone, leaving only a froth of white bubbles in starlight.

Nothing was said, no tears were shed, and that night the papers would be safely on their way to Moscow, to Patricia and Arkady.

Violet let out the throttle and the nose of the boat lifted a little from the water. Corfu Town was much closer now, and there, just in front of it, Vidos Island, the lights of the villa beckoning them home.

PART I

Vidos, Corfu, November 1995

I.

DAWN ON SPYLAND. A watery sun filtered through the mist and the island emerged hesitantly, like a ship coming into port: first the ruins of the church, then the umbrella pines, then, finally, the ivy-covered villa. Mist lingered on around the cottages and outhouses, the cliffs and beaches, the unseen sea, slowly churning. Further out, from the direction of Corfu, a fishing boat came to meet the island through the mist, rising and falling with the waves.

The boat had seen better days, a relic of the island's former life as headquarters of Britain's Secret Services in the Mediterranean. If you looked very closely, you could see a faint red motif inscribed around the gunwales.

Three passengers: Costas and Angelos, possibly brothers, certainly Corfiot, employed by MI6 as their fathers had been, for their silence and strength, their ability to ensure that potentially embarrassing episodes such as this were over swiftly and decisively. Today they wore blue fisherman's jumpers, black watchcaps. Costas steered the boat carefully up to the dock that jutted from the island's western shore.

The other passenger was Edward Lane, formerly H

Europe, a tall, angular man in stiff tweed, his white hair a halo above a wretched face. Lane was one of many sent to the island since the fall of Communism, his skills no longer relevant in a world that had slipped half its moorings. Too much an insider to function on the outside, Lane had been packed off to Vidos to enjoy a well-earned retirement.

As with so many of the inhabitants of Spyland – which was what those who lived there called Vidos – he'd found the secret world difficult to leave behind. Yesterday, he'd disappeared from the group during a shopping trip to Corfu's Old Town, discovered by Costas in the small hours of the morning trying to force his way into the freight-handling depot at the airport. He'd been waving a cigarette lighter shaped like a revolver at a baffled-looking nightwatchman, shouting that he'd come for Malkin and would not leave until he had eyes on the bastard. Costas had tried to calm him down, taking the gun gently from his hand and using it to light his cigarette.

Lane had seen Malkin in Cofinetta Square, he told Costas. He'd followed him here, to the airport, where he'd lost him among the crowds of tourists arriving for the day's last flight. The Russians had always envied the British presence on Corfu, Lane said quietly, as Costas steered him towards a taxi where Angelos waited. He'd not been surprised to see Malkin, Lane went on, his oldest foe. What was important now was to understand how much the Reds had learnt about Vidos. Costas shushed him, wrapped a blanket over his shoulders against the 6 a.m. chill, and told the driver to take them down to the harbour.

II.

NINA WOOLF LAY awake. She had not fallen into what she remembered as the comfortable blankness of sleep for months, not since her arrival on Spyland. The nights burned with memories, everything ablaze. She heard the boat that brought Edward Lane back from the main island, the creak of the front door, then footsteps and Lane's querulous voice.

She heard his bedroom door open, a moment of muttered conversation, the heavy steps of the men who'd brought him home heading back to the staff quarters. After this, something like silence: the occasional gust of wind, the wash and suck of waves on the beach below. Nina turned over in bed and faced the wall, her eyes open.

She'd learnt the danger of closing her eyes. When she did, half-recalled episodes played like a cinema reel in the blackness, each more monstrous than the last. She was looking for a child, her own, in a dark wood. Then *she* was the child lost in darkness, stumbling and gripped by the awful knowledge that she was alone, with no one to rescue her. She felt as if she were falling through the rotted floorboards of her mind. She would find herself panting and sobbing until one of the genial Greek wardens would arrive, or Mrs Samways, and she'd feel a sharp prick in her arm and a wash of easiness, of forgetting.

She still didn't sleep, though. Not even when, in the muddy half-light of sedation, Mrs Samways held her hand and sang lilting songs from her childhood in Wales.

There was something in Nina's head – although it felt deeper, closer to her core – that was watchful, waiting for the moment that she let her guard down. And when she lay there, with grey-haired Mrs Samways humming *sleep my darling, on my bosom, harm will never come to you*, there was a moment something within her began to loosen, when it felt as if she might finally sleep. Then all the dread would rush in again, and she'd sit up straight in her bed, her shoulders rising and falling, and she'd know that it was possible for a life, even one as young as hers, to be irretrievably shipwrecked.

III.

AFTER AN HOUR, sun came in through the crack in the curtains of Nina's room. It came into Edward Lane's room, whose curtains were open. He lay outstretched on his bed, still in his herringbone suit from the night before, eyes wide and furious, his white hair, over-long and very fine, splaying on his pillow. On his bedside table was a packet of Karelia Slims, an ashtray, and the cigarette lighter shaped like a pistol.

Nina stirred, hoisted herself up and out of bed, and threw open the curtains. The sun had lifted the mist and now sparkled on the sea, on the peaks of the Albanian mountains just a few miles to the east, on the green slopes of Mount Pantokrator on Corfu.

The villa – faded pink, crumbling in places – had been built some hundred and twenty years earlier on a rocky outcrop at the northernmost tip of Vidos. It was shabbily elegant, framed on two sides by the sea, on the others by a terraced garden with an immaculate lawn marked out for crown green bowls.

In one corner of the garden there was a bowls shed painted in bitumen, such as you might find sheltered by leylandii hedges in town parks from Weymouth to Wigan. Nina's room looked out over the bowling green, a little patch of England, a reminder – like the cricket pitch in the middle of Corfu Town – that this was once Empire.

Vidos was almond-shaped, protected by the curve of Corfu to the west. The southern half of the island was forest: umbrella pines interspersed with olive and scrub oak. To the north it was more open, although the buildings that stood or half stood there always seemed at risk of being swallowed by the jasmine and oleander, plumbago and ivy that grew wildly all around and over them. Vidos had been, briefly, along with the rest of Corfu, a French island, then British, then an animal sanctuary run by an eccentric English dowager. Still its mornings were unusually bright with the sound of birdsong. There were coveys of grouse, bevies of quail, warblers that sang well into winter. Some said that strange beasts lurked in the island's dense southern woods: tapirs, warthogs, jaguarundis.

There were more birds here than elsewhere on Corfu; that, at least, was undeniable. Even now, in November, a wash of song mixed with the whispering of the pines and the distant tolling of bells that came across the water from the Old Town. Large white rabbits, great-great-grandchildren of the sanctuary, had taken up residence in Agios Stefanos, the church whose ruins sat on Vidos's highest point. They looked down now, the rabbits, over the low white bulk of the sanatorium, past the sheds and workshops, to the villa, glowing pinkly under its ivy mantle.

Just to the west of Vidos, at the mouth of the Gouvia Marina, was another, smaller island: Lazaretto. This, as its name suggested, had been a leper colony and then a concentration camp in which the Italian occupiers had imprisoned and then executed members of the *Ethnikí Antístasi* – the Greek Resistance – during the war. The presence of a prison island so close by highlighted the ontological fuzziness that surrounded the residents of Spyland. Neither detained nor precisely free, not inmates nor patients exactly, permitted certain liberties but with the sense that these might, at any point, be revoked.

Nina, for instance, after brushing her teeth and pulling on black jeans and a black Sonic Youth t-shirt, was able to stroll without impediment into the rising light, down to the beach that stretched along Vidos's eastern shore. She could, if she wished, take a boat to the main island of Corfu, explore the Old Town, or ride a bus down to the tourist bars of Benitses and Kavos, or up into the wild and rocky north. But if she should try to board a ferry to Athens, or a plane from the dust-blown airport, she knew – although she was unsure *how* she knew – that she would be denied boarding, pulled into an airless room, reprimanded by figures who existed out of sight but were certainly there, in the shadows, waiting. She would be hauled back to Spyland, repaired and replanted, to serve out her time.

Nina came out of the woods and onto the beach. It was a mixture of pebbles and sand, jetties stretching out at irregular intervals. There were other properties here: a collection of waterfront cottages that had first been fishermen's huts, then a half-hearted attempt at a holiday camp, but which were now known as the village. The residents of the village would come up to the villa for tea or medication, but otherwise lived much as retired Brits lived in quiet Greek fishing resorts all over the country.

The only difference was that these retired Brits had all been at one time or another employees of what they referred to between themselves as 'the Office' but which was better known as the Secret Intelligence Service, or, informally, MI6.

IV.

NINA'S HABIT WAS to swim each morning, regardless of the weather. It was a discipline, ingrained since childhood by her father, who believed that any stretch of water — icy, murky, or treacherous — was worth plunging into. *The colder the better,* he used to say, claiming that the resistance itself made the immersion meaningful — a lesson, he promised, she could one day apply to life.

Her father had been an erratic presence, drifting in and out of her childhood. Swimming became a way of keeping hold of his shadow, of clinging to the idea of him. But even that idea had grown ragged, a collage of fragments: fleeting memories of his rare visits home between assignments or unexpected appearances at her school, massive and distracted.

If she and Colin had had children, she thought, they might have remembered her the same way — distant, elusive, defined by absence as much as presence. During her sessions with Mr Drinkwater, this had become a quietly disturbing truth: she was, after all, her father's daughter. She would face life's battles armed with his strength, encumbered by his frailties. She'd inherited his charm and intelligence, along with his prominent nose, and also, more regrettably, his casual disregard for his own safety — and for the feelings of those who loved him.

Now she walked out on the jetty at the end of the beach nearest the villa. She pulled a pair of goggles from a pocket, slipped them over her dark mass of unruly hair, and then took off her clothes to reveal a severe black one-piece, the choice of one who was definitively here to swim. Her body, which had been a source of pride to her when she was an agent, hard-sprung with muscle, was finally returning to something like its former shape. Her time in the cell in Srebrenica had ruined more than just her mind.

On her shoulder, just above the clavicle and half-concealed by the strap of her costume, was a pucker of scarred flesh, a permanent reminder of what went before, of why she was here. Further down, on the same arm, a small but angry blotch of red skin — she scratched it at night, or when her mind curled back to Bosnia — as much a relic of her time there as the bullet wound.

She dived into the water without much of a splash, the whole process as swift as vanishing. She began to swim towards Albania, seemingly untroubled by the choppiness of the waves, the coldness of the water. Below her, caught in the clear winter light, a vast, turquoise realm revealed itself: great rocky involutions of the seabed, stretches of sand interrupted by corals and swaying sea-grass, darting shoals of fish in iridescent colours. It was never winter under the sea.

Nina's morning swim had become something of a conversation topic in the village. She hadn't ever thought of herself as being observed – her head mostly in the water, her mind empty of everything but the sound and taste of the sea – but several pairs of binoculars were trained on her that morning.

Violet Davenport – an elegant and precise woman with carefully coiffed auburn hair – watched Nina wistfully, thinking of her own youth, of warmer seas and limbs that never hurt, but wanted only to go charging about the place, or to wrap around other limbs. Violet stood on the veranda of their cottage and leant towards the sea, towards Nina. Harris was not yet awake, sleeping off the bottles of Theotoky and ouzo he'd put away the night before.

These were the hours Violet cherished most, when the sun just crested the distant hills, and the world, still half-asleep, shimmered. The pebbles glistened with dew, and the veranda's table and chairs were jewelled with droplets that caught the early light. She picked up the glass ashtray and emptied the cigarettes – Harris's, not hers, she had given up years ago – into the oleander that grew in profusion around the village. She heard the bark of Harris's cough, the groans with which he greeted consciousness.

She gave a last look out to where Nina, very distant now, was sending up pearls of water with the motion of her legs and arms. She might almost have been a dolphin leaping through that ancient sea.

In the next cottage along, Humphrey Musgrave and Benedict Pierce stood at the window of their drawing room, each with a pair of binoculars pressed to his eyes.

Humphrey was large and Benedict small. Benedict was quiet and studied while Humphrey was boisterous and expansive. Both were immaculately dressed: worsted suits, white shirts, matching yellow cravats. They had taken a shine to Nina, as they often did to Spyland's younger guests, seeing them, perhaps, as a means of making touch with the secret world that had for so long sustained them, to which they had devoted their lives, and from which they were now exiled. Benedict had discovered that he and Nina had both been at Hertford, and, years apart, had doted on successive incarnations of the college cat, Simpkin. He seized on it with delight, as if the shared affection, the shared quadrangle, spiralling stone stairwell and ersatz bridge, were proof of some quiet design: fate, nudging them towards each other.

It had become part of Nina's morning routine to take tea with the couple after her swim. Benedict picked up the robe she had adopted, even though she was still a long way out, barely visible in the chop of the waves, and set off to meet her. Humphrey went to the kitchen to boil the kettle.

Nina turned now and headed back for shore. The sun was higher, the world beneath her a deep and endless blue. She saw needlefish and flickering shoals of anchovy, a solitary octopus huffing his way between shards of sunlight. She didn't feel cold, or tired, and her head was empty like it never was empty on land. The faces of those left behind – dead, damaged, betrayed – dissolved into blueness. She kicked hard for home, saw the seabed first indistinctly, like a happy memory, then rising to meet her.

She reached the jetty and pulled herself up onto the ladder, feeling the wind sweeping up the channel from the south, cold on her skin. Benedict – mouse-like, apologetic – was hurrying towards her, the robe held before him like a matador's *muleta*.

She shook out her hair and stepped into the robe, stooping to collect her clothes. Benedict smiled at her proudly, as if he'd just invented her, then offered his arm. Nina took it, giving him a little squeeze as she did so.

They proceeded down the jetty, nodding to Violet and the saturnine figure of Harris Davenport, who had just emerged behind her in his nightshirt, glowering darkly. He always looked, thought Nina, like a handsome, ruined actor, hauled off stage after forgetting his lines one too many times. Violet waved back.

There was someone else watching them. High on the hillside, in a chair on the sanatorium terrace, sat a man in the white shirt and trousers of that institution. His skin was very white, his hair a deep red, almost luminous. He was smoking hard as he watched Nina, lighting one cigarette from the butt of the last.

Other than the motion of hand to mouth, he was entirely still, so still that a white rabbit, appearing snufflingly out of the undergrowth, came to sit close to his feet. So they stayed for much of the morning, man and rabbit, transfixed by the view, by the water, by the memory of Nina moving through it.

V.

'IT IS, IN the end, unforgivable,' Humphrey said, pouring the tea into Nina's cup, the cup she always had: bone china with a golden meander running around the rim.

She and Benedict were seated on either side of Humphrey at the table, all of them looking out through the long front window to the sea. 'Edward Lane, more hazard than man,' Humphrey continued. 'To be frank, he always was. Do you remember, Ben' – here he laid a large hand on Benedict's arm – 'how he was during the business in Krasnoyarsk? Utterly feckless. No judgement at all.'

'And now, poor soul, his mind . . .' Benedict's voice was reedy where Humphrey's was rich. 'You heard about last night, my dear?' He turned to Nina.

'I was awake when they came in. Must have been six or so.'

'He left us after supper in the Old Town. Went barrelling off, ranting about Malkin.'

Humphrey took up the story now. 'They practically had to straitjacket him. He'll be pinned to the bowling green for the next few months, I shouldn't wonder, right where they can see him.'

'*Right* where they can see him,' Benedict said.

'Should be up in the san with the incurables, if you ask me.' Humphrey smiled lightly, trying not to betray the pleasure he took in such scandals.

Nina sipped her tea. Spyland had always existed to her as a warning, a destination for those who weren't able to deal with the pressures and double-think of life in the Office. It was spoken of as racehorses must speak of the slaughterhouse: a potential outcome, certainly, but not to be mentioned, or even thought of, when life was all gallops and grandstands.

'How long has he been here, Lane?' she asked. 'His name is familiar.'

'It should be. He was the coming man for a long time.

Never quite reached his destination, though. H Europe for a time, but only in name, and briefly.'

'And then, with the Fall, he was lost,' said Humphrey. 'Swiftly and dramatically. He would have worked with your father, I'd imagine. Your dad joined the Office in, what, the Sixties?'

The residents of the island knew that Nina was the daughter of the notorious Lucan Woolf, although Benedict and Humphrey didn't seem eager to speak of their professional interactions with him. Unsentimental, dogmatic, prone to violence – what they shared only confirmed what she had already gleaned as a child. And yet – and this, she supposed, was the familial machinery driving so many quiet tragedies – she could not extinguish the longing for his approval, or at least a fleeting sign that he remembered her, here where people were sent to be forgotten.

Benedict rose and refilled their cups, milk first, then the tea. 'We were at Oxford with Edward Lane. He was a pal, for a time, but then we rather lost touch – he was in counter-espionage, I think. Ran into him once or twice in Siberia. He played a small hand in our getting sidelined.'

'One doesn't hold it against him, of course,' Humphrey interjected.

'*Of course*. But I must say I watched his own defenestration with some minor satisfaction. He didn't see the change coming, you see, and, like so many, he was axed in the Christmas Massacre.'

'He wasn't in the *première vague* of that cohort,' Humphrey added. 'But one began to hear his name in the same breath as Spyland.'

'*Wasn't adjusting,*' Benedict whispered.

Benedict, Humphrey and Harris had been here the longest of anyone, Nina knew this. They'd seen the villa repurposed from its former operational role, had witnessed the sanatorium being built and the cottages reclaimed from the rampant oleander.

'How many are still here?' Nina asked. 'The Christmas Massacre lot?'

Benedict looked at Humphrey. 'It felt like a flood, didn't it, *carissimo*?'

'A deluge of the disappointed and deranged.'

'There were, what, twelve, thirteen in all? They came all through that spring and summer. It was '93, wasn't it? Two years ago. Time here . . . so strange.' Benedict looked out over the sea as he spoke, a wistful note in his voice. 'Amazing how swiftly some of them turned up their toes. Heart attacks, strokes, *felones-de-se*.'

'Drink,' Humphrey said.

'*Mainly* drink. Problem with having a job that's also your life. You lose one, the other soon follows. McGill went first. Smuggled a revolver out here with him.'

'Lucy Fellowes was next,' Humphrey said. 'She was the best of that SovBloc gang. They shouldn't have let her go and she knew it. She used to swim, just like you, Nina.'

'Beautiful woman, even at fifty, fifty-five . . .'

'And one day she didn't come back. Lost to the depths.' This last with a delicious shudder. 'Then there were three or four dreary analysts whose names I never cared to learn. Drunks before they came and once here—'

'*Corfiot ouzo,*' Benedict mouthed. '*Mavromatis.*'

'Much to their taste, my dear.'

'So that leaves Lane at the villa, the Pottinger brothers and Dennis Robertson in the san, Struan McKenzie and Deirdre Chung down here in the village. Six of them. And we're, what, twenty-five on the island just now, thirty perhaps, if you include the incurables?'

Nina remembered visiting the thirteenth floor in her first year at the Office, when MI6 was still based at the crumbling Century House on the Lambeth Road. It was September '91, everything basking in the glow of the Fall, but there, on the thirteenth floor – SovBloc – panic and paranoia clung to their posts. She recalled the fog of cigarette smoke in the air, the drawn blinds, whispered conversations in corners.

Even the clothes had had a faded history about them: brown suits and plaid skirts, Burberry trench coats and kipper ties. One long wall of the room was taken up by a map of the Soviet Union, with a rash of coloured pins around Moscow, Leningrad, Minsk and Kiev. No Commonwealth of Independent States here. There was something tainted in the air of that place, the rash ever darkening, and she'd always been happy to leave, to head back home – to the Balkans, on the fourth floor.

She'd been one of a group of new junior officers under the formidable figure of Clara Sinclair. Nina and her colleagues idolised Clara. They shared her optimism at the prospect of a bright and federal Europe, with the independent Balkan states as important members, freed from the rusty shackles of Yugoslavia. When Clara was named Chief and whisked up to a wide mahogany office, none of them were surprised, although they were sad to see her leave. She brought light and energy as C where her predecessor, Rupert Locke, had been all whispers and tweed. Now Clara was spoken of as a possible foreign secretary, a prime minister, even. She was replaced as H Balkans by a very different character: Boyd Lawson, more a legend than a reality for most of them, although it was Boyd who'd recruited Nina to the Office in the first place.

They finished their tea now and sat in companionable silence for a few minutes. Then Benedict drew out an exercise book and a pen while Humphrey went into his study to read. This, too, had become part of their routine: soon after Nina had come down from the san to the villa, while she was still very raw, far too thin and prone to shivering fits, Benedict had suggested she become his teacher. He was a *furious* linguist, he told her. He was fluent in Albanian, he'd said, gesturing across to the mainland, but had *shameful* gaps in his Serbo-Croat.

Nina liked to feel the language on her tongue, the way the words tipped her straight down a childhood slide to Korčula, her father and grandmother in the kitchen of her grandmother's home, dropping into Croatian together, the language seeming to emerge from the landscape of Korčula, to speak with the accent of the island.

Her grandmother was English, but, when her husband died at Monte Cassino and she'd found herself in a grey and lifeless post-war London, she had come out to Yugoslavia on nothing more than a whim and made it her life. Lucan, in short trousers, had accepted the move with equanimity. Her grandmother had spoken immaculate Croatian, was deferred to by mayor and priest alike, and had become as vehemently Korčulan as she had once been English.

Nina's father had lived on Korčula until he was packed off to Rugby. He'd gone back to live there for a while as an older man, she knew this – there were photographs of him in his twenties at the harbour in Vela Luka, and on the veranda of his mother's house, young and skinny, looking up with large, wounded eyes at the camera. Her father's past was hazy to her, its dates and places difficult to construe, its signal moments mysterious, itself a secret world. She'd loved him though – and it surprised her, the way this was half-phrased in the past tense in her head. Not that she no longer loved him, exactly; rather that she did not know now if the person she loved had ever, really, existed.

VI.

As NINA MADE her way back up to the villa, three elderly patients walked past her, smiling distantly as if they'd known her once upon a time, in a different life. She didn't recognise them, but then there were many characters like this on the island: ghostly, medicated figures who seemed to drift about the place, mumbling and shuffling from the villa to the village, from the beach to the san.

Humphrey called them the incurables. They would often be found sitting in the villa's long dining room, staring out over the water, their eyes misty with memory, or on the bowling green, playing game after solemn game, cradling their bowls and contemplating their next roll as if they were deciding on the invasion of a hostile territory. Nina knew that some of them had been prominent figures in MI6, names once spoken of carefully in the smoking rooms of White's and the Travellers Club.

Now, though, they were lost, abject souls, knowing too much to be allowed to mix freely in the wider world. Snagged on history, as her grandmother had been at the end, living more in the past than the present, a wandering, translucent figure.

Nina had been on Vidos for twelve weeks. As long, she calculated, as she'd ever spent on Korčula. Her father used to take her and her sister to visit their grandmother, beginning with a few days just after Nina's fifth birthday – Sadie had been seven – followed by a succession of summers when time on the island had seemed to stretch forever. Their mother was already ill at this point and stayed at home. That period of Korčulan summers had ended with her father one side of her, Sadie the other, in the small chapel by the harbour, then the walk under a baking sun to the cemetery on the hill and the white mausoleum. She'd felt very close to her father in his silent, angry, tearless grief. This was how she, too, was sad.

She sensed the kinship between the islands, Korčula and Vidos, had felt it since she'd first arrived: familiar ground. It was fitting that she should be sent here to recover after her ordeal – that was the phrase Drinkwater used for Bosnia. She knew the healing power of the constellation of pines and saltwater, thyme and sunlight. It was just that, so far, her inner life was an all-consuming fire, her heart so battered and broken that she thought it quite possible that she might never recover. She felt just as damaged now as she had been when, three months earlier, she'd arrived: empty, mute, and as if a great dark wave were rearing over her, always on the verge of crashing.

The villa was quiet when she went inside. She was late for her medication. The other patients had taken their Valium and lithium, their downers and flatteners and straighteners, and had retreated back to their rooms. She went to the dispensing window, where Mrs Samways stood with her back to her, carefully counting pills from one jar to another.

'Won't be a moment, love,' she said. 'Nice swim?'

Nina was always one of the last to pick up her meds. It gave her a few moments to chat with Mrs Samways, who was otherwise perpetually busy, taken up with the more demanding patients in the villa or called to help with a difficult new arrival at the san.

'Cold,' Nina said. 'Beautiful, though. There was an octopus.'

Mrs Samways shuddered. 'Frightful,' she said. 'Don't know how you bear it. How are our friends by the water?'

'I only saw the boys. Benedict's Croatian is coming on well. He'll be teaching me before long. Oh, and Violet and Harris, but they were just stirring.'

Now Mrs Samways turned towards her, tapping out three pills into her palm and passing them to Nina. 'There you go, love,' she said. 'Let me give you something to take them with.' She handed Nina a glass of water. Nina swallowed the pills, bracing herself for the strange electric jolt that came each time, moments after, somewhere in the front of her brain, just above the eyes.

'Is Edward all right?' Nina asked. 'I heard him come in last night.'

Mrs Samways lowered her voice. 'Embarrassed more than anything. Won't be allowed off the island for a good while, I shouldn't wonder. Lucky that Angelos and Costas found him after he wandered off.'

'I might go over myself later,' Nina said. After almost a month in the villa and longer, hazier weeks in the san, trips to Corfu were still an excitement. Those first weeks on Spyland were muddy in her head: arriving at the airport on Corfu in a rattling military plane, the drift and wash of a white, medicated san.

She'd met Drinkwater on her third day. He'd come in while one of the nurses was changing the dressing on her back, cleaning the entry wound before turning her over to inspect the exit, just below her clavicle.

Drinkwater was a small, neat man in his fifties with blue-black skin and a clipped moustache. It was rumoured that he had been a soldier in Oman. Special forces, they said, involved in anti-insurgency work. He struck Nina from the first as the most reserved and controlled person she had ever met, his movements slow and deliberate, as if he and gravity were in complex negotiations.

'You'll want to be hurrying, then,' Mrs Samways said. 'Boat leaves in twenty minutes. I'll let Mr Drinkwater know that you won't be there for your appointment this afternoon. You'll miss the new boy, too.'

'New boy?'

'Boyd, I think. Not a youngster like you, but not old. Not sure of his story. Straight from London. He's been up at the san for a week.'

'Boyd Lawson?' Nina said, feeling a sudden tightness in her chest.

Mrs Samways perused a chart, tutting. 'Lawson, yes. Do you know him?'

'Yes. Yes, I do.'

Mrs Samways raised her head, her eyes, large and alert, behind thick glasses. 'Is there anything I should speak to Mr Drinkwater about?'

Nina stood in a bar of sunlight on the parquet, one hand clasped in the other. 'I . . . I used to work for him. That's all.'

'He'll be glad to see you, then,' Mrs Samways said. 'A familiar face.' She collected some papers, drew down the blind on the dispensing window and came through the door, locking it behind her. 'I must get up to the san now,' she said. 'And you hurry along, you'll miss the boat and there isn't another until after lunch.'

VII.

NINA WALKED OVER to the western side of Vidos, to a dock by an abandoned restaurant. The building was little more than a shell, its roof gone, Fix beer bunting still fluttering across the terrace, a board with a list of specials leaning in one corner.

At the dock, two boats were moored. It was Angelos skippering today. She preferred him to Costas, who was more obviously solicitous to Nina while somehow conveying a fundamental mistrust of her and all those on what he called *nisi ton kataskópon*: the island of spies. Angelos was silent beneath his pile of dark, salt-cured hair. Nina was dressed as she had dressed ever since she'd been released from the institutional apparel of the san: black jeans, her black Sonic Youth t-shirt, black boots.

The boat was an old Albanian fishing caïque, used by the island for as long as anyone could remember, right through the Office's Mediterranean adventures with the CIA. It was marked with the flag of Sarandë, the large seaside town more or less visible at the foot of the Albanian mountains across the strait.

As they made their way into Corfu's old harbour she wondered, as she always did on this boat, how many of the Pixies – this is what the British and American Secret Services had named the Albanian insurgents – had sat just as she sat now, under the awning at the stern, feeling the smoothness of the wood beneath, the roughness of the sea-worn handrails, awaiting their deaths.

Now Nina walked up from the harbour to the road, where she boarded a bus. She slipped a tape into her Walkman, put on the orange foam earphones and leant her head back on the seat. She let the music wash over her – a difficult comfort, each note a loose thread tugging at some particular memory, all of them tied to Colin. Music plunged her into a body she no longer inhabited, one that had once known how to feel, how to breathe, when songs spoke for her better than words ever could. Thurston Moore's drawl, Bob Mould's guitar – they had been a code between her and Colin, a common language wrapped in feedback and fuzz. Now *Daydream Nation* sounded fractured, brittle, as if each chord had been corroded by contact with her past.

It was Drinkwater who'd told her about the path that stretched the full length of Corfu's varied and tortuous coastline. She'd begun to follow it, walking for six or seven miles and then taking the bus back to Kerkyra to catch the evening boat to the island. The next time, she'd rejoin the route where she'd left it, continuing north and west, coming first to the new harbour at

Gouvia, then to a series of closed-up tourist towns, then villages clinging to the cliffs below the dark slopes of Pantokrator.

Today, she was heading for Kassiopi, a town whose name struck her as absurdly beautiful, so beautiful that she'd dreamed the place into being even before she'd seen it. Maybe it would be the saving of her. She stepped from the bus at the White House, Lawrence Durrell's home. His wife, Nancy, still lived there, but the place had a forsaken, haunted air about it, perched like a smooth white skull on the rocky hilltop. She made her way past it and down to the shore, where she picked up the path, here little more than a goat-trodden track through the rocks and scrub that grew beside the sea.

Just as with her swim that morning, she found self-dissolution in the process of forward motion, the putting of one foot in front of another. Physical exhaustion was good for her, she acknowledged this. Although it didn't help her sleep, nor stop her scratching the raw patch on her arm, it released something that cleared the reeds of her memory, and permitted her to lie in her bed at night without the constant jolts of guilt and panic.

She could feel herself falling, most days. The months in Srebrenica, which had come so close to destroying her, were just the most recent of a whole battalion of reserve traumas waiting for the immediate crisis to recede. Beirut and Doha, of course, but also Colin, poor Colin, and the many times over the course of her brief career in which she'd felt far, far out of her depth, and drowning.

Much of that battalion had been trained and led by the man who would soon, she assumed, be sharing the villa with her. Boyd Lawson didn't look like a spy. He had the swagger of a rock star or Hollywood actor, a kind of rakish and disreputable air about him with his ruffled red hair and washed blue eyes.

She'd been impressed by him when first they'd met: in her tutor's study, a Wednesday evening in February. Boyd had worn a dark suit and tie, something imposing and adult about him, but also a sense of *sprezzatura*, of the outside world, adventure and opportunity. Dragan, Professor Dolunc – her tutor – had been trying to persuade her to stay at university. An MA, a doctorate, even All Souls. There was another possibility, though. And that was where Boyd came in. MI6 was looking for speakers of Serbo-Croat, and with her father's name behind her, she would advance in the Office easily enough.

She came to a small cliff, the path running close to the edge for about a hundred metres before dropping down to a beach. She looked at the map she carried folded in her bag. This must be Kerasia. A small shrine sat at the highest point of the cliff. On Korčula they would have called it a *grotto*, she thought: set into a rough stone shelter was a wooden image of Mother and Child, each of them warped and desiccated by the salt spray, blenched by the sun.

She went to the edge of the cliff and looked down. Jagged rocks, rock pools, the churning sea. It was higher than she'd reckoned – perhaps fifteen metres up – and she had a sudden vertigo, as if the sea below had rushed up towards her and spread out its arms. For a moment she thought about jumping, or rather she thought how easy it would be to fall. Few would miss her. She imagined the moment of impact, the sudden and efficient wiping away of everything she was, all the love and memories and regret dashed on those sharply inviting rocks. All the books she had read, all the secrets she had kept, all the scraps and shards of self that made her . . . She pictured Aegeus, waiting on the cliff, eyes narrowed against the sun. The black sail, the black sail! Then the dive, the long falling, the bloody embrace of the rocks. The way we disappoint our parents and the way they anticipate that disappointment. Nina felt horror rising, the dark wave cresting.

There was a similar cliff top, far from the sea. It had appeared unexpectedly and illogically at the end of a Srebrenica alleyway. She'd been running, her breath tight in her chest, her heart loud, blood pulsing in the corners of her eyes. She had held the girl, Samija, under one arm. Samija was scarcely more than a baby, perhaps two years old, but under-nourished, and Nina had carried her easily. She remembered the girl crying, but the noises of that time were scrambled in her head, the whole period in Bosnia – both in the field and then in captivity – ringing with a long and mournful sound she heard still, sometimes. It was Amar who was holding her up. He was too big to carry – almost five now – and a little lame in one leg. He was such a lovely boy, no complaining, despite what he'd seen.

But he couldn't keep up with Nina, who was running with extraordinary, almost pleasurable power in her legs. She felt the sweet summer air on her face, and she snapped at Amar to move faster. He tripped, and when he did she turned and saw that they were closing in, the men, their guns holstered, recognising there'd be no great struggle ahead of them: just a young woman, a lame boy, and a baby.

It was then that Nina had darted down an alley between two bombed-out houses, hoping at least that there might be a place to hide in the rubble. The walls on either side of the alleyway were still standing, though, and she could see no way of getting over them. She carried on running, sobbing, practically dragging Amar along the dusty path. She'd come to the cliff: the path just ended, no warning or dropping away of the land until this – a great emptiness before her. She'd turned and seen the men, four of them – Scorpions, she knew their black uniforms – blocking any possibility of escape.

She'd scooped up Amar, as much a mother as she'd ever felt with the little one under one arm, the boy pressed to her chest. Looking evenly back at the Scorpions, she'd stepped off the cliff into the warm evening air.

She hadn't thought before stepping out into nothingness. It was, if anything, the opposite of thought, moving before her mind had a chance to catch up. She remembered, as she left the earth, the feeling she used to have, as a child, when she'd let go of a kite. It only happened three, four times. Her father stopped buying her kites after that, but she loved feeling the tension on the string as the wind picked up, the way the kite would whip through a frantic series of coils in one direction, then another, like a creature begging to break its bounds. Then, with everything fluttering and shaking, and with the eyes of her parents and her sister upon her, she'd let the kite go, and she'd laugh and laugh as it fluttered up into the wide and fragile emptiness of the sky.

She and Amar and little Samija, like kites let loose

that early April afternoon. Nina had almost thought they'd carry on going, that the wind would seize them and send them spiralling up, over the fortress, over the mountains, and to safety. As it was, gravity did what gravity does.

She'd not been heroic in Srebrenica – several times she'd been the opposite – but at that moment, when they began to fall, and she curled herself around the two young ones in mid-flight, putting the soft parts of her body in the way of the rocks and branches they encountered on the way down – that was a moment to weigh against all the lies and conniving. Then, when they landed, and the baby began to cry, Amar looking up at her with his large, dark eyes, she'd folded herself over them again, as the bullets rained down from above.

Now, almost eight months later, she stumbled back from the edge of the cliff into the lee of the shrine. As the waves pounded below she said a prayer, the words coming to her in Croatian – unexpected and unbidden. *Izbavi nas od zla . . .*

She wondered, leaning there against the ancient and weather-beaten shrine, if the two of them were still alive, the children, Amar and Samija. And, if they were, whether that was enough, whether it justified all she had been through in Bosnia.

This was the question for any spy, she supposed: whether it was ever worth it. Whether the wreckage of one's own life, the misery inflicted on others, could be justified by some abstract good, by the evils left undone. She had been too green to ask it at the start – others had made the grand calculations, leaving her only the tyranny of small choices.

Jump, or face the Scorpions.

Then, once the bullets stopped, whether to lift the children – both of them screaming now, though Amar's wail was for her, for the sudden bright bloom of blood at her shoulder. Whether to press on, through thinning trees, to the stream below, to kneel there in the silvered water, drinking in gasps, washing the wound, as if cold and current alone might undo what had been done.

And then what?

Find a way out. If there was one.

VIII.

SHE DIDN'T GET as far as Kassiopi. The land dropped around her as she neared the north-eastern point of the island, and then she was at Erimitis, wild and reedy, so close to Albania that she could almost reach out and caress its rocky shoreline. The wind blew loud and chill here, and the path became a wooden walkway through marshes. A desolate place, the few plants bent and salt-scoured.

The road appeared over to her left and, there, a bus stop. The light was fading from the sky – not dusk yet, but rather a leaching of the day into the dullness of a November afternoon. She headed for the bus stop, clapping her hands together for warmth.

It took twenty minutes for the bus to come chuntering down the hill towards her, black smoke belching behind. She was the only passenger. She reached for her Walkman – music as medicine, as memory – hoping to find some thread that might lead her back to who she used to be. She swapped out Sonic Youth for the Cocteau Twins, the sound cascading through her mind like mist, dissolving edges, blurring thought and time.

She wondered if her father would come out to see her for Christmas. Her mother was ill, had been so for years, an illness defined largely by what it was not – neither cancer nor heart disease, nothing wrong with her liver or kidneys. Her father had surprised all of them by the solicitude he had shown towards a wife whom, in health, he had appeared to take for granted. Between assignments in the field, he would come back and care for her ostentatiously, eager for praise, bearing gifts from Samarkand or Porto-Novo that she'd look at carefully, turn over in her hands, and then place on the bedside table.

The house in Kensal Green in which Nina and her sister had grown up held a particular sadness in their childhood, when their father was away for long stretches at a time, and their mother, Nelly, jangled with nerves, leaping up whenever the phone rang, chiding them for the most minor infringement of the strict code they used to speak of him, their father, the spy. Then, when Lucan was back, there was a false jollity, a hectic energy that brought a flush to their mother's cheeks, a glassy brightness to her eyes.

Christmases were hell. The girls had been packed off to boarding school at seven – paid for by the Foreign Office – and swiftly became strangers to each other, to their parents, and to their home. Now home was sad in a different way: their mother spent her days watching television, or being helped up to bed by the nurse. When he was around, Lucan sat at his desk in the spare room, whispering into a telephone.

Her father had flown out to see her once, early on, when she was still in the san. The hallucinatory muddle of those days – Colin, Srebrenica, Beirut, and Doha parading through her fevered mind – had made everything feel unreal, but his arrival cut through the haze like a blade of light. He came in wearing his old trench coat, still smelling faintly of rain and tobacco, and sat by her bed without speaking. At some point, he took her hand in his – a rare gesture but steady, firm, unmistakably him. When he left, he'd tucked a slim, worn book beneath her pillow: e.e. cummings, a poet she barely knew. Scrawled on the flyleaf in his untidy script were a few words: *i carry your heart with me (i carry it in my heart). Dad.* It made her sad in a different way, this brief glimpse of the father he might have been.

Two months later, on the bus, she found herself missing him, just as she missed Colin, missed all the solid points of her old life. Thoughts like this always brought in their wake a hopeless, bleached feeling. She looked out at the landscape trundling past – the coves and beaches, the rocky hills and olive groves – but she could take no pleasure in this beauty. It was as if she lived now in a gallery from which the paintings had been removed, leaving only patches of discoloration on the walls, reminders of the love that had once been there.

When she was little, her father told her often that he hadn't planned to have children – they would only get in the way of his work – but then he'd met her mother, Nelly. They were agents undercover together, first in Moscow, then Yugoslavia, working to drive further wedges between Tito and Khrushchev.

He'd fallen in love – this struck Nina only then, on the empty bus growling its way past the great Venetian fort of the Old Town. Her mother had been made to quit the service when she married Lucan – until quite recently, female officers were forced to choose between their careers and their hearts. Her cynical, grizzled, battle-hardened father – love had caught him by surprise. Nina's mind leapt, as it was wont to do, from this thought – from any thoughts of love and devotion – to Colin.

She had refused to sacrifice anything for him, had believed – and isn't this one of the invidious fantasies of the young, she thought – that she was sufficiently bright and magnetic to live several lives at once: the dutiful girlfriend and the wandering spy, the garrulous confidante and the tight-lipped dissembler. Perhaps it was only when it all fell apart, when she herself fell apart, that the great tragedy of the single path, the one liveable life, became clear to her.

Angelos was waiting in the boat when she arrived at the harbour in the Old Town. Humphrey and Benedict were already on board. They had been shopping in the market: Benedict surrounded by bags, a loaf of bread under his arm, Humphrey wearing a smart new felt fedora. Benedict saw her and waved, dropping the bread. Humphrey reached up to help her on board and they pulled out into the choppy water of the sound. As she sat down, he passed her a pastry he'd bought for her – an orange honey cake that she shared with him, the sweet and floral taste of it clashing with the dank weather and rough seas.

Angelos and Benedict were engaged in some kind of good-natured argument. A change came over Benedict's whole body when he spoke Greek, just as it did when, in the middle of a conversation, he broke into Italian or Russian or Farsi. It was strange and shamanic, his ability with languages, as if he were channelling some foreign spirit as he spoke. Nina and Humphrey sat back and watched him as the lights of the island rose up out of the gloaming.

IX.

A WEEK LATER, a Wednesday, the sort of Corfu November evening that might easily have been mistaken for spring. The sun was moving slowly towards the horizon as if reluctant to surrender the beauty of the day, while the moon was already moored in the lemony heights. A scattered handful of pink-bellied clouds sat in the western sky. To the east, the Albanian mountains were dark.

Nina and Benedict spent the afternoon immersed in language, their voices rising and falling softly. Between phrases, silence pooled around them, dust hung, the faint rhythm of waves beating the shore. She was beginning to see that these lessons were not really for Benedict; they were for her. A quiet structure to her days, a shared purpose crafted with precision, like everything Benedict did. On the veranda, Humphrey slumped in his rocking chair, holding a book but mainly sleeping, snoring, like a retired working dog, letting out an occasional stifled grunt or yelp.

Towards six, Benedict removed his spectacles, polished them, and took a last swig of the verbena tea they'd been drinking all afternoon.

'Shall we go for a stroll?' he said. 'So glorious out there. Seems a shame to huddle inside with all that light in the world.'

They made their way quietly past Humphrey, who, despite the obvious depth of his sleep, seemed able to keep the rocking chair moving with the rise and fall of his breath.

They walked up towards the villa, then past the san to the ruins of the church on the island's highest point. The pink clouds had begun to fray, settling into a thin line over Corfu, from Pantokrator in the north to the salt flats around the airport to the south.

Nina saw herself and Benedict as someone watching might see them: an unlikely pair, she was wearing a Hüsker Dü t-shirt and black jeans, black boots on her feet, Benedict in houndstooth tweed and yellow cravat. Nina was slightly taller, still too thin, Benedict owlish, round glasses and wisps of swept-back hair. She took his arm.

'Let's walk down to the south,' she said. 'I feel like a bit of wild.' Just then, over the water, the bells of the Old Town began to toll the hour, the deep-throated gong of the cathedral, peals from the other churches. As they moved through the scrub that grew around the ruins of Agios Stefanos, they sent up a flock of sparrows, twittering chidingly.

The land dipped into woodland, following tracks that barely deserved the name. The air was sharp with the tang of pines, the ground a carpet of red needles. It was dark among the trees now; the sun had fully slipped behind Corfu, and with the night came November – an icy breeze threading through the woods, setting the pines to quiver and raising goosebumps on Nina's arms.

Benedict seemed all of a sudden on edge, darting ahead then looking backwards, peering through the shifting trunks of the trees.

'I was sure there was a clear path through here,' he said, his voice barely a whisper. 'But I haven't been down this way in years.'

She could picture him as an agent in the field: a small, forgettable man, propelled by nervous energy, his mind never quite permitting him safety. There were two types of agent, she thought: those who felt fear and negotiated with it, and those who felt no fear at all. She used to be the latter. She wondered if that had changed.

Finally, the woods began to thin and they came to a clearing from which they could see, through a final copse of bent pines, the shore ahead, shimmering in the light of the moon.

'You must be cold, *carina*,' Benedict said. 'Would you like my jacket?'

She wondered for a moment if it would even fit her.

'I'm cold-blooded,' she said, shaking her head. 'You've seen me swim.'

A bullet.

A bullet fizzed past her, skittering off branches in the thicket ahead.

She'd been under fire recently enough to know that it was the fractions of the seconds that counted. 'Follow me,' she said, pushing Benedict, who seemed frozen in wonder. She bent low, running in zig-zags towards the coppice on the far side of the clearing.

Another bullet. So close this time she felt the breeze of it. She reached the trees and stood for a moment, breathing, her back hard against the scaly trunk of a pine.

She had been cycling through possibilities in her mind. Identify your enemy – she heard this in the voice of the former SAS staff sergeant who'd trained her, high in the Welsh hills. If you could pinpoint who was after you, you had a chance, an edge. You could anticipate their next move, spot a weakness, and exploit it.

No one from Bosnia, she thought. There was too much chaos there, she was too small a part of the story. Her mind went to Tamim, lying dead in Doha. One of his fanatics, perhaps, or his large and vicious family.

It was Kadyrov she settled on. She had come close to exposing his operation in Beirut the year before: a seemingly unending supply of guns and ammunition flowing from Chechnya through Iran to Hezbollah, repeated attempts to destabilise the fragile peace in Lebanon.

The mission in which she played a small but occasionally effective role had, in the end, been a failure – a source had betrayed them, or someone in the Office had been less than careful with intel. It had concluded in farce: Kadyrov had attempted to snatch her in broad daylight from a Beirut café, appearing at the door when she'd been expecting one of the agents MI6 was running inside Hezbollah. She'd escaped then, darting out through the back of the café, pulling a niqab from her bag and disappearing into the women's section of the Masjid al-Zahra. She knew things about him, though, secrets that wouldn't play well with his Iranian backers. And he knew that she knew. If it was Kadyrov, that was bad news for them.

Benedict came wheezingly into the cover. An explosion of pine chips and sawdust just beside him. Nina grabbed him by the arm and pulled him deeper into the woods, downhill. She almost stumbled once, regained her footing, helped Benedict clamber over a mound of knotted roots.

This went through Nina's mind: life is inescapable. She had come here to heal and recover, to put the chain of catastrophes that was her career behind her. But the chain had tightened around her, and there was no island in all the oceans of the world distant enough to escape it.

They came out of the copse onto the edge of a low cliff. The lights of the Old Town were visible off to the right, the moon over the Albanian mountains to the left. Ahead of them, the wide channel: unseen, far to the south, the islands of the Ionian strung out like jewels on a necklace. Nina was breathing fast, more bullets flying, shocking her back to a former life. She looked at Benedict, surprised by the almost placid look on his moon-silvered face.

To the right, the cliff sloped downwards to the shore, which curved out of sight, round to the dock and the abandoned restaurant. Immediately to their left, a rocky prominence. She took Benedict's arm and pulled him towards the outcrop.

Whoever was following was not being careful about it. The sound of a large body moving through the woods. Broken branches, snapped twigs, the liquid burst of a bevy of quail sent up in fright. Nina climbed the rocks and turned to offer Benedict her hand.

She hauled him up and then, careful in the dim light, lowered herself onto the far side, where boulders heaped down to the water.

Pebbles scattered from where her feet sought and found

footholds. The sea seemed very far below them, but she reckoned that, if they could get to the water, they would be only a short distance from the village, from safety. She looked back to see Benedict, frowning in concentration as he made his way along a thin lip of rock. She lowered herself over another boulder and saw that there, where the land levelled off to form a narrow platform, was the mouth of a cave.

Benedict dropped down beside her and gave a nod.

'Yes, I thought we might be here,' he said. 'Come on, then. I imagine we don't have all that long, *liebling*.'

The darkness inside was total. They walked back together for some distance. Nina could feel things at her feet: sticks or bones, a stool or a small table, something metal that rattled when she kicked it and made her bite her lip. Benedict seemed to judge that they had gone far enough. He sat down, Nina lowering herself beside him.

The entrance glowed behind them, dazzlingly silver. Nina strained her eyes and her ears, remembering the staff sergeant again. Use moments of rest to plan for the moments of action. Slowly, she felt her tension lifting. She allowed herself to breathe, reached out and took Benedict's hand in hers. It was small and cold and she squeezed it tightly.

The question of her own bravery was something she thought about often and with a giddying sense of being a stranger to herself. She had done brave things – this was true – and had always prided herself on her courage. But the forces that drove her were mysterious. Her father had, quite literally, encouraged her as a child. A memory came to her: a holiday in Wales, the family at the top of a waterfall, looking down into the dark pool below. Her father took her hand and she was aware of her mother turning away, unable to watch. Sadie had taken one glance down and then backed off, shuddering. Nina hadn't wanted to jump, but there was such pride in her father's face, such confidence in her. Our lives are shaped by such moments. The fall, when it came, stretched her thin in the high Welsh air, until the cold snap of the water, the exhilaration, her father's whoops, the sight of Sadie, above, looking down at them.

An hour passed in the cave. There was no sound from outside other than the slap and wash of the waves. Benedict sat so silent and still that she wondered if he had fallen asleep. Then, all of a sudden, he got to his feet, pulling her up beside him. He was surprisingly strong, wirily so.

'I think we're probably safe to move on now,' he said, the briskness in his voice almost convincing.

They went out onto the platform, clambered down over another formation of jagged rocks, and were soon on the beach at the southern end of the village. Nina turned things over in her mind. Perhaps, after all, she hadn't been the target. The bullets had certainly felt intended for her, but then, she thought, we are always the heroes of our own tales. She knew only a little of Benedict's history, but reasoned that if she'd collected a handful of enemies in five years at the Office, he could surely call on a greater selection. Someone wanted one of them dead, that much was certain.

Now Nina could make out Struan and Deirdre's cottage, set back a little from the shore, then the rest of the village, lights winking. It felt like another world, one in which nothing could befall them but language exchange, chess, and lemon cordial. They walked the final stretch to where Humphrey, glass in hand, stood on the veranda, watching them approach.

X.

AFTER TELLING HUMPHREY what had happened – he was sympathetic, horrified, insisted they both have a glass of brandy – they marched up to the villa, demanding to see Drinkwater. He'd appeared after some minutes, in striped pyjamas, barefoot in the cold entrance hall, aware of how this diminished his authority and clearly uncomfortable.

'It's really *not* how we do things here.' His voice was peevish. 'There are office hours. I trust this is an absolute emergency.'

'There was someone in the woods. He was after us. It was a hunting rifle, I think. You need to send someone out there now. You must let the Office know.' Nina's words came out in a frantic stream. Benedict was quiet beside her, only nodding here and there.

She was aware that she sounded slightly unhinged, but she felt the dark wave rearing over her, a desperate need to lay the responsibility at the feet of someone else, some calm authority.

As it was, Drinkwater seemed largely uninterested in their news. Every so often, he said, poachers would come over from Corfu, or even from Albania. 'They're wild for slaughter. And we are blessed with eatable bird life here.' The more that Nina protested that it had been a clear and targeted assassination attempt, the more Drinkwater shushed and patronised her.

'We'll send Costas up to have a look around. I do try to persuade people not to go yomping about in the evenings. We are here somewhat on licence, you know. Rather a bad look to be telling the locals how to live their lives, even if such activity seems . . . distasteful to us.'

Nina looked to Benedict for support, but he said little, and seemed to agree with Drinkwater that they hadn't seen the man's face, didn't even know that it was a man, indeed. They would be more careful when wandering on the island in future.

Nina sensed that there were currents of meaning lying just out of sight, buried in what was said and unsaid between Benedict and Drinkwater. Benedict tried to place his arms around her when they said goodnight at the door to the villa, but she stepped back, then watched him walk down the path to the village in the moonlight, a small, sad figure.

In bed that night, she tried to establish some perspective on the events in the woods. When you live in a world in which threats, when they are made, are intended, it's hard to accept happenstance. She kept asking herself whether it was possible that bullets that had felt directed with such intent, such a clear impulse towards the soft and fleshy parts of her, had been grapeshot meant for quail and pheasants.

She wondered if, all along, Benedict had known that all of their fieldcraft, all of the movement and desperation, had been mere play-acting. If they had really in the end escaped not from Kadyrov or some dark spectre of Benedict's past, but from a Corfiot poacher bent only on putting food on his family's table.

By the time she had sunk into the waking doze that was the closest she would get to sleep, she'd persuaded herself that maybe Drinkwater was right. She was, after all, not entirely sane.

XI.

THE NEXT MORNING, she sat in the pale coolness of Drinkwater's study, counting the bars of shadow cast by the Venetian blinds.

She liked morning sessions with him, the little rituals of two carefully placed glasses of water on the coffee table, how he'd always be working at his desk with his back to her. 'Come in, come in,' he'd say, and then continue to work for a minute or two before turning to look at her. He had eyes that were dark and deep and she always felt seen, in that moment, all the goodness and wrong in her made acutely visible, as if judgement and mercy could exist in the same gaze. The meetings were meant to heal her – part of a process, they said. She had disintegrated in Bosnia; reintegration would take time. Yet healing, she realised, was not a destination but a distance, a horizon forever receding. The dark wave was there, always above her, stretching its back, grubby foam yellowing the crest.

Drinkwater was wearing a khaki suit and a white shirt open at the collar. There were flecks of grey in the close-cropped hair of his head and moustache and she supposed he was older than most people thought. Fifty, perhaps. He had a leather-bound notebook, the scratch of his pen and the muffled sounds of the villa part of the silence rather than disturbing it.

She remembered the first time she'd had a session with him, when she was still up at the san. His office was different there, more institutional. She'd looked at his dark, knowing, sympathetic eyes and she'd begun to cry. He'd sat there, occasionally passing her a tissue or writing a note on his pad. She'd said nothing in that session, just a gurgled 'thank you' as she left. She'd cried the rest of that day and much of the night.

Now, unusually, Drinkwater spoke first. 'Boyd Lawson,' he said. She'd thought that he might mention the events of the previous evening, but instead he went straight to Boyd, and she felt her mind refocus, swing round to the figure of her former boss.

'Yes.' She looked at the glasses of water on the table. He never drank from his and so she never drank from hers. She wondered if the glasses were left there from patient to patient, or even day-to-day, objects deployed for the aura of calm they radiated.

'He replaced Clara Sinclair as Head of the Balkans desk, correct?'

'Yes.'

'And he recruited you.'

'That's right.'

Silence. She heard Mrs Samways chiding someone. A shared laugh.

'You're aware that he's now with us? Up at the san?'

'I'm aware.'

'And how do you feel about that, about him being here?'

'I feel . . .' The problem was that she felt so many things, and these things overlapped and contradicted one another. A single statement would not only not suffice, it would take her further from the truth. 'Why is he here?' she said.

Drinkwater cleared his throat in two soft syllables, something he did when he was discomfited. She still read people like this, drafted in her mind the tics and tells she might one day rely upon.

'I can't give you details, of course.'

'Of course.'

'But I can say that he is in a bad way just now and we're doing all that we can to help him recover.' A pause. 'He wanted . . .' Drinkwater looked at the Venetian blind, then stood and opened it with a jerk, so that sunlight poured into the room. She was dazzled, held a hand up to her eyes. The sky outside was very blue, Albania very green in the distance. 'He asked if he might apologise to you, Nina,' Drinkwater said in a low voice.

'For what?' she said, but in her mind was Doha, emanating a sinister, prickly heat. She saw, as if piling up at her feet, the broken bodies of Amar and Samija. She saw Pigeon Rocks rising from the sea. She saw Kadyrov.

Here was the truth of it: even at the worst – *especially* at the worst – something in her craved the fall. In the café in Beirut, when Kadyrov stepped through the door and she knew she'd been played; in that hotel room in Doha, with Tamim panting his last breaths; even there, she recognised it – a thread of wanting that ran beneath the fear. She'd felt it, that brief, blinding lightness – this was the centre of the world, the axis on which it all spun. The closer she edged toward the abyss, the more she glimpsed the terrible symmetry of things.

'My grandmother,' she said now, as if they'd never spoken of Boyd, 'sat me down when I was twelve, thirteen. She told me something that I've never forgotten. I think the reason it stuck was that she'd said the same thing to my father when he was young, or at least that's what she told me. The greatest mistake that people make in life, she said, is to confuse excitement for happiness.'

A moment. 'She was wise,' Drinkwater said.

'It was more than that, though.' Nina paused for a moment. 'My grandfather was long dead by that point. He'd died in the war. My father was three, four when his father was killed. But she warned my father because she saw it in him. Something she'd feared in her own husband.'

She stopped speaking, but she called to mind a photograph of a couple outside a country church in winter: her grandfather, tall and film-star handsome, with dark hair and wild dark eyes, her grandmother smaller but also beautiful. Nina remembered as a child looking at the photograph and hoping that one day she'd grow into her own face, that her nose would be smaller, her emotions less immediately readable in her expression, that she might achieve the serenity of her grandparents in that photograph.

'And you think she told you . . .'

'Because she saw the same in me. A sort of desperation, a need to push things to their limits.'

'A long line of risk-takers.'

'That's how I've always thought of it.' There was a defensive note in her voice that she wasn't quite able to disguise.

'A lot to live up to.' She didn't like it when Drinkwater did this: making statements that were too obvious, challenging her to push back. It reminded her of the Office's negotiation training, or the sparring sessions she'd had with Professor Dolunc in his cosy study at Hertford, the sense of a mind moving ahead of hers, perceiving weaknesses in her argument that she would only come to see in retrospect, on her way back to her room, her university days spent in constant *esprit d'escalier*.

'Boyd Lawson,' Drinkwater went on. 'He was also a risk-taker. Notorious for it, I believe.'

'He was a hero. We all knew the story. That's the thing about the Office – there weren't that many like you, like Boyd, like my father, maybe. Men who'd been in the field, who'd done the kinds of things we all imagined doing when we dreamed about being spies. Most of us were tied to a desk.'

'You don't view your time in Bosnia, in the Middle East, as proper action?'

She sat back in her armchair, closed her eyes and was silent for a long moment. 'I suppose, but I never felt quite in control of it. It was so . . .' She flicked through the possible words in her mind. 'Sullied . . . debased . . . When Boyd talked me through an operation beforehand I imagined I'd feel noble, that there'd be a kind of old-world valour in laying myself down in the service of Queen and country.'

'But . . .'

'But nothing ever went to plan. There was always that lurching sense of improvisation, of reacting rather than acting. Or – more often – of being acted upon. I was always on the back foot. Or on my back.' She riffled through memories, each image slick with shame. 'The sex was never explicit in the briefing notes, but it was always there, humming beneath the surface. The Service trades in frailty, in pressure points and humiliations. If there was something a man wanted, something that could be leveraged, then we would find a way to offer it to him. The calculation was always cold. But to be the calculation? To be the thing offered? No one ever quite prepared me for that.

'This, I suppose, is one of the great contradictions of our world . . . the Service wades through the filth of human behaviour, deals in its darkest secrets, its most sordid kinks. It operates in a realm where morality is not just irrelevant but actively dangerous. And yet, it remains a government department. A bureaucracy. We file our reports in triplicate. We sit through ethics briefings delivered by men who have never been in the field. We are expected – required – to maintain an essential integrity while the people we fight are not only unburdened by conscience but actively weaponise its absence. I have sat across from men who could take apart a body as methodically as a clock, who spoke of suffering the way a chef speaks of seasoning, and yet I was the one bound by policy, by restraint, by the illusion that we must not become them.' She realised that her voice was rising in pitch. She drew in a deep breath. Drinkwater noted something in his diary, cleared his throat. She continued, her voice lower.

'I entered every encounter at a fatal disadvantage; not just because I had something to lose, but because I still believed, somewhere deep down, that losing it mattered.'

Drinkwater collected his papers and then cleared his throat again. An ending, this time. It always seemed that they were on the verge of a breakthrough, and this breakthrough was forever forestalled. In fact, she thought, in that long moment before he spoke, the therapy was both a help and a trap. The more they spoke, the more she felt that she couldn't exist anywhere else. That her life would be this: endlessly cycling through her mistakes, the dark wave poised but never breaking.

'Thank you, Nina,' Drinkwater said. She stood, feeling horribly observed as she walked across the room to the door. He sat watching her as she turned and gave him an awkward smile, then she was out of the door and into the echoing central hallway of the villa.

XII.

SHE HADN'T BEEN expecting to see him. This was how she explained it to herself afterwards. The intake of breath that was almost a sob when she opened the door to Humphrey and Benedict's cottage to find him, Boyd, sitting there on the high-backed sofa, looking smaller and older and more defeated than he'd been when they'd last met at VX — this was what they called the Office's new headquarters at Vauxhall Cross.

It was evening, the last of the day's light draining out over the sea, and she'd come down to have supper with Humphrey and Benedict. A Sunday roast. Sometimes Harris and Violet would be there: Harris insisted on bringing his own bottle of ouzo with him, which he'd drink in silence, while Violet and 'the boys' — that's what Violet had called them since Oxford, half a century earlier — spoke of old times and dead friends.

Struan McKenzie and Deirdre Chung were there tonight. He was a lean and ascetic Scot, a cryptographer, while she was tall and wore her grey hair headmistress-short. They occupied the generation between Nina and her hosts – she put them at forty-five, fifty at a push. They had worked in signals intelligence – SIGINT – and both seemed more at home in the world of numbers and symbols than in conversation.

Why they were here, on Spyland, had never been made clear, although this didn't stop people speculating. Benedict had intimated that, in the wake of '89, their names had appeared on a 'naughty list' that emerged from the Soviet embassy in London. Violet's explanation was simpler: they had been driven mad by numbers, she said, had spent too long wandering the occluded pathways of cryptology, now seeing all existence as a kind of semiotic game, every word spoken part of an endlessly referring system of signifiers and hidden meanings.

Boyd was sitting between Struan and Deirdre, but he stood when Nina came in. 'Hello,' she said in a soft voice. Boyd didn't reply but instead turned and held his hands out towards her, as if in supplication. It fell very quiet then. Harris refilled his glass of ouzo, the waves lapped at the beach, a little owl peeped in the woods above.

No one spoke as Boyd came to stand just in front of her. She saw how thin he was, how diminished, the way his face seemed to droop beneath the red flame of hair. He looked as old as her father, where once he had seemed both absurdly young and ageless, one of those for whom the years extracted no toll. He fixed his bleak blue eyes on her and, for a moment, she met them.

Benedict came and placed a glass of wine in Nina's hand. He gave her arm a squeeze and then made his way to the record player that sat on a sideboard at the back of the room. Soon Jane Birkin was warbling gently and Humphrey and Violet picked up a conversation in which they were trying and failing to remember the name of a restaurant in Addis Ababa they'd both loved. Harris stared in furious accusation at his empty ouzo glass until Benedict brought another bottle. Deirdre was humming along to the music, occasionally breaking into a rush of French at the chorus. Boyd still stood before Nina beseechingly, his eyes wide and swimming. Time took a long breath. Then, very slowly, he lowered himself down onto his knees and bowed his head.

Nina's first impulse was to laugh. The conversation died, and it was only Jane singing 'Que C'est Triste l'Amour'. Boyd lowered himself further, until his chest was pressed to the floor, and it looked as if he were praying. He was pitiful, ridiculous, and so Nina reached down and laid a hand on that familiar red hair, ruffled it.

'Come on,' she said. 'Let's have a drink.'

So it was that she found herself sitting out on the balcony with the man whom she had long blamed not just for the specific agony of her time in Srebrenica, nor just for the fiascos in the Middle East, but for the slow shipwreck of her life: for Colin, the collapse of her career, and the erosion of the person she'd been just a few short years ago. That bright, impulsive girl who had once moved through the world as though it were an extension of school and university, a game she'd believed herself uniquely destined to win.

They stood looking out into the darkness for a time.

Her wine was very cold and very good. Boyd was drinking whisky and soda. She could smell it in the air, mixed with the tang of the sea, the night flowers, the cigarette he had produced from somewhere and whose intermittent glow cast brief, fleeting light across his face.

She could see his past self too: an evening at VX, just her and Boyd still at their desks. His face haloed by a lamp. It was 1992, early in the war, a time of uncertain alliances, rumours of atrocities by one side or the other. They had an agent in Sarajevo who had suddenly and inexplicably broken off communication. Another source in Mostar spoke of mass graves, ethnic cleansing, forced sterilisations of Bosniaks by the retreating Serb forces. She remembered a feeling, then, scarcely two years into her time at the Office, that she was at the centre of something decent and hopeful, a force for good in a fallen world. And part of that feeling was Boyd Lawson.

'How are you?' Boyd's voice in the darkness brought time racing to the present.

She was quiet for a moment and her words, when they came, were soft. 'I'm okay,' she said. 'All good.' A pause. 'What about . . . What happened? To you, I mean?' Affection and guilt. The strange and familiar sensation that she was both closer to and further from this man, her boss, her former boss, than she should be.

Boyd sipped his drink. 'Your guess is as good as mine,' he said. 'I was uncrackable, that's what I thought, at least. I didn't break in Colombia, even when they lined me up to shoot me. Didn't in Tripoli or Tehran. Then, in September, I was sitting in a meeting of the Joint Staffs in Whitehall. We were on a call with the White

House and Zagreb. They were talking about an incident – a bomb dropped on a children's hospital in Goražde. I started sobbing. I tried to stop myself, tried to pass it off as allergies or whatever, but it was as if something had been breached, and rather than getting control of myself I started spiralling out. I rushed to the door and found an empty room and I just fell apart. I didn't stop for a week.'

He pulled out a pack of cigarettes, offered her one – she declined, then changed her mind and took it. She liked the idea of cigarettes more than the taste of them. As a teenager she had imagined her future self leaning against a motorbike in leather trousers and Ray-Bans, smoking. Boyd lit hers and then his, their faces close and bright for a moment in the light of the flame.

'And Sarah?' she asked. 'The kids?'

He sighed out a stream of smoke. 'Sarah and I have been a mess for a long while now. The kids were an attempt to fix that but, honestly, it was past any kind of saving.'

'I'm sorry. I liked her,' she said, remembering whispered telephone conversations, the small, nervous, pretty woman who sometimes waited for Boyd in the lobby of VX in the evenings.

'The job takes it out of everyone, in the end. I need you to know that I regret what happened to you, that I thought about you all the time you were there, in Bosnia. If there was anything I could have done differently, some way of getting you out sooner . . .'

His words sounded shop-worn, as if he'd played them over too many times already. And she was nowhere close to forgiving him. She had spent five months in the cell.

Although time wasn't the right way to think about it, because the person who had gone there, unconscious and bleeding, remained there still.

She'd woken after the fall down the cliff in Srebrenica, the bullets, the tumble into the stream, to a dull pain in her shoulder, a badly applied bandage bright with Betadine, the children nowhere to be seen and pale light seeping through a high, barred window. There was a stained mattress in one corner, a jug of brackish water, a bucket. It was a room stripped to essentials – just as she'd been stripped, pared back to the raw, to the place where survival and self become indistinguishable.

She'd expected to be interrogated, spent the first days rehearsing techniques of resistance and obfuscation, preparing herself for the familiar rhythms of questioning, for torture, reminding herself of the lies she'd learnt and the half-truths she was willing to disclose. She'd tried hard not to think of the children, of where – if anywhere – they might be now.

No one had come, though, not on the first day, nor on the second, and only when the bucket was almost full, the reek of it enough to bring water to her eyes, and she was so hungry she was half-mad with it, did a man appear at the metal door. The noise of the bolts shooting back made her leap up from the mattress, where she'd been dreamily tracing the cracks in the plaster on the wall, imagining them the delta of a wide and beautiful river.

The man had a mask over his head and the black uniform of the Scorpions. He waved a pistol in her direction until she crouched in the corner and then he stood looking at her for a long time, only his dark eyes visible. He'd picked up the bucket and hefted it outside, returning with a bowl of rice and meat, a new jug of water. She'd eaten like an animal, scooping the food into her mouth with her hands, almost crying at the pleasure of it. Then, when she'd eaten, he gestured for her to take off her clothes.

That man – whom in her head she named Bogdan – wasn't the last of them to come for her, but he was the most persistent. She had braced herself for the brutal rituals of power, for bruises and broken skin, for threats spat into her ear. But nothing could have prepared her for the slow corrosion – how Bogdan seeped into her bones, twisting her flesh into something foreign, something vile. In that airless basement, her body ceased to be her own. By the end, she could no longer see herself in the mirror of her memories; the person she was had been burnt up in a conflagration of shame and fury. She was the smoke that remained.

'Dinner is served.' Humphrey poked his head through the doorway, his smile worriedly sympathetic. Boyd threw back his drink and they made their way inside.

XIII.

THE DINING TABLE was low and long: Humphrey and Benedict were bookends. Nina took a place beside Humphrey, Harris on the other side of her, his head already wobbling dangerously. There were candles, everything cast in a warm yellow glow. Harris turned to her. 'Nina,' he said. Her mouth was full and she swallowed too quickly, choking so that Harris clapped her on the back. She tried to remember if he'd ever spoken to her directly before. He was usually a man who addressed a room in the abstract, rather than the particular. 'How old are you? What? Twenty-four?'

'Twenty-five,' she said. 'Twenty-six in May.'

'Had you joined the Office by then, by the Fall?'

'No. I started just after, in 1990. It was all still going on, the whole edifice still falling, if you like.'

'Ah.' She saw him looking around and reached to refill his wine glass. 'Thank you, my dear.'

'I worked on the Balkans desk,' she said. 'On the fourth floor. Initially under Clara Sinclair.'

'Dear Clara,' he said. 'Admirable lady. I knew her mother.'

'Patricia? Wasn't she also in the Office at one time?'

'Indeed. Patricia was in my year at Oxford. Just after the war.' He lowered his voice. 'Extraordinary how many of us from that era went into the Secret Services. I suppose it's a reflection of the time – all of us marked by the war, a world order utterly changed, the wish to be doing something meaningful.' He looked dreamily upwards, caught for a moment.

'We have a daughter a few years older than you, Violet and I,' he said. 'Katherine. Writes to her mother every once in a while, but appears to have decided that the organising principle of her life will be animosity towards me and all that I stand for.'

'I'm sorry,' Nina said. 'Where does she live, your daughter?'

'In London, with her partner. He's an anarchist. And an architect.'

'Do you ever go back to England? Could you not try to see her then?'

He swilled his wine in his glass and took a long swig. 'As you know,' he said, his voice lower still, 'the choice of whether to leave Corfu is not entirely up to us.'

Nina thought for a moment. 'I suppose it makes sense. We've already cracked under pressure. Who knows when we'll crack again.'

'I can see you have suffered,' Harris said, taking her hand for a moment, a gesture he seemed at once to regret, placing it down. 'At first,' he went on, 'it wasn't at all like it is now. When we arrived here, some of us fifteen, twenty years ago, there was no sanatorium, no medication. It was much more of a prison. Positively enlightened now. Although, of course, many of us had been here before, when it was operational.'

'You worked here, on Vidos?'

'Yes, briefly, in the late Forties. Most of us did, to some extent. Violet and me, Benedict and Humphrey. Such wonderful, hopeful days. Even though the operation was an unmitigated debacle. That was largely down to Philby, of course.'

A silence. He looked suddenly wretched, his face long and pale in the light of the candles.

'We were, all of us, seduced by him, by the promise he seemed to hold out to us of a brighter, fairer world. I frittered my life away on that dream. Neither a decent agent nor, in the end, a useful Communist. And the shame of being turfed out. Your pa, bless him, was one of those leading the charge to oust us. Not that I blame him, mind. I'd have done the same in his place, chucked out the whole rancid lot of us.'

'Hold on, you were a Communist?'

'A double agent. Not a terribly good one. I'm afraid

you're rather outnumbered here. All of us were, to some degree, compromised. We were swimming with the current back then, all the hopeful shimmer on the surface. It was only afterwards that we saw the blood in the water. History is like that, you know.'

'Lived forwards, understood backwards.' She looked around the table, recognising a strange rearrangement of her feelings towards her friends, the traitors.

'The owl of Minerva flies at dusk. Benedict would know who said that.'

Nina took a sip of her wine. 'Were you sent to prison?'

'I was given a choice: a public trial in the UK or exile to Spyland. The villa had been shuttered as a centre of operations after Valuable collapsed. They needed something to do with the place.'

'Valuable – that was the operation in Albania?'

'Mm. With the Pixies and King Zog, Philby the puppet master behind it all. Anyway, they sent us out here more to bury us than anything else. A handful of liabilities to the Service, all of us knowing too much: Benedict, me, Violet, Humphrey, and a few dreamy socialists George Blake managed to finger.'

'Blake!' Humphrey had overheard them and spat the name down the table like a curse.

Harris raised his voice a little, drawing Humphrey and Boyd into their conversation. 'I was just explaining to young Nina how we came to be here. A touch of Philby, a dash of Blake, and a good measure of our own naïveté – that about sums it up, wouldn't you say?'

'And Nina's papa,' Humphrey said. Boyd raised an eyebrow, suddenly interested.

'Yes, well, quite. Always Lucan.' Harris continued. 'The

C at the time, Esmond Harrington, was a grasping, political type, and he leapt upon Vidos as a way of manoeuvring people out of his way. Avoiding the humiliation of another Philby. He even came up with the name – Spyland. The island of spies. Rather good. As the Seventies became the Eighties, the prison turned into a retirement home. Our little group grew into a community, a very English, crown-green-bowls-playing community. Many of us were genuine Communists, others just fellow travellers. We drank a lot in those days. Some of us still do.' He spat these last words and stood up, seizing his glass and stomping down the room to stand beside Violet, who looked at him with a sweetly distracted smile.

'Harris, *carino*, no coffee?' Benedict said.

'It's late, we must go.' He bent down, filled his glass to the brim and took Violet's elbow. She muttered something to Benedict and rose from the table. Harris downed his drink and marched out.

Later, as Nina put on her jacket at the door, Benedict came and stood beside her. His eyes were worried. 'Listen, love,' he said. 'I probably should have told you, about our past. About Philby. When you arrived, it felt like a new beginning. I didn't want you to think less of me, of us.'

'Don't worry,' she said, smiling at him. 'By the time I knew my own thoughts, Communism was already a dream the world was waking from. I might've believed it too, if I'd been there at the beginning, when it seemed like the future.'

XIV.

DUST MOVED IN the light that came through the slats of the blinds and settled on their glasses of water. Drinkwater was making notes at his desk. Nina wondered for a moment about his name, about whether the glasses of water on the table were in some way a challenge, his name an instruction. She remembered her Oxford interview, when Dolunc had invited her to sit down with a curt nod, then hurled an orange at her. *'Naranča? Ne halva,'* she'd said, tossing it back to him. Now Drinkwater stopped writing and closed his notebook.

'Tell me about Colin,' he said.

'He was . . .' She summoned him to her mind. 'He was just a boy, really,' she said, unhappy with this as a way of beginning, of the distance between words and reality. 'He was clever and terribly serious. Not made for the world. Not like me.'

She had first noticed him sitting alone in hall, their second night in college. His hair fell in front of his eyes and he'd had to sweep it aside to see her properly when she sat down across from him. He looked a little abashed – already she'd made something of a name for herself: a riotous first evening in the college bar, an ability to hold her drink, but, more than this, her beauty, a thing she couldn't see herself – her nose got in the way – but which she had been told about sufficiently often to recognise as fact.

'He was the first person I loved,' she said. 'The only person.' Not her first lover, not by any means. At thirteen, she'd been the only one of her friends to have a boyfriend

– a mechanic in the village who occasionally drove the school bus. He was twenty-four. Next, she'd seduced her French teacher, then a diplomat friend of her father, then a merchant banker, the father of a girl in a younger year, whom she'd met when his car broke down on the road leading up to her school. She'd seen him from the window of her maths classroom and went to help him change his oil – she'd learnt something from her mechanic – then had him drive them to a quiet lane. He'd had regular car trouble throughout that autumn, until she grew tired of him and would just watch with a kind of weary sympathy as he wandered forlornly up and down the driveway, eyes turned towards the school's high, blank windows.

She wasn't faithful to Colin, not even at the start let alone during that long and spiteful ending when they had taken turns to hurt each other as if it were a sport. They were the first couple to get together in their year, her choice immediately elevating this shy English student to something like a celebrity. And as the first and most glamorous couple in college, they took on a symbolic value, as if the hopes of their year group were somehow vested in them.

'We were together all through university,' she said, wondering as she spoke if this kind of thing bored Drinkwater, who must have been more accustomed to hearing about failed dead drops and compromised agents. 'He was very much in love with me. And with the obscure Middle English poets he studied. We lived together. In a college room in our second year – his was bigger than mine so we just moved all of my stuff in there. Then we rented a flat at the top of a house off the Iffley Road.'

She stopped then, seeing clearly the low slope of the flat's ceiling, the stained and flaking plasterwork, the narrow bed they'd shared. She remembered how, one Valentine's Day, he'd made her a crème brûlée, the sugar burnt into a bronze heart on top, and brought it to her in that bed.

'We made a pact,' she said. 'That we wouldn't stand in the way of each other's success. But my ambitions were so much clearer and more fully formed than his. He applied to do a PhD at Magdalen. I helped him prepare for his interview, celebrated with him when he got it. I joined MI6 without telling him.'

'Nothing at all?' Drinkwater said.

'I sketched out the job in terms that were generic enough to be meaningless. We agreed we'd carry on living in Oxford, in the same flat, and that I'd commute down for my job at the Foreign Office. He'd do the shopping and make dinner. It felt like the sort of story we'd tell our kids. Early years of making do and striving. Sacrifices. Small luxuries.'

She found to her surprise that she was crying now, tears flowing hotly down her cheeks. 'But of course I got dragged into the excitement of the job. Two friends from college started with me, Fergus and Nandini, all of us cycling from one desk to another, understanding the trade we were being asked to make: sacrifice our twenties for a place on the inside, at the secret heart of things, deep in the gears when others only saw the machine. Fergus played cricket with Colin, and so it didn't seem so strange that I started staying over at his place. Colin didn't blame me – the hours I worked, rising before dawn to get the same coach back to London. It was, I suppose, a failure of planning above all.'

She smiled, drew a sleeve across her face and looked over towards Drinkwater, hoping now that he'd collect his papers together, give his spoken cough, and draw their session to a close. Instead, he peered at her over the rim of his glasses. 'Young lives are chaotic, are they not? You did your best.'

'I could have done better,' she said. 'I could hardly have done worse. I started sleeping with Fergus not because I particularly fancied him, not even because we were so often drunk, but just because he was there. And then there were the men I was encouraged to get to know — that was their phrase for it. In Russia, they called them swallows, the honeytrap girls. First Clara Sinclair, then Boyd, sent me in pursuit of sad little diplomats with their expensive watches and bored wives, and they'd take me out to the same dimly lit hotel bars where prostitutes would look at me with complicity and I'd feel myself better than them, although God knows why. At least they were clear about their job.'

'And you and Colin drifted apart?'

'It wasn't as simple as that. At the weekend, or the evenings I made it up to Oxford, we'd go on as if everything was fine, even though there was this space growing between us, a space that became vaster and more desolate with every passing day. Of course, what I didn't realise, because of who I was, who I am, was that as I was drawing away from him, he was drawing away from me, too. And, honestly, it seems insane, but I do think that part of the reason we stayed together so long was because we had become a point of reference amongst our friends: the couple who got together in Freshers' Week, a picture of what love might be.'

A V of gulls moved from one slat of the blind to the next, the perspective skewed and dizzying, and Nina felt a sudden lurch. Partly, it was that she knew what was coming next. She understood that this was the point of her sessions with Drinkwater: the ordering of her life into narrative, the comforting structure of story. But stories can be shaped and sculpted, endings forestalled or subverted, whereas this one unfurled over her like the sweep of a dark and monstrous wing.

'It was after the mess in Doha,' she said, her voice low and flat. 'I was shaken up. I didn't tell Colin I was back in London for a while. There was a man I was seeing. It was all pretty sordid.' She was scratching at the skin on the inside of her arm, picking at tiny scraps until she saw bright and stinging blood beneath.

'Go on,' Drinkwater said.

'There were a couple of nights that I hardly remember at all, so much booze and coke and awful, awful sex. And after one of those nights, I took an early coach up to Oxford. Dawn on Magdalen Bridge, memories everywhere and just this deep sense that my life had taken a wrong turn.' In her mind: faint ripples breaking the river's surface, the toll of distant church bells, and a pair of swans gliding downstream, watery reflections in the early light.

'I turned up at the flat about eight in the morning. I let myself in and crept down the hall, up the staircase – it was an old Victorian place and had a big central area, lots of poky flats and bedsits leading off it. We were at the top of the house and I remember thinking how much I was looking forward to seeing him, that we'd go out for breakfast on the Cowley Road and we'd talk and I'd feel better about everything. I found Colin there, in our bed, this pretty little slip of a thing asleep beside him. It turned out – and this after an almighty shouting match – that as part of his PhD he taught a class of undergrads, and this girl was one of them. Eighteen, she was, and you know how far away that feels for us at – what were we then? Twenty-two? As if she were a child. He begged and grovelled and swore it would never happen again.'

Here she drew a jagged breath. She could feel that their time was almost up. She wanted to present what happened next in a light that would reflect – if not well on her – then not as badly as she knew she deserved. She realised that she wanted desperately for Drinkwater not to despise her.

'I only meant to give him a scare, you know,' she said. 'And the fact was that I had been doing so much worse, so much more awful and unforgivable things than him. There was something almost innocent about his little dalliance. That gawky girl in the underwear her mother had bought for her.'

'We punish others the most harshly for the faults we recognise as our own,' Drinkwater said.

'Perhaps. I played the role of the wronged woman with gusto, throwing handfuls of his shirts out of the window, packing up a box of his books and CDs and hurling it out into the street. He was crying and I was shouting that I hated him and never wanted to see him again and there were people looking out of their windows. Iffley Road's propriety shattered.

'I washed the sheets and cleaned the house and did some work I'd been putting off for weeks. I thought he might come by that evening with a bunch of flowers, but I wasn't worried. If he had to spend a night or two on a friend's sofa, that might teach him a lesson. And all this time I made resolutions myself. I wasn't so much of a hypocrite that I didn't see what I'd done – with Fergus, in particular, but everything, really. I planned in my head what I'd say to him, how I'd make it all okay. I cooked myself dinner and had an early night and resolved that next day would be the first day of the rest of our lives together.'

Here Drinkwater collected his papers together, gave his little cough and a regretful smile. 'I'm afraid we will have to continue with this next week.'

She stood and walked from the room, through the villa and out into the bright morning. All that day, before her, still as the dust on Drinkwater's water, was the image of Colin as she'd found him the next morning, lying on the landing outside their door, a serrated kitchen knife in his hand. He'd made a mess of his wrists, although it looked worse than it was. She'd called an ambulance, done her best to stanch the bleeding, begged him not to die. He didn't. When he came round, he wouldn't look at her, perched sleepless and strung out beside his hospital bed, her hair a fright.

He told the nurses that he didn't want to see her: they said this to her, with great kindness, in the blue light of the corridor outside his room. He sent the child, his student, round to collect the rest of his possessions from the flat. Since then, they hadn't spoken, not even once, although Nina knew from friends that he was still with the child, that they were happy together, living small, comfortable, academic lives, with cats. She missed him.

XV.

It was Christmas Day and it was cold. Nina had swum as usual that morning, but it was an act that required grit. *Grit makes pearls* – her father's voice, forever in her head. She hadn't stayed in for long and her hands and feet were purple and pulsing when she emerged. A party of them were going over to the Old Town that morning for a service at the Anglican church. Nina sat at the prow of the boat, looking back as they made the short journey across to Corfu. Vidos was dwarfed by the Albanian mountains behind it. Many of these mountains had snow on them now, and even here, as they cut across the water, a few soft flakes drifted in the air.

Humphrey wore a huge camel-hair coat and muffler; Benedict's head was almost hidden inside a white fur hat. Arctic hare, he told her, given to him by a man in Moscow. Boyd had decided to come with them at the last moment and sat talking to Harris and Violet at the other end of the boat. Boyd had now been moved to the villa, and while Nina had not fully resigned herself to his presence, she had begun to see his actions in a new light – rather than the architect of her trouble, he was, perhaps, just another victim, albeit one who had lasted longer in the Office than she had. Drinkwater and Mrs Samways were coming on a later boat with Deirdre, Struan and Edward – it was the first time he'd been permitted off the island since his lapse the month before. A Christmas trip to the Old Town was tradition for the long-time residents of Spyland, part of the rhythm of the year.

Nina had received a letter from her father a few days earlier. He had been hoping to come and see her in the New Year, but her mother had taken a turn for the worse and he was involved in a very complicated piece of business for the Office. He simply couldn't get away. He sent her his love and looked forward to seeing her back in England, soon, fully well again. She felt an obscure but definite censure emanating from him, as if he had judged her and found her wanting.

She thought about writing back, to explain herself, although how, exactly, she wasn't sure. She wasn't good at letters. She had begun and discarded so many to Colin over the past few years, but the words never seemed sufficient, the sentiments always weak or weaselly. In the best of them, one she'd almost sent, she had imagined what would have happened if she'd never joined the Office, conjured up their quiet, bookish lives, the children running between their legs. She hadn't sent it largely because she imagined that he now lived that life. She was the tragic one.

The Anglican church sits at the far side of Corfu Town and was almost empty that day – the island's expat community tended to wither in winter. The priest was a young, studious-looking man, visibly delighted to have been posted to Greece. He did his best to imbue the service with a degree of festive jollity and the congregation gave back: Humphrey's voice was beautiful, a bass that rattled the windows. Benedict stood beside him, as if basking in the wall of sound, his own reedy tenor almost swallowed up entirely. Drinkwater and Mrs Samways sang pleasant harmonies, while Harris and Violet swayed in time to the music.

After the service, they went for lunch at Humphrey's favourite restaurant, a little place near the synagogue where the food was good and plentiful, the waiters more than usually handsome. Retsina was brought out in large, cold jugs and Benedict produced paper crowns and party horns. Drinkwater had become tipsy very early in the meal and began to sing carols in his rolling, mellifluous voice, Mrs Samways warbling along with him. Nina realised that they must both be lonely out here, their lives made small by the impositions placed upon those they were charged to shepherd.

Humphrey had a gift for Nina. He took her aside as they were serving coffee at the end of the meal and presented her with a box, a ribbon tied around it. 'I wanted you to have this,' he said. 'A girl like you shouldn't have Christmas without a present from an admirer. This was given to me by someone very special. Someone who made his own mark on the Service.' She opened the box and drew out a silver pen, glittering in the dim light.

'It's beautiful,' she said, and threw her arms around his neck, breathing in the familiar, ripe smell of him. He smelt of her father.

'And deadly,' he said. He took it from her and, sliding the pocket-clip with his thumb, produced a wicked-looking blade from its shaft. 'I'm certain you'll be back in the Office before long,' he said. 'Just as certain that I won't. I'm glad that it's going to a good home.'

There was warm raki after the coffee, and one of the waiters brought in his guitar and they sang in a mixture of English and Greek: high, happy songs of the season. Drinkwater and Mrs Samways began to dance, then Humphrey and Benedict rose to join them – immaculate and graceful in the way they held each other, the way they moved apart and then together, as if they could read each other's minds. Soon they were all dancing, the tables moved aside, and Nina, very naturally, found herself with Boyd. He was a good dancer, she less so, but they were both drunk now and the owner of the restaurant kept bringing out raki and sweet Mavromatis. Soon the songs became slower and more melancholy, the waiter plucking notes from his guitar as if he regretted every one, and Boyd held her close to him, his body strong and hard beneath his clothes.

There was a moment that Nina remembered very clearly, much later, when everything had unravelled and she was trying to piece it all together again. Benedict and Humphrey had been dancing with a kind of frantic energy. The jitterbug, she guessed, or the Charleston. Lots of shaking of the hands and kicking up of the feet. A jazzy 'Jingle Bells' – someone had found a trumpet. As the others – Mrs Samways and Drinkwater, Harris and Violet, Nina and Boyd – collapsed into chairs along the edges of the room, exhausted and breathless, Benedict and Humphrey kept dancing.

It was mesmerising to watch them – a picture of love in its final chapters, when every dance feels like it could be the last, and to keep moving is to hold off something darker, more final. When the song ended and the room burst into applause, Benedict and Humphrey stood there, chests heaving, eyes locked on one another as if the rest of the world had fallen away. They embraced, and tears sprang to Nina's eyes, unbidden.

It was quite dark when they made their way out into the night. The snow that had come in little flurries earlier fell more heavily now, giving everything a smudged, dreamlike air. They tipped the waiters and the owner insisted on embracing them one by one, telling them that, as friends of the great Humphrey, they were now his friends, also. Harris was stumbling a little as they walked down the passageway that led past the synagogue, all the snow melting as it hit the ground. Nina found herself with Harris and Violet, who were talking of Christmases they'd spent in far-off places during their time in the Office: in the wilds of Siberia or the mountains of Oman, in Jeddah with a lecherous emir or hidden in the life-raft of a Turkish magnate's yacht. Nina loved hearing them: a connection to her father, to a life she still hoped to make her own.

It was only when they reached the dock that they realised that several of their party were missing. Drinkwater tried once, then twice, to count them, collapsing into a fit of laughter. Harris was leaning heavily on a bollard, his eyes narrowed in furious concentration. 'Where is everyone?' he barked.

Now others began to arrive, appearing out of the darkness like ghosts: Struan and Deirdre, Mrs Samways, Benedict, then, breathing heavily, Edward.

'Here we all are,' Mrs Samways said, then her face fell when she realised this wasn't quite true. 'Where's Boyd?'

'Where is Humphrey?' Benedict looked suddenly concerned – something in his voice causing Nina to sober up.

'I haven't seen either of them,' she said.

Nina, Violet and Benedict headed back to the restaurant, while Drinkwater, Deirdre, Mrs Samways and Struan hurried along the front to the Spianada, figuring the two men might have stopped for a final drink in one of the bars along the front, or an unseasonal ice cream at Papagiorgis.

Edward and Harris stayed with Costas by the boat, Harris mumbling about damn fools keeping him from his evening Scotch. Edward looked dreamily up towards the great fort.

The streets were empty, the locals inside with their families, or over on the mainland, celebrating. The snow had become rain, a cold, insinuating rain that flattened Benedict's hat on his head. The restaurant had closed its doors by the time they got there, and there was no one else to ask: it was as if the town had been emptied of its inhabitants by some swift and silent plague.

As they turned and headed back to the dock, Nina could see that Benedict was becoming increasingly frantic. 'He simply doesn't wander off,' he kept saying, as if Humphrey were a child. Violet held him very tightly by the arm and murmured soft, comforting things. They found Costas and Harris smoking together on the boat, huddled under the tarpaulin roof. Edward had elongated himself on the prow, seemingly unconcerned by the rain. 'Look,' Benedict said, pointing down the dock, in the direction of the Palace of St Michael and St George. There, coming towards them, they saw four figures, indistinct in the misty drizzle. Slowly, they came closer: Deirdre and Struan first, then Mrs Samways, leaning heavily against Boyd. Drinkwater was nowhere to be seen.

Benedict almost ran to meet them, Nina struggling to keep up. 'I'm so sorry, my love,' was the first thing Mrs Samways said, and Benedict fell into her arms and it struck Nina, not then, but later, when she thought back over the day in bed that night, that it was as if Benedict had been waiting for something like this to happen, that his actions were those of someone who had rehearsed his responses in advance. They walked swiftly back towards the Spianada, to the rusticated walls of the oldest part of the harbour.

Drinkwater had seen him first, Mrs Samways said, the camel-hair coat unmistakeable, floating in the lagoon just below the Palace. He'd dived in, Drinkwater, notwithstanding how sloshed he was, how cold the wind and the water. The police were already there, Nina saw this now, a car with its light flashing on the promenade. As they came closer, she saw Drinkwater with a blanket pulled around him, a tall policeman bent over him and there, laid out on the flagstones, the bulbous figure of Humphrey, breath in the air from everyone but him.

XVI.

THE DINING ROOM of the villa had been converted into a sort of interview room, in which Nina now sat, facing the man she'd first seen standing over Drinkwater on the dock. His name was Inspector Metallinos. He was tall and angular, dressed in a dark suit and tie, his black hair swept back from a high forehead, spectrally elegant. It was three days after Christmas and the inspector had come to Vidos to speak to those who had been with the man he called 'Poor Mr Musgrave' in the hours before his death. Metallinos's English was careful and correct, his voice low and mournful, his hands folded on the table in front of him, still as a priest's.

'What would you think in my position, Miss Woolf?' His words were softer than his eyes.

'I don't quite know,' she said. It was funny, she thought, how quickly she dropped into the role of the reluctant interrogatee, giving as little as she could, making him work for every morsel of information. She found her mind drawn back to the night in November with Benedict. The splintering of wood under rifle-fire, Benedict's mixture of serenity and fear. She had put it from her mind with what now seemed to her unnatural haste. She wondered whether she should mention it to the detective.

'I have been speaking to Athens, naturally,' he went on. 'A British expat is found dead on a tourist island, there's a sense of . . . expediency. It is very much hoped by my superiors that Poor Mr Musgrave, despite his unusual past, is simply the victim of the strength of our drink.' He drew a cigarette case from his pocket, opened it and selected a cigarette, looking around for an ashtray. Finding none, he replaced the cigarette in the case and put it back.

'I ask you again, Miss Woolf, what you would think in my position, where a man living on the Island of Spies, a man who has likely made enemies during his time working with your MI6, is found dead in the town for whose safety I am responsible?'

'I have no idea,' she said, 'what particular pressures are brought to bear on you. But please, inspector, know that Humphrey wasn't the sort of man to fall prey to some silly accident. He was too much alive, too vital for that. Something isn't right here.'

'Perhaps,' said the detective. 'This, too, is my instinct.'

He thought for a moment, drew out the cigarette again and lit it, tapping the ash dismissively on the ground. He tossed the packet onto the table. 'What can you tell me about this man Lawson? He was the last to see Mr Musgrave alive, I believe?'

Nina picked up the packet of cigarettes and placed one in her mouth, leaning forward for Metallinos to light it. She kept having to remind herself that the detective was not some enemy agent trying to extract information, but rather, potentially, an ally.

'He was my boss. If you're asking if he had anything to do with Humphrey's death . . . I can't imagine what motive he'd possess. What he might want from Humphrey, or from Humphrey not being around. But then, not much makes sense to me just now.'

Metallinos placed his cigarette in his mouth and then took one of her hands in both of his. His hands were smooth and cold. 'You, I think, were very fond of Mr Musgrave. I will do what I can to get answers for you.' He let go of her hand.

Nina flicked ash on the floor and blew a plume of blue smoke towards the ceiling. 'What I keep thinking about, you see, is that Humphrey hadn't been in a position of power since the Seventies. The whole point of this island is that people are put here to be forgotten. Humphrey was exiled to Vidos so that he couldn't say anything or do anything to harm the Service. But who knows? We have long memories in the Office.'

'The Office?'

'The Secret Intelligence Service. MI6.'

'Ah. Litotes — this is what you call it, I believe? Deliberate under-exaggeration. Very British.'

'Humphrey was certainly involved in some of the Office's trickier chapters. You'll have heard of Kim Philby?'

'Of course.'

'And George Blake?'

'Perhaps . . .'

'But why now, after all this time? I simply can't think.'

'That is what I intend to ascertain. I am not perhaps versed in the ways of intrigue and subterfuge for which your organisation is so celebrated. But I am dogged. This is the word, I think.'

'Thank you,' Nina said.

'Thank *you*, Miss Woolf.' Metallinos looked at her through the smoke, his dark eyes warm and intelligent. 'And if you should think of anything else you wish to tell me, I will be here later. I am here now, of course.'

'So I see,' Nina said.

She went, still holding her cigarette, out of the dining room, through the villa's entrance hall and into the bright and ice-spangled day. She wore an old pea coat that had once belonged to her father – it was big on the shoulders but still smelled faintly of him. He'd given it to her during a visit home, after Colin and Doha but before Srebrenica, when she'd been granted a few days off to recover. She had told Boyd in his office in VX that she was ready to return to her duties. With the war in Yugoslavia growing more brutal and uncontrolled by the day, she was needed back at her desk and then, swiftly, out in the field. She'd not been ready. That much was clear now. Sometimes she felt like her life was an exercise in seeing how much a person could take. She strode down the path towards the village.

She had spent much of the time since Humphrey's death with Benedict. He did not know what to do with his sorrow. Violet and Nina had passed that first, sleepless night in Benedict and Humphrey's cottage. They took turns to stay up with him, not speaking or consoling, just walking the floor with him, listening to him sob and call out, flinching along with him when he spotted a scarf, a cane, a well-thumbed book: evidence of the absence of one who had been so jovially present.

Now she found Benedict sitting on the pier, a plaid blanket wrapped about his shoulders, his little legs dangling over the water. Violet stood behind him, looking wretched. Nina embraced her and then sat down beside Benedict, taking his cold hand in hers. Violet gave Benedict's shoulders a squeeze and then went back down the dock and along the beach to her cottage.

They were quiet for some time and then Benedict spoke, his voice lower and calmer than at any time since Humphrey's death. His eyes, behind round glasses, were watery and red.

'You saw the detective?'

She nodded. 'I didn't know what to say. Or how I could help.'

'He suspects everyone. Seemed to think that Boyd might have had a hand in it.'

'Surely not. Not Boyd.'

Benedict turned to look at her. 'Humphrey was murdered, Nina. I'm sure of it. Whoever was after us in the woods that night, they got him. They got to my dear, dear Humphrey.'

PART 2

Oxford, November 1945

I.

BENEDICT WAS WAITING to use the telephone. He had held it off as long as possible, not because he did not wish to speak to his mother, but rather because he knew it was doing them good, this empty air between them. Since the news — delivered by a softly spoken officer on the doorstep of their home in Marlow — of his father's death, Benedict had been living a kind of double life, at once the dutiful son, helping his mother through a nervous breakdown of quite historic proportions, and the panicked student, a boy falling into manhood, preparing himself for Oxford interviews in French and German which filled him with dread and a higher than usual sense of his own unworthiness.

He had prevailed, astonishingly, and when he told his mother the news he saw three things in her face: joy for him, then sorrow that his father was not there to witness it, and finally and most overwhelmingly, a recognition that this would be the end of their time together, this strange and fragile period during which he had been forced to restrain his grief and care for hers.

Not quite care. Rather he became something like a replacement for his father during the final years of the war, bringing his mother tea in the mornings as his father had done, managing the household accounts, even — and this he would tell no one, ever — sleeping in her bed.

There was a young woman using the telephone box outside the Sheldonian this Tuesday evening. He recognised her — not so young, in fact — as Patricia Sinclair. She was in Somerville, in his year academically but a good three or four years older in age.

She had done something glamorous and dangerous during the war. She was a FANY, dropped into France by the SOE, some said, others that she'd held her family's palazzo in Venice for six days against first the Italians, then the Germans. She was tall and square-jawed and handsome in a way that made Benedict feel quite muddle-headed. Catching his eye, she smiled and made a small, inscrutable gesture — perhaps to say she'd be finishing soon, or perhaps nothing at all.

A fine drizzle began to fall, swirling in flumes around the lamps of Catte Street, pearling on Benedict's eyelashes. He had come out without a hat but the weather suited his mood and he looked up at the gothic vastness of the Bodleian and was hit, as he was at least daily, by a sense of astonishment that he, a young man from a single-bookcase family, should now brush knees with next years' novelists and prime ministers.

He felt an upwelling of gratitude for the university authorities and their new passion for applications from state school students. His headmaster, a wise and gentle man who had seen something cultivable in Benedict and had pressed on him books by Turgenev, Goethe, Flaubert. His parents, too, had been more ambitious for him than they'd ever been for themselves. Perhaps because his skills were so literally foreign to them — this ability he had to absorb languages and move between them despite never having been further from Britain than the Isles of Scilly.

Patricia came out of the telephone box, smiling down

at him. She was wearing a beret and a black jumper so soft and expensive that for a mad moment he thought of sinking his face into it. She looked from him up to the drizzle and shuddered.

'I *am* sorry,' she said, perhaps to him, perhaps to the weather.

'Can I fetch you an umbrella?'

'Would you?' She smiled. 'I'm only going to the pub.'

He scampered through the rain to the porter's lodge, stepping carefully over Simpkin the cat, who was stretched in the doorway contemplating every untelephoned mother in the world. Len, the porter, had struck up a kind of friendship with Benedict based on geography – he was from Maidenhead – and class. And, because this was Oxford, Benedict found that they shared a love of the paintings of Stanley Spencer.

'All right, Ben?' he said.

'Very good, Len.' Six weeks into his time at the college, this call and response was their shtick. 'Might I borrow a brolly?'

Back at the telephone box, hair damp and glasses fogged, Benedict unfurled the umbrella and held it up for Patricia. She was tall but, with a stretch, he managed to shelter them both; she took his arm as they walked across the road to the King's Arms. His mother, he thought, could wait – although even as he thought it he doubted the truth of the words.

Inside the pub, it was warm and smoky. Patricia took off her beret and shook out her hair, which was magnificent. Benedict leant on the umbrella, feeling foolish, looking at her.

'You're Benedict Pierce, aren't you?' she said, her voice

raised over the hubbub. 'You're supposed to be terribly clever. A linguist.'

'That's right,' he said, 'the linguist part. I'm not sure about clever. May I buy you a drink?'

'That's sweet, but I've got a crowd over there waiting for me.' She gestured at a riotous table in the corner. Benedict recognised several of them – Humphrey Musgrave, Violet Chisholm, Harris Davenport – names that existed for him in the same realm as Spencer Tracy or Greer Garson.

He saw how the students at other tables observed and reacted to the actions of this group, as fishing boats will bob and jostle when a cruise liner comes into harbour.

'Why don't you come and join us?'

There were several bottles of wine on the table and someone found him a glass.

'This is Benedict Pierce, he's frightfully bright,' said Patricia, and very quickly he was talking to a smart-looking Russian student whose name was Arkady Malkin and who was studying English Lit. at Merton. He and Arkady moved between English, French and German, and then Benedict felt brave enough to try a little Russian, which he'd been teaching himself.

'*Ya chuvustvuyu, chto Turgenev, bol'she chem kto-libo, zakhvatyvaet istinu russkogo dukha.*' Arkady roared with laughter, insisted that he repeat and translate it for the rest of the table. He then murmured something about Turgenev expressing the wintry truth of the Russian soul.

Everything was golden: the lights in the smoky air, the wine in their glasses, the laughter and warmth of the company. It was the sort of evening Benedict had dreamed of back in his bedroom in Marlow, swotting over the Méthode Gouin.

At one point, when they were all quite drunk, Patricia reached across the table and removed Benedict's glasses. He blinked at her.

'You see?' Patricia turned towards Violet, a small and intense mathematician who had worked at Bletchley Park during the war. 'He's very handsome.'

Benedict felt himself blushing. No woman had ever looked at him like this before, his mother excepted.

'Of course he is,' Arkady said in his drawling voice, his English almost too studiedly perfect, his moustache quivering with his smile, his blue eyes bright. 'Now stop embarrassing the boy.'

By the time they spilled out into the night, where the rain had blown over and a crisp half moon hung like a sail above the Sheldonian, it was too late for Benedict to telephone his mother. He said goodbye to his new friends – surprising himself that he was daring enough to call them this, even in his head – and made his way back towards college, swinging his umbrella. As she strode up Broad Street, arm-in-arm with Arkady, Patricia called over her shoulder.

'I'm giving a lunch at mine on Saturday. You will come, won't you?'

II.

PATRICIA LIVED IN a grand house in Jericho, looking over the river and the railway track towards Port Meadow. Benedict turned up on time, which was much too early; Patricia and Arkady were still in bed. He had spent an agonised morning dressing, finally hanging out of his window and asking Len, who was weeding the rose beds in the quad, to pick between two ties. Now, at half past twelve, he stood at the door holding a bunch of freesias and a bottle of Bulgarian wine, his father's tweed jacket scratchy through his shirt. Patricia answered the door in a silk negligée, her wonderful hair all over the place.

'Oh, my darling, is it that time already? Come and sit down. Freesias! These are delightful. You shouldn't have. We'll be down in a jiff.'

That jiff stretched to almost an hour. Benedict spent the time thumbing through the books — a brilliant and thoughtless mixture of English and Russian full of intricate notes in the margins. By the time Humphrey, Violet and Harris arrived at the door, Benedict had learned to distinguish between Patricia's notes — in blue ink, sharp and critical — and Arkady's — appreciative, in pencil.

Soon they were sitting down to lunch in the bright dining room, the damp beauty of Port Meadow spreading out before them.

The day passed in a haze of drink and conversation. Arkady was a Communist, of course, but so were the rest of them. The talk over lunch — partridge with bread sauce, rustled up by Patricia in a tiny kitchen — was very earnest and intelligent, Arkady telling them of his war, of the bond he felt with his comrade soldiers, the sense of a collaborative effort to build a new world out of the ashes of the old.

It wasn't so much his words that stirred Benedict as the way he delivered them, with his ardent blue eyes. Patricia and Violet sat forward in their chairs when Arkady spoke, leaning towards him hungrily, like plants leaning towards light. Harris and Humphrey seemed more interested in the bottles of wine and port that Arkady brought in – 'Courtesy of the USSR,' he said – than in the need to reclaim the means of production from the corrupt elite, but they hummed in the right places and clapped particularly hard when Violet spoke about the iniquity of Empire and families starving in India.

Benedict hadn't really thought much about politics before. He loved Russia for Tolstoy, whom he hoped soon to read in the original, but Communism seemed to have signalled the end of great Russian writing.

This afternoon, though, he glimpsed the first fierce hope in it – the belief that Communism, through the sheer force of its ideals, would sweep away the sclerotic old order, razing the rot and remaking the world into something dazzling, something new.

'Russia perfected the novel,' he offered shyly, 'now she might perfect the world.' They looked at him quietly, Patricia and Violet contemplating this new light to lean towards. Basking, Benedict saw that embracing this doctrine would enable him to spend more time with these captivating people, and the fact they had invited him into this select and secretive group was in itself a mark of distinction.

'I have one question, though,' he'd said towards the end of the afternoon, light dropping over the poplars on the far bank of the river. 'There's any number of societies you could join.' Harris moved about the room looking for dregs, the others lolled on the furniture, a sense of woozy companionship between them. 'There's the Leninist Society and the Marxist Forum, the Oxford Revolutionary Circle and the People's Union. Every other day I see a new face on Cornmarket telling me to abandon selfish individualism and embrace the brave collective dawn. Why don't you join them? Why all this secrecy? Doesn't it go against the very thing you're trying to foster? A world without divisions?'

He saw Patricia look towards Arkady with an arched eyebrow. Arkady nodded, almost imperceptibly.

'Benedict,' she began, pausing to allow Humphrey to light her cigarette, 'we're not *above* that lot. We're all taking different paths up the same mountain. At least, that's how I see it. But when I met Arkady during the war . . .'

'I was in Venice,' Arkady said. 'Cultural attaché to the Soviet delegation there, although in truth I was only halfway through my studies at Leningrad. It was decided that my skills would be better employed in forging links with the Communist and Socialist groups in Italy.'

'Your uncle decided . . .' Patricia said.

'Yes. My uncle Vasiliy is fairly important in Moscow. No children, so he's been shepherding my career. First it was Venice and now Oxford.'

'Arkady and I spent time together in Venice – have you been, Benedict?' He shook his head. 'Well, it's glorious and my family's had a house there since the Romans or something. Anyway, we talked and drank and I told him that I'd had a place at Oxford that I'd deferred in '42 so I could do something useful in the war.'

'Something *bloody* useful,' Humphrey added.

'Well, yes, it was enormous fun. Arkady's ears pricked up and he said, listen, why don't we go there together, to the university? He got his uncle to pull some strings and a year and a half later, here we are.'

Benedict looked from her to Arkady and back again. Harris was asleep on the sofa, Violet was staring quizzically at them all over her glass of wine. Humphrey continued to loll, unperturbed.

'But what is here, exactly?' Benedict said.

'We are here – you are here, Benedict. Look at us. The future beckons. Diplomatic roles are newly open to women . . . Violet came out to stay with me in Venice this summer just gone. She knew Harris from Bletchley Park, another bloody genius. Humphrey had his own pedigree from the war . . .'

'SOE Massingham, in Algiers,' he said. 'Dropping Jedburghs into France.'

'So,' Patricia went on, 'we decided we'd take things on from the inside. Rise as swiftly as we could within the system so that, when the revolution comes, we can help steer the ship. We just want to be very sure that when the moment arrives the right sort of people are close to the heart of things, primed to seize control.'

Benedict, himself by this point definitively drunk, smiled groggily at them all. Patricia leant forward and placed a hand on his knee. 'We think you'd be a wonderful addition to our team,' she said.

As he lay on his bed that evening, still quite tipsy, it occurred to Benedict that he may have been chosen by Patricia as the closest thing the university had to a member of the working class. A bit of proletarian rough. But then he remembered the way Arakdy had gripped his hand at the end of the day, Patricia's arms around his neck when he said yes, he would rather like to attend another of these gatherings, and he saw ahead of him a future in which he and his friends helped to forge bonds between the peoples of all nations, bonds which meant that a war like the one that had taken his father from him could never happen again.

III.

BENEDICT WOKE TO the splash of water, and for a long moment he was entirely unsure of his whereabouts. Then, with a rush, he remembered: the night train from Victoria, smoking with Humphrey on the deck of the ship in the cool morning as they chugged into Calais, then Europe rolling by, everything looking post-war. Urchins selling cobs of corn at the stations, vineyards marching away through France, the heat as they approached the coast.

They spent a night in Nice, eating bouillabaisse and drinking rosé on the Promenade des Anglais. Patricia had booked them rooms at the Negresco – she and Arkady shared one, Harris and Violet – whose relationship was, Benedict understood, something old and complex – took another.

He and Humphrey stayed late in the bar talking and looking out at the lights of the boats in the harbour. It was extraordinary to hear French all about him, to use a language that had existed for him until that point only in the classroom and in books.

'*Je prendrai un petit verre de Chartreuse pour terminer,*' he said to the dark and hawkish barman, his choice of drink a years-long promise to himself. '*Et remplissez le pastis de mon ami, s'il vous plaît.*' They sat in silence now, sipping. Humphrey wore a soft linen suit, a yellow cravat around his neck that matched the yellow rose in his lapel. His cheeks were pink from the drink and he occasionally and absent-mindedly turned the signet ring on his finger.

It was May: Mods were over and life was all friendship and adventure. Benedict's mother had come to see him off at Victoria, the early summer sun filtering through the station's high windows, casting fleeting patterns around her small, anxious figure. Her drab and functional coat, her stern haircut, the careful powder dusted over her lined face — all of it made her look like a relic from a world long past. He felt a rush of shame and hated himself for it, so he embraced her with a fervour that felt more like penance than affection. Patricia approached with her practised elegance, speaking to her with a condescension so polished it nearly passed for warmth. She asked about her summer plans, murmured regret over her husband's death, and assured her, with a smile that barely touched her lips, that Benedict would be well looked after.

This last part was true. Where the money came from, he didn't know, but when he expressed his fear that he might run out of cash before they even reached Patricia's parents in Venice, the matter was resolved almost without words. Even now, as he reached in his pocket to pay the bar bill, Humphrey wafted a handful of francs towards the bartender and patted away Benedict's protests.

They lurched up the stairs together, Humphrey pausing to dance a little jig with the statue of Napoleon III on the landing.

There was a large, canopied bed in their room. Benedict stood for a while looking out over the dark Mediterranean, up the esplanade where a few couples still wandered in the night, a solitary drunkard stumbling homeward in broad zig-zags. He could hear Humphrey brushing his teeth, heard the loud stream of his piss, something animal about the vigour of it. Humphrey, it seemed, did not wear a nightshirt, jumping into bed in a blur of pink flesh.

Benedict changed in the bathroom, pulling on his pyjamas, taking off his glasses and splashing his face with water, feeling a stir of anticipation that he did not care to name or examine too carefully. He extinguished the light and climbed into bed.

Humphrey's warm hand, when it came, was not unwelcome, moving down from the waist of Benedict's pyjamas to where he was, to his surprise, tumescent. Humphrey helped him out of his clothes, moving deftly in the darkness. Benedict's breath came fast and he felt his pulse in the corners of his eyes.

Then, when Humphrey moved his lips and tongue from Benedict's neck, down to his chest, then to his stomach, then further down, everything became blank and shimmery, his consciousness no longer centred in his mind, but rather in a place of no language, deeply internal, without judgement, guilt or morality, only pleasure.

He'd woken to find sun streaming in through a crack in the curtains, Humphrey's unfocused face looking down at him.

'We need to go,' Humphrey said. 'The train leaves in an hour.'

Benedict rose awkwardly from bed, made his way to the bathroom and found his glasses. Humphrey was still naked and came and stood behind him, draping his arms over Benedict's shoulders.

They looked at each other in the mirror appraisingly. Benedict was small and pale, Humphrey large and florid. Benedict's ribs were visible, a thin line of hair leading down from his navel. Humphrey's body was almost entirely hairless, his muscles large and well-defined. Benedict could suddenly imagine him as a rugby player at Harrow, or with the Jedburghs in North Africa. A man of palpable strength.

'You're awfully sweet,' Humphrey whispered in his ear.

They'd scooped up Patricia and Arkady – Violet and Harris were already down having breakfast – and then they were on the train for Menton, across the border and along the coast, bouncing from one Riviera resort to the next.

Something in Benedict lifted that day, as they chugged through Italy. This was happiness, he thought, stealing a glance over at Humphrey. Patricia took his hand, thoughtlessly, and pressed it to her lips.

'We do love you, Ben,' she said. 'And you're going to love Venice.'

They changed trains in Florence – the splendour of the Duomo visible as they came around the long curve into the city, bells ringing and light funnelling down the valley from Fiesole. Finally, just after midnight, their train pulled into Santa Lucia Station.

In the watery light, Benedict rose from his bed, remembering the night before: a gondola ride through lamplit canals, the gondolier singing to himself in a voice low and sonorous, the sense of a city so beautiful and otherworldly that it ought not to exist. He had leant back against Humphrey in the boat, had seen Patricia notice this and shoot them a smile that felt like a blessing.

They'd pulled up next to a large and gloomy building down a narrow inlet off the Grand Canal. The Palazzo Alba d'Oro, home of the Sinclairs. Patricia's father, Sir Reginald, a tall and nattily dressed man of seventy or so with carefully styled white hair, greeted them at what he called the *porta d'acqua*.

The palazzo was dusty and faded: they went up the majestic staircase to the first floor, where Patricia's mother, Honoria, as tall as her husband and with the same jutting chin and hard eyes as her daughter, glided towards them across the chipped parquet.

Over a late dinner in the long, gloomy dining hall, their faces candlelit, their shadows dancing on the frescoed walls, Benedict gleaned that Sir Reginald had been Ambassador in Spain, a sinecure given in recognition of his heroics at the Battle of Estaires. With the coming of Franco, he'd been over-zealous in his support of the Republicans, siphoning cash and weapons to the International Brigades. As the British sought to ensure Spain's neutrality in the war with Hitler, Sir Reginald's presence became an obstacle, one which was solved, he said in the voice of a man used to being listened to, by the concoction of a scandal.

What this scandal was, he didn't reveal, but Benedict saw Patricia's mother drain and refill her wine glass as he spoke. They were here in exile, stewing in resentment.

Benedict had hoped that he and Humphrey would be asked to share a room again, but as it was, they were shown to their bedrooms scattered across the palazzo's many and dizzyingly arranged floors.

Benedict was in what must once have been a boathouse, its floor clearly below the level of the water. There was a strong smell of damp, creeping patches of mould on the walls, but the bed was large and comfortable and he slept swiftly and happily, delighted at the turn his life had taken.

IV.

BENEDICT WAS CONVINCED that Venice was heaven, particularly with Arkady and Patricia as his guides, its every sinewy canal and mossy balustrade imbued with tender decadence. He understood how it was possible to fall in love with a city, the way Venice had made its liquid way into his bones.

They went from gallery to restaurant, from church to workshop, and everything seemed like a local star in the great constellation of *La Serenissima*. Benedict's Italian was only passable, but he found himself welcomed warmly at the cocktail parties in neighbouring *palazzi*, where people arrived by gondola wearing masks, whispered unspeakable things to their hosts, and the drinks were strong and endless.

One evening, they went to the Cannaregio palazzo of a Russian émigré businessman, Nikolai Ostroverkhov. It was a fine, balmy night, a gentle breeze blowing in off the Adriatic. Humphrey had helped Benedict choose his outfit from one of the costume shops in San Polo. He was in a harlequin's motley, looking more like an upstart stable boy in diamond-patterned silk than a commedia dell'arte rake.

The mask sat bumpily over his spectacles, completing the general awkwardness of his get-up. Humphrey and Arkady were satyrs – their tops bare, their faces obscured by wild, horned masks. Violet, Patricia and Patricia's mother, whom Benedict had learned to call Lady Sinclair, were naiads – river spirits draped in gauze and sparkles – while Harris and Sir Reginald wore the cloaks and beaked masks of plague doctors.

The landing stage of the palazzo had been transformed into a kind of platform, garlanded with lights, onto which gondolas and vaporetti disgorged their extravagant passengers.

Ostroverkhov had acquired the palazzo in the early Thirties, when even properties as grand as this could be bought for a song. Since then it had provided a home for such luminaries as Maxim Gorky and Leon Trotsky, and was now, Arkady told him, the home of the renowned Countess von Benckendorff, the Russian Mata Hari and at one time the Soviet Union's most renowned and fearless secret agent.

Inside, the palazzo's central courtyard was lit up with flaming torches and busy with couples dancing, a gypsy band playing guitars and violins, masked waiters circling with champagne and tureens of caviar.

Wearing a mask seemed to unleash something in Benedict – he became very drunk, very quickly, throwing back glass after glass of Select spritz, gin and tonic, or whatever came his way. The night took on a garish, nightmare quality, with Sir Reginald and Harris the plague doctors leering at Benedict one moment, Humphrey and Arkady prancing goatishly the next, their faces wild and alien.

Patricia tried several times to speak to him, but the music was too loud, and she, even masked, so obviously beautiful that she was rarely out of the grip of one of the young men circling wolfishly about the place.

Benedict felt a sudden urge to be alone and made his way up the ornate staircase to the *piano nobile*, where older guests sat along the balconies overlooking the courtyard below, remembering their own dancing days, the way a hand had crept down the back of their dress, or the softness of a young bosom pressed against their chest.

Benedict weaved between chairs and took another flight of steps to the *altana* – the bedrooms and servants' quarters in the palazzo's higher reaches. Then he was out on the roof terrace in the moonlight, the music coming up in drifts and snatches. He looked out over the lit domes and spires of the city towards St Mark's, the tower of San Giorgio like a pillar of flame in the distance.

It took a minute or two for him to realise that there was someone else on the terrace, a man with his back to Benedict, looking up the Grand Canal towards the Rialto.

Benedict cleared his throat and the man turned. He was wearing a mask in the shape of the sun with a halo of radiant beams. At the mouth, there was carved a cruel smile, the man's thin lips just visible within. The man was not tall – only a few inches on Benedict – and he wore a well-cut black suit and a white shirt open at the collar.

'You're Benedict Pierce, are you not?' The voice was warmly British, with the hint of a stutter.

'That's right,' Benedict said, taking a step towards the man, not sure whether to hold out a hand. He felt suddenly foolish in his costume with its gaudy diamonds and frills. The man turned back towards the canal, watching the arrival of a group of guests below, then staring again at the Rialto.

'My name's Philby,' the man said. 'I was told you'd be coming *en arlequinade*.'

'I know your work, sir. My mother takes *The Times*. You write frightfully well.'

'That's kind,' Philby said. 'Your friend Patricia speaks very highly of you, Mr Pierce. She says you are quite the coming man at Oxford.'

'She's decent. I do enjoy languages, but, honestly, she knows so much more than me. She's seen so much more.'

'I rather imagine that's why she's brought you out here. To get a sense of the world. Of its beauty and its cruelty.'

They looked out over the canal, where vaporetti vied for the handful of tourists coming out of restaurants, the businessmen going home to their wives in Giudecca and Castello.

Philby drew out a packet of Senior Service and offered one to Benedict, who took it and removed his mask to light it. Philby, too, took off his mask, and Benedict found a man in his thirties, his face a little lined, his hair streaked with grey.

There was intelligence in the pale blue eyes, humour too, as if you were in on the joke and he liked you for it.

Philby lit his own cigarette and took a deep drag. 'I hear you have embraced Patricia's political *Weltanschauung*,' he said.

Benedict looked sharply at Philby, unsure how to answer. 'I'm not sure . . . That is to say, I'm not entirely clear . . .'

'Tush,' Philby waved a hand at him. 'Patricia and Arkady and I have no secrets. The plan is mostly mine. Arkady is wonderfully resourceful and seems to know everyone in Moscow.'

'I'm not quite sure I should be speaking to you about all this,' Benedict said.

'Now listen here,' Philby leant in, his voice low and confidential. 'You should know that our lives have followed remarkably similar paths. Cambridge, for me, but otherwise . . . We understood, all of us, that flows of information would be critical in deciding the outcome of the great struggle. That we could tip the balance by managing that information.'

A new group of masked revellers arrived on the pontoon below. Laughter came up to them on the breeze, young voices raised in delight.

'Of course I write for the newspapers, but I report to the Office. London, Istanbul, occasionally Beirut. And that – my life as a spy – is simply another form of cover. Because the Soviet Union is where my true loyalties lie. I can trust you with all this, can't I, Benedict? Patricia assured me that you were one of us.'

'Yes, sir.'

'Good lad. I knew it. You may call me Kim. I imagine we're going to be seeing rather a lot of one another in the future. We must go back down.'

He carefully reattached his mask; Benedict did similarly. 'One thing, though,' Philby said, placing a hand on Benedict's shoulder. 'I want you to know what a bond it will build between you. The secrecy, the danger. The five of us – myself and those who travelled with me – we are closer than any husband and wife, any father and son. Secrets bind tightly. Your life from now on will be lived in service not just to a great and noble cause, but also to Patricia and Arkady, to Humphrey, Violet and Harris. They are worthy of your devotion. You understand me here?'

'Yes, sir,' Benedict said. 'Kim.'

When they came down the stairs, Benedict saw Patricia and Arkady sitting at one of the tables along the *piano nobile*. Patricia's eyes were on them and Benedict raised a shy hand. Patricia smiled and waved and when Benedict turned back to Philby, he had vanished.

In his watery bedroom late that night, or perhaps in the soft, uncertain hours before dawn, Benedict woke to find a man in pyjamas tiptoeing across the parquet floor. His head was woolly with drink and exhaustion, the edges of the room blurred in the dim blue light filtering through the blinds, the canal's reflection rippling softly against the walls. Humphrey moved like a shadow, caught briefly in that liquid glow, and then he was beside him, sliding into the bed with a whisper of breath – warm and quick, close enough for Benedict to feel. Their hands found each other first, tentative, searching, and then their mouths, and then they were dissolved in one another, grasping and thoughtless, until the sun stood high in the Venetian sky.

PART 3

Corfu, May 1996

I.

FIVE MONTHS HAD passed. Nina sat on the same pier, looking down into the blue depths. It was already hot at 8 a.m., but not the oppressive heat of summer; rather it carried a softness in it, a memory of night and spring. Benedict came to sit beside her. He was wearing an old-fashioned-looking pair of striped swimming trunks, pulled up too high at the waist, and a black diving mask. He looked much older bare-chested: a few white hairs around his nipples, ribs jutting out above a stomach dusted with liver spots. He'd started swimming with her at the end of March, when the first good weather arrived, although the water was still icy. Nina had worried about his heart at first, but it seemed that immersion served the same purpose for him that it did for her. In that moment of breathless shock, all the world was narrowed to the body, to desperate life, and loss and pain and the past were all but forgotten.

Benedict stood up, took a deep breath and flung himself into the water. It was one of the images Nina would remember, in years to come: the little man just weeks before his seventieth birthday flying through the air, legs akimbo, arms windmilling, sending up a white explosion and a whoop as he disappeared beneath the surface. Nina slipped into the water less dramatically than her friend, but soon she was swimming alongside him, slowing her pace to a gentle glide so that they made for the bay together. She kept watch for jellyfish – they had both been stung the previous week — but there were only the usual shoals of curious minnows, the wicked spines of urchins on the rocks far below.

She liked to swim far enough out that she could see the whole of the island and could feel, for a moment, that she was an outsider, looking in. They were over the channel here, the green had become the deepest blue, and she and Benedict stopped and turned back, treading water. They saw the pale pink villa hanging out over the sea, ivy snaking up its sun-bleached walls, the white and blue cottages of the village. They saw the san stretching halfway up the island and the ruins of the church at its peak. They saw Corfu behind, huge and hazy in the early morning light, a small cluster of clouds above Pantokrator. Spyland was home, Nina thought to herself, perhaps the closest to a real home she'd ever had.

When they came in from their swim there was always a sense of emptiness. Violet took to delivering their robes just as Benedict had once done for Nina. Then they would go and sit on the veranda of Harris and Violet's cottage, watching the day rise over the water. Nina was touched by the solicitude these old friends showed Benedict, the way they took every opportunity to place a hand on his shoulder or give his arm a squeeze. Harris's thoughtfulness in particular moved Nina more for how unexpected it was.

'We miss him, you know, old chap,' Harris said that morning, breaking a silence during which Benedict's face made clear the path his thoughts had taken.

Benedict turned towards him wretchedly, then stared back down at his mug of tea. 'It's a very special form of torture, being trapped here, in the home we made together.'

'I'm sure we could ask them to move you,' Violet said. 'You could go back up to the villa.'

'I'm afraid that would be worse,' Benedict said. 'Really I just want to be off this island, away from all of it. Incarceration was just about supportable with Humphrey. There was so much life in him, you know? It was impossible to feel hemmed in with him around.'

At this point Nina had an idea, one which she outlined to Benedict as they made their way back to his cottage. 'Why don't you come and walk with me?' she said. 'It will do us both good.'

II.

THEY SET OFF early next morning. It was another exquisite early summer day, the swifts pouring through the sky, joyful to have made it home from their African wintergrounds. As Angelos nosed the boat into the harbour in the Old Town, Nina saw Benedict's eyes dart along the promenade to the place where Humphrey was found. She took his hand and squeezed it. Then they were out on the dockside and making their way to the bus station by the market. Benedict was in sturdy hiking boots and long woollen socks, a tweed jacket and yellow cravat. Nina could see that he was already sweating and offered to put his jacket in her bag. They sat together on the bus, looking out at the farm stalls and factories, the fields and holiday camps: fleeting scenes of other lives slipping by.

They descended from the bus at Corfu's westernmost point, Cape Kefali. Nina had walked the island's north coast over that winter and early spring, basking in the isolation, the wildness. Now they stood for a moment, looking over the cluster of rocks that marked the edge of the island, towards the toe-tip of Italy, Sicily, Africa. Benedict drew in a deep breath and let it out. The sea seemed to sigh back at him.

'Right,' he said, turning sharply and setting off at a clip. The path here ran along the road, hewing close to the shore, passing through a handful of sleepy tourist villages with their supermarkets selling footballs and inflatable toys out front, their shuttered barber's salons and scooter rental shops. Nina had been worried about whether Benedict would be able to keep up. As it was, she had to break into a trot every so often. He was buoyed by a kind of manic energy, interested in everything as they walked, stopping to point out a church on a hillside high above, or naming the flowers that grew in the rocks beside the path: chamomile, bee orchid, wild fennel. After a while, the path turned away from the sea and climbed the spine of a cliff. They stopped for a moment at the top to catch their breath and take in the view: olive groves rolled away to the sea, while behind them the land reared up steeply, stepping in flower-strewn terraces to the rocky ridge of mountains that strung between Mount Kourkoulí here in the west and Pantokrator in the east.

'I say, love,' Benedict began, and when Nina looked at him she could see little red patches on each of his cheeks. He was wringing his hands as he spoke. 'You've been very sweet to me. You were a dear thing before Humphrey happened, but I really don't know what I'd have done without you this last winter. Your father and

I, we had our run-ins over the years, but you're a gem. He should be very proud of you.'

There were a few strands of hair in front of Nina's face and she blew them away. 'I'm not sure he is,' she said. 'I'm not really sure that he thinks of me at all.' She drew out a salami from her bag and cut it with the knife that Humphrey had given her, flicking the small blade out from the shaft of the pen.

Benedict smiled when he saw it. 'He was so excited to give you that,' he said. 'I think he imagined you plunging it into the neck of some monstrous Serbian warlord. He had great belief that you'd return to the Office some day, Nina. You should know that.'

They ate some of the salami and then carried along the path, tracing the edge of the cliff and then higher, up through the meadows towards Mount Kourkoulí – the dry mountain, she'd heard local people call it. It grew hotter and they walked in companionable silence. Benedict had picked up an olive branch and was using it as a walking stick, although his pace was still sprightly and every so often he'd stoop to inspect an ants' nest, or name a bird flying over: 'Bee-eater . . . hoopoe . . . red-backed shrike.'

Nina found, as she usually did when walking alone, that the rhythm of movement loosened her thoughts, enabling her to examine what in the sleepless air of her bedroom was merely a jumble.

Boyd had come to see her late the night before, sitting on her bed and talking to her deep into the night. Now that he was in the villa, these visits had become a regular thing, and although she could still make herself angry at the situations he'd put her in, she was not good at holding grudges. Nor did she believe, as she knew that some on the island did, that Boyd was in any way responsible for Humphrey's death. He said he'd lost Humphrey soon after leaving the restaurant that afternoon, had been wandering through the alleyways looking for a favourite bar for one last drink, when he'd come out on the steps leading down from the Liston to find Mrs Samways in tears, Drinkwater soaked and shivering, and Humphrey dead on the dockside.

This did not mean that Nina believed that Humphrey had merely stumbled to his watery death. She'd been interviewed again by Inspector Metallinos, who was as softly determined as he had been on their first meeting. What, he asked, was Humphrey's particular role in the Service? Whom, specifically, had he worked with, and against? Who amongst his enemies might have been waiting, with great patience, for the opportunity to bring an end to that expansive life? The inspector was polite but implacable and had become a regular visitor to Spyland over the course of the spring.

Last night, in her room, the windows open to the breeze and the crickets, she and Boyd had spoken of the cell in Srebrenica. She had already gone over it with Drinkwater – the desolation, the feeling of her mind and body being separated by the terrible things that were done to each of them in turn – but talking about it with Boyd was different. In part, of course, because it was to a great extent his fault that she was there at all, ridiculous to send her so green and naked into the heart of enemy territory, her eventual unmasking as inevitable as it was brutal. But it was also that he'd been there himself.

'I remember,' he'd said. 'Colombia. Not as bad as you,

of course. But they led me out in the yard every morning and lined me up in front of a firing squad. They didn't need anything from me. Just wanted to make my life hell. Sometimes it was blanks, sometimes they'd fire over my head. It destroyed me, really. You don't come back from something like that.' The story of Boyd's failed attempt to infiltrate the FARC guerrilla group in Colombia was well-known in the Office. He had been rumbled almost immediately and then held prisoner for a year deep in the Amazon. It was why his career, which had until that point been on a resolutely upward trajectory, had stalled, why he had been exiled to the fourth floor and the Balkans when he'd previously been spoken about as a future C. The Office was full of people like Boyd, who because of chance or a single mistake had found their prospects irretrievably scuppered.

Nina and Benedict had been climbing for some time, moving through the shade of an olive grove and then out into another meadow, the grass humming with crickets, the wildflowers like jewels scattered in the sward. Finally, they were at Lakones, looking down over Palaiokastritsa and the sweep of the island's west coast beyond. They sat on a rock, breathing in the sweet air and the beauty of the world, of Greece. Nina turned to Benedict and saw that his eyes were bright with tears. She put an arm around his shoulder and they rocked gently there, Benedict sobbing, the woods below them loud with birdsong.

III.

THEY MADE THEIR way down the hill towards Palaiokastritsa. It was steep, and they sent rocks tumbling before them as they walked. Benedict still had his olive stick and occasionally whipped at a head of wild fennel or rapped on the trunk of a tree as they descended. Nina could see the way the town narrowed to a point, its shops and tavernas fanning out along its two beaches. It was a beautiful town, perhaps the most beautiful of all the places she'd visited on her self-guided tour of the island. And she was happy to be there with Benedict, for whom the trip seemed to have freed something that had been trapped since Humphrey's death.

'Palaiokastritsa was the home of the ancient Phaeacians,' Benedict said. 'From the *Odyssey*. It's here that Homer begins his tale, on Corfu. So you could say that the island is where literature began.' Nina liked it when Benedict's voice took on this professorial air. It made her think of him as an earnest young man in lectures at university, or how she imagined him in his early days at the Office, full of vim and idealism. 'Odysseus would have washed up on the shore just there,' he said, pointing to the turquoise waters of the bay, the long white curve of the beach. 'Nausicäa and her friends were playing a ball game in the waves when this naked man landed at their feet. They, too, were naked. I always imagined them playing cricket when I was young and reading the *Odyssey*.'

They entered the town now, passing from a fish restaurant to a laundromat, then a tourist shop selling buckets and spades. More inflatables, a constant votive offering to the island's buoyancy. The bay here curved round to a point where, on the rocky headland pushing out into the sea, there stood a monastery surrounded by dark green pines. It reminded Nina of the villa, perched there over the water. They went and stood on the sand together.

Nina took off her rucksack and placed it at her feet. Benedict sent his olive stick spiralling into the water. They paused for a moment. Salt and pines.

There were clusters of tourists further up the beach, some of them swimming in the turquoise water, some lying on the hot sand. Nina always found it strange meeting English people, travellers from her world but impossibly distant. As she and Benedict continued along the beach, she heard an English father barking at his children, the long Home Counties vowels of a group of gap-year girls, a laugh that reminded her, absurdly, of Colin. The young man looked nothing like Colin, but as he stood there in the water, glancing up shyly at the girls, she felt a familiar pain, imagining a different life for him, for her.

They had lunch in a taverna on the waterfront, watching tourist boats come in, listening to the happy prattle of the holidaymakers, the drawl of expats. 'Everyone's English,' Benedict said. 'It's like being in Malta or Gibraltar.'

'Corfu was British, I suppose.'

'Only for about a week and a half,' Benedict laughed. 'Says something, I think, about the mark we leave on a place.' He had taken on his professorial air again and was speaking loudly enough that a young couple at the next-door table had stopped their conversation to listen.

'Corfu was a great naval power in antiquity. At the time of the Peloponnesian War, only Athens, perhaps Corinth, could rival her.' The waiter had brought them a bottle of retsina. Benedict stopped to taste it and nodded. 'Important trading post for the Romans, too, all but destroyed by the Ostrogoths in 500 or so. The new city was built then, called Corfu or *Korphoi*. Byzantine for twin peaks.'

'After the two hills in town?'

'Exactly, the *Castel a Mare* and the *Castel a Terra*. Corfu was part of the Theme of Cephallenia. Byzantine until 1200 or so, followed by another 500 years under the Venetians.'

'Is that why it feels like Venice in the Old Town? You expect to see a gondolier poling past the Spianada.'

'It's why the island takes such long breaths. Half a millennium at a time.'

Their food arrived – Benedict had ordered for both of them in Greek, quizzing the waiter and pointing out to the sea and then the kitchen. There were plates of calamari and aioli, sardines and octopus, prawns in a rich tomato sauce. Benedict continued between mouthfuls. 'So, yes, after the Napoleonic Wars, Corfu became British for less than fifty years, capital of the United States of the Ionian Islands. The Brits built roads and schools, turned the Ionian Academy into a world-class university. Put in half-decent plumbing. They still refer to the north-east coast as Kensington-on-Sea.'

'I knew I'd seen Princess Di in a rubber ring.'

'We did good things, here and there,' Benedict said, smiling, 'we British. When Corfu asked for independence, we gave it with our blessing.'

Nina didn't think of herself as a patriot but had worked with plenty of men who wore Union Jack boxer shorts. Benedict, like many of his generation, she supposed, had grown up at a time before nationalism had been tainted by its worst proponents, people who'd run out of their own luck and took their country's, hung their lives around it like bunting. There was, with Benedict though, a further complication: the red-and-blue paradox. He was both Communist and patriot. A man who saluted the flag while quietly eroding the soil beneath its pole.

There had been times in Bosnia that she had convinced herself that she was on the right side of history, that her country's politicians and diplomats were driven by something humane and generous-hearted. And it was clear to her that the forces she'd been sent in to fight had been monstrous. But she found it hard to link this impulse to something broader, something that made her feel as Benedict now looked, tethered and woozy, and faintly honoured to be so.

He was drunk, she thought – the jug of retsina had been refilled once already – and spoke even more loudly. 'Of course Britain, then, was Empire, high Victoriana. A very different place. Byron was your man. He'd stoked up philhellenism to a rousing pitch and there was a kind of panache about the English. We lost that over the course of the Great War, the Thirties.' She realised that Benedict was playing the kind of role that would once have been performed by Humphrey, had he been here: the bon vivant, the charmer, the raconteur. But there was darkness here where Humphrey had been all light. 'Civilisations need to re-energise every so often, break apart and reform. Britain put its feet up, got comfortable.

Stagnant. Look around.' Here he gestured to the room, to the craggy retirees and tanned bankers, the pretty gap-year girls who had followed them up from the beach. 'I thought Britain could lead the remaking of the world, I had such hope for us. But these are not leaders, they are sheep.'

There was silence when he finished. Nina watched a bead of sweat travel down from Benedict's forehead to his chin. She signalled to the waiter for the bill and finished her own glass of retsina. 'I'm sorry,' Benedict said to her, then, more loudly, to anyone still listening: 'So sorry.' They paid and then wandered out into the blazing day. 'Let's go to the monastery,' Benedict said. 'They have a whale.'

IV.

NINA COULD HEAR the waves on the rocks below, the breeze rustling above. It was cool and cave-like under the pines, the road almost invisible beneath a scurf of cones and needles. Benedict took her arm as they climbed. At one of the bends in the road, there was a clearing in the trees and they looked down on the town, saw the gap-year girls filing out of the restaurant, making their way back down to the beach.

'Darling,' Benedict said. '*Fíli mou*. I'm awfully sorry for my little outburst in there. I find myself getting terribly cross about things, especially history. It's all so horribly muddled in my mind – where we went wrong, how we ended up such a selfish, graspy country. I had such optimism when I was your age. But then history took one wrong step, then two, and now it's all so dreadfully tarnished that I worry that no one will ever be decent again.'

Nina knew that Benedict hadn't been back to England for a couple of decades, wondered what he'd make of the City boys in their blue suits and red cars roaring around Chelsea, the sleaze and self-satisfaction of the political classes. What could you feel in a country that was all surface? He broke away from her and marched up the road, his head down. She had to hurry to catch up with him. They stood aside to let a tourist bus pass on its way back to the Old Town, or to one of the cruise ships that was moored at the docks near Lazaretto.

The monastery sat in a wide clearing in the pines, a sprawling complex of buildings around a central church, its walls painted the colour of honey, an elegant bell tower rising in the centre. They made their way across the dusty parking area, then through a set of wooden doors and into a courtyard of low lavender hedges, bees humming in the heavy air. In the church, Nina took a thousand-drachma note from her wallet and bought them both candles to light. 'For Humphrey,' she said.

'Naturally,' Benedict replied. They found the shrine of St Spyridon and lit the candles there, placing them on metal spikes where they flickered in the sea breeze that climbed to find them. 'We came here often, Humphrey and I,' Benedict said. 'Years ago. To look at the whale.'

They sat together in the pews in the candlelight listening to the wind and the sea. Then Benedict stood. 'Follow me,' he said. They walked through another courtyard and into a large building that served as a kind of museum. In the entrance hall, hanging above them, was the skeleton of a whale. 'Isn't it wonderful?' Benedict said, laughing, with the brightened eyes of a child. 'It was caught by a monk in the 1840s. Hauled up on the beach here.' On the walls were icons and mosaics, some of them very old, all shining with the peculiar golden light of the place. The whale swayed very slightly above them. They stood in silence, looking up at the bleached bones of the vast creature, imagining the seas it had swum through, the world that had played out above it.

They walked back through the courtyards, through the wooden doors and out into the clearing in front of the monastery. There, in the shadows on the other side of the wide parking area, almost hidden by the overhanging pines, was a black Mercedes, engine idling, windows dark. A man and a woman stood beside it, their backs turned to Nina and Benedict. The couple leant towards one another in conspiratorial conversation. The man wore a Panama hat, the woman had a silk scarf over her head. Nina looked idly at them, then up to where a bird was calling high in the trees. It was only when she turned to Benedict that she saw that something was wrong. His face had emptied of colour save for two hectic spots on his cheeks, his mouth hanging open. She thought for a moment that he was going to fall and reached out for him. His hand was clammy, tremulous.

'What is it?'

He was still looking across the wide sunlit square of ground to the shadows and the car, where the couple had stopped their conversation and were getting into the back seat, the driver revving the engine now. The door slammed and the car roared off.

'I could swear,' said Benedict, 'that was Patricia Sinclair. And . . . and . . . Nina, it was your father.'

Nina felt her blood singing, her t-shirt suddenly too tight around her neck. A wave of recognition: the man in the car, the man with the Panama hat, the broad shoulders squared as if about to give – or receive – a blow, that man had, indeed, been her father.

V.

THEY MISSED THE bus to the Old Town and took a taxi, Nana Mouskouri songs playing on the car's tinny radio. Nina had, at first, tried to run after the black Mercedes, had started down the hill after it, cutting between pine trees, hoping to reach one of the hairpin bends before the vehicle that was carrying her father. But the driver was moving at speed, spinning his wheels on the pine needles and then roaring off across the causeway and through the town. She stood there panting for a while, before jogging back up to find Benedict.

They had sat on the low wall in front of the monastery for some time, gathering their thoughts. When they spoke it was in a rush of questions, scarcely formed conjectures about what they could be doing here: Patricia, whom Benedict had not seen for years, and Nina's father.

'Perhaps,' Benedict said, 'they're here to get to the bottom of Humphrey's death.'

'Perhaps,' Nina said dejectedly. For her, the question of why her father might be on Corfu was less pressing than another, more wounding mystery: why had he come without telling her?

Angelos was sitting in the boat when they arrived, talking to Boyd, who had been shopping in the Old Town. Boyd tried to engage them in conversation, asked them to admire a new linen shirt, but neither of them wanted to talk, and so Angelos took the boat out into the narrow stretch of water that lay between the harbour and Vidos, and they sat without talking, listening to the slap of the waves and the calls of the birds. The birds were all about them: it was dusk and the violet heights were awash with Alpine swifts, shrieking and wheeling over the town as if casting spells. Above the sea, Nina could see terns and gulls coming back from their fishing trips, while on Vidos itself, crows and jackdaws cackled and chided.

Benedict walked with her and Boyd to the doors of the villa, waited for Boyd to go inside, then gave Nina a peck on the cheek. 'I must speak to Violet and Harris,' he said. 'They'll know what to do.'

She stared after him, wondering what anyone could do about the appearance of these figures from each of their pasts. She had to consider that the apparition of her father and Patricia Sinclair might merely be the latest piece of evidence that she was, at some deep level, quite mad, and Benedict with her. She went inside and saw, in the dining room, the figure of Edward Lane, reading. He was concentrating very hard on a sheaf of papers in a brown folder, a cup of coffee perched on the table, but seemingly untouched, at his elbow. Edward looked up when she came in.

'What ho,' he said. 'How was your walk?'

The tears caught Nina by surprise. She sat down opposite him and put her face in her hands, crying so hard now that her palms filled with tears, which then seeped down between her fingers.

'Oh my dear,' Edward said, offering her a handkerchief. 'You poor old thing. There, there, now.'

She looked up at his kind and narrow eyes, his mop of white hair, and smiled in thanks, blowing her nose noisily.

'Why don't you tell me all about it,' he said.

She did so, moving shakily through the events of the day and then slowing when she reached that moment, darkly glimmering, in which they had seen the couple across the parking lot. When she said Patricia Sinclair's name, something in Edward's face changed, a hardening that made her think of what he must have been like, years ago in the field, a man to be reckoned with.

'How sure are you of this, Nina? The mind can play tricks on us, you know.'

'I'm sure. As sure as I can be of anything.'

His eyes narrowed further. He stood up and went to the window, looking out to sea, to Lazaretto – the prison island – and the mainland behind it.

'You know about your father's history in the Service?' He didn't turn as he spoke. Nina could see a boat cutting through the channel, its sails big in the breeze.

'I know a little, I suppose.'

'He appeared in the early Sixties, your pa. Always in Benedict's shadow, at first. Made me suspicious of him, but then he was in the field, first in Moscow, then Yugoslavia. Came back a quite different man. It can do that to you, operational life. MI6's reputation was in the swamp at that point. Burgess and Maclean in '51, Blake in '61, Philby in '63 . . . Blunt and Cairncross after them. We'd shared so much with them – information, secrets, names who trusted us with their lives. A poison that infected us all. But, worse, we'd only just begun to work closely with the Americans. We looked precisely the fools they'd believed us to be. Degenerate fops leaking like Eton Mess on a warm afternoon. When your father came back to Century House, he was just the fellow to shake things up.'

A man with a bald head and protuberant ears came into the dining room. 'Game of bowls, Edward?' he said, his voice all breath. He held up his bowling bag as if tempting a monster from its lair.

'Sorry, Hugo. Tomorrow?' The man beamed delightedly, gave a salute and turned about. 'Right on cue,' Edward said. 'Hugo Poynton. Your father sent him out here. Dyed-in-the-wool Communist. Lovely fellow, but hopelessly compromised. Fell in love with a GRU agent and kept him well-supplied with information about the Berlin Tunnel. Which lines we were going to tap and when. Still, water under the bridge. Decent game of bowls in him, in fact.' Edward took out one of his slim cigarettes, lit it with the revolver lighter and sent a stream of blue smoke upwards. He tapped his ash in the coffee cup.

At that moment, a memory surfaced in Nina's mind. She was on the balcony of her grandmother's house in Korčula, sitting with her father one heavy summer night. She must have been twelve or thirteen. Her sister and grandmother had already gone to bed, leaving her alone with him as he smoked a cigar and sipped brandy, the familiar drunken slur softening his words. A hurricane lamp flickered on the table, drawing moths in frantic spirals. Her father began to speak – low, conspiratorial – about the spies he'd rooted out: double agents, Soviet moles, traitors turned against their own. There was pride in his voice as he described how he'd swept the Office clean, sending the turncoats into exile or snuffing them out entirely.

With each declaration, he'd punctuated his words by flicking his lighter, catching one of the moths in its flame. They flared up, the moths, momentarily incandescent, before crumbling into ash and disappearing into the night. When he fell silent, Nina quietly rose from the table, walked to the French doors, and turned back to watch him, the click and flare of the lighter, his face cast in the trembling light, while the flaming moths drifted up into the darkness.

'It was your pa who exposed Benedict and Humphrey,' Edward continued. 'Violet and Harris, too. Presented the C at the time, Esmond Harrington, with evidence they'd been involved in espionage for the other side. Your pa worked alongside fellows called Snow and Smith. Everyone dreaded a knock from the three of them. Patricia's secret army.'

'He was, I think, quite wounded himself.' Nina felt an obscure need to defend her father, twinned with a strange kind of guilt-by-association, that he should have hurt these people she loved, even so long ago. She had to remind herself, from time to time, that these people, her friends, had been traitors. Seduced not by money, but by a beautiful lie. What unsettled her wasn't the betrayal, exactly, but the sense that she and they, in some abstract way, belonged to the same tribe: intelligent, idealistic, reaching for something beyond themselves.

'Of course your pa and Patricia were in cahoots with Arkady Malkin every bit as much as Benedict and the rest of them. I was sure of it. I could just never get anyone to believe it. I wasn't popular, that was my problem. Never have been, truth be told.'

'Malkin? The boys were talking about him the other night.'

'That is because I'm quite certain that he, too, is here on Corfu. I knew him vaguely at Oxford. I was there with Benedict, Patricia et al. He was a vain, preening type, the last man you'd finger as one of the revolutionary proletariat. But he was certainly a Soviet agent, perhaps even then. Someone quite important in the KGB, the Director at one point. Now, he's just another gangster. But he has power and money, and a direct line to the top table in Britain and elsewhere.'

'You think my father was one of them, a Soviet agent?' It struck Nina as absurd, but then all of this was absurd. The essential incongruity of life was one of the things she'd learnt during her time on Spyland.

'Not at first, I don't think. Although there were rumours about his time in Moscow. Your father has always been a man out for himself. It's a kind of idealism, I suppose. Not a patriot, though.'

Edward nested his fingers and looked at her. He had eyebrows she'd heard described as beetling, though to her they were more like the caterpillars on the olive trees in her grandmother's garden in Korčula. *Bitelbrouwed*, she heard Colin correcting her. *Middle English for jutting or overhanging.*

'So how did you come to be here?' Nina thought Edward extraordinarily lucid, notwithstanding his late-night peregrinations in the Old Town.

'I carried on kicking up whatever fuss I could about Malkin and his network of double agents. I was shuffled from one dusty frontier post to the next, from Benin to Balochistan. Over the course of the Eighties I moved into that daydream of semi-retirement that failed spies inhabit, waking up in the middle of my own talks at Chatham House, falling asleep in my chair at the Reform Club, taking adventurous holidays on my own or with one of my increasingly small number of friends.'

'Sounds like fun,' Nina said.

'Sometimes I'd lose my passport just to have a problem to solve, a border guard to flummox. Then the Wall fell and we had access to anything KGB we could want, vast archives. Lucy Fellowes was our first pair of eyes on the paperwork. Reams of material on Malkin, on Patricia, leaks going back decades.'

'And she came to you with it?'

'She went to the C first, of course. Rupert Locke, by this time. He didn't last long. No spine. He sent her away with a flea in her ear. She tried Esmond Harrington, the former C, but he didn't want to know. Tried Smith and Snow, but they simply informed Patricia that someone was on her tail. Patricia had had years to sew it all up, you see? So she finally came to me, dear old Lucy. I called in a favour with the foreign secretary, marched into Whitehall with Lucy at my side, presented the material to a panel of Foreign Office tuppenny tyrants.'

'What happened?'

'The next evening, your father turned up at my flat in South Kensington, told me to pack my bags. That I'd be going on a long journey. I met Lucy at RAF Northolt, thought we might be going involuntary skydiving together, if you catch my drift. They brought us out here. Spyland. Lucy, of course, they dealt with soon after. She was smuggling out letters to the press, to politicians. A watery silence.'

'And you really thought you saw Malkin the other night, at the airport?'

'Sure of it. And if your pa and Patricia are here, maybe they're with him. I'd heard word that Malkin had fallen on his feet in the post-Communist gold rush. Suddenly managing director of this oil company and chairman of the board of that Siberian engineering conglomerate. Worth billions, they say. Why he'd be on Corfu, I have no idea. But I intend to find out.'

VI.

'WHY DON'T WE go back to Srebrenica, to your period in captivity? It's almost a year now since you were there. How has that passing of time helped you?'

It was almost dark outside. Nina sat in Drinkwater's study, the windows open to jasmine. 'I'm not sure it has helped at all,' Nina said, after a pause. 'We all think we're strong until we're tested, don't we?'

She couldn't look at Drinkwater; she spoke to her feet, her words ending up in a pool by her Doc Martens. 'Listen,' she said. 'There are people who've crawled out from darker places, I know that. But the cell – it didn't just hold me; it remade me. Unstitched what I was and sewed something else together. You can turn it over and over, drag it into conversation, dissect it until the edges blur, but in the end, it becomes part of your inner landscape, a creature with yellow eyes crouched in the shadows of every quiet moment.'

Silence fell. She thought back to the cell, to the way the hours seemed to expand in there. Time developed a kind of weight, pressing on her chest, her cheeks, on the joints of her bones. She fashioned a grammar of shadows, a mythology of light. She remembered a whole day spent scratching at the smear of red skin on her arm, and then, in the dimness, watching the wound weep and shimmer. How the crickets grew so loud that the sound was almost visible in the air about her.

Bogdan was gentle with her, respectful, even, despite what they did together – although she had no agency in the act, refused to look at him but instead fixed her eyes on the bars on the window, light falling through greenery beyond. She imagined herself as one of the kites her father used to buy her, playing out the line that was strung between her mind and the body to which these things were being done. She would see how far she could take her consciousness away, up through the canopy of leaves, through the drifting summer clouds, into the high spheres of the air. Sometimes she let go of the line altogether, allowing herself to disappear into the immensity of space, hurtling through an infinite diorama of turning planets and nebulae, black holes and ancient, dying stars. When Bogdan finished, he would ask her questions about her mission, her colleagues, her operational history. The questions were half-hearted, though, and soon he'd be telling her, in his melodious Belgrade accent, about his childhood in the city, his love of James Bond films, his time at university, ended early by the war.

She remembered one night, afterwards, he stayed for a while, sitting at the end of her bed, smoking. She was in the corner, knees pulled up to her chest. 'I love watching your Mr Bond,' he said distantly. 'It is never serious for him. His world is not just different from the real world, it is the opposite. He knows who the enemy is, knows who is good and who is evil. He is always in control. You never see Mr Bond kill a child, or a mother, you never see him awake in the night. I turn on the films then, when I can't sleep. They have become for me a kind of dreaming.'

Some nights, Bogdan didn't appear, and that was worse. The waiting, everything jangling, and then, eventually, a different man would come in. Each of them wore some variation of the Scorpions' uniform: black jacket with the golden emblem, combat trousers and boots. Some even kept their berets on. Most reeked of booze and cigarettes. Some couldn't perform and so hit her instead; some sobbed in her arms. When they did manage to finish inside her, she'd mop at herself with a fold of her sheet, trying to get rid not only of the physical evidence, but of the memory.

She was always on her guard, always watchful. She knew that there would be a moment when a chink of light appeared in the darkness, a gap through which she could squeeze. So every time her door was open, and particularly when her visitor was drunk, or stoned, or both, she kept herself completely alert, sharply vigilant.

When the other men stopped coming and Bogdan became her only point of contact, this possibility seemed to narrow: he never reeked of the slivovitz that his comrades seemed to drink with every meal; what's more, he appeared to sense her watchfulness, her coiled potential, and he was particularly careful to lock the door behind him when he came in, to keep his pistol well out of her reach. He radiated a kind of brutal and unflinching self-possession.

She had been marking the days on a brick in the corner, scratching the passing of time with a chip of stone. It was almost September. There was a mellowness to the light outside her window that had not been there in the heat of summer. She imagined the work that was being done at home to get her back. She knew that her father, maybe Boyd, maybe others in the Service, would be pulling whatever levers they could. But she also knew that the war was at a delicate point and that her position in Bosnia under non-operational cover left them with precious few options. From an official perspective, she did not exist, was not being held captive, had never set foot in the country, was less than no one.

By September, she turned in her bed like a blank page and had almost forgotten a world in which she once moved about with freedom.

'You escaped,' Drinkwater said, as if he had been following her thoughts. 'Tell me about that.'

She paused for a moment, worried the skin on her arm, took a deep breath.

'I realised that no one would come for me. I needed to make my own way out. Although by this stage I wasn't really thinking. I was pretty unhinged.' Here he gave a slow nod. 'I'd been aware of sounds – gunfire, shells – that hadn't been there before. I knew that something was happening, and some part of me told me that I needed to take advantage.'

She wasn't going to tell Drinkwater about the specifics of that night. Bogdan had come to her later than usual – it was past eight, the evening fading outside. Her dressing hadn't been changed for several days and was giving off a rank, meaty smell. Bogdan was wearing a t-shirt with the Chetnik skull and crossbones on it, she remembered that. He looked like he'd been out in the dirt of the day. As he pulled down her trousers, her pants, there was an explosion, nearer than any other she'd heard. He looked up at the window, at the plaster dust hanging in the air. He was more hurried than usual, rougher with her, his gaze darting up again to the bars. She could tell when he was about to climax – the quickening of his breath, the low moan, the eyes closing for an instant. It was then that she rose and jabbed her fingers forcefully into his throat.

It was a move she'd learned from the staff sergeant in the Brecon Beacons. The target was the slight hollow just below the Adam's apple, the fingers braced and thrusting up and into the soft tissue. This was the second time she'd used the move in the field. The first time, she'd felt triumphant, the sense of having turned the tables decisively, but as she watched Bogdan grasping at his throat, struggling for air, his breaths coming in frantic wheezes, she felt something like pity. He reached blindly for his gun, which he'd left on the floor by the bed. Nina rose and stamped very hard on his fingers and then, taking the gun by the barrel, she brought it down three times, sharply, on his head.

Now she moved quickly, searching his pockets – keys, a wallet with a few thousand dinar in it, a knife in a sheath at his ankle, a golden scorpion on its handle. She tucked the gun into her waist and let herself out into a narrow passageway to a flight of stone steps. At the top, a metal door. She edged it carefully open and stepped out into a courtyard. It was empty, the only sound that of gunfire crackling in the hills, the occasional boom of a shell. She drew the pistol with the knowledge that she'd never fired a weapon outside a range, that her firearms training had been basic, introductory, not intended to prepare her for a moment like this.

'I was on the run for five days,' she told Drinkwater. 'I was defeated by geography, or politics. A bit of both. I followed every rule of tradecraft, covered my tracks. But I hadn't counted on the war moving on while I was in the cellar. They'd been keeping me in a village near Šid. I managed to scavenge some food and water in the town that first night, headed north-west, towards Croatia. It was harvest time and there were crops I could eat. I rationed my water. You wouldn't believe the flatness of the land there — like a hallucination, these fields that seemed to stretch on forever under the moon.'

'You were picked up in Krajina, were you not?'

'I thought I'd reached Croatia. Safety. But the borders were shifting so much at that time. The sentry posts on the old frontier were empty — I'd been planning to go through the fields, but it was a ghost-town, the border post. I realised all this time that I was moving towards the fighting, that I needed to get on the other side of it, to Hungary or deeper into Croatia.'

'You kept walking?'

'Four more nights. Flat, desolate field after field. I made it as far as Beli Manastir, only five kilometres from the Hungarian border. I was hiding in a hay barn, waiting for nightfall to make the crossing. Someone must have seen me go in, because a Chetnik squad arrived and surrounded the place. I thought about fighting, took the safety off the pistol, but there were too many of them.'

'And yet you were released into UNPROFOR custody in Knin a week later.'

'That's true. Why I was released, I still have no idea, although this was right in the middle of Operation Storm, the Croatians making these extraordinary gains. It may just have been that I was a problem they no longer had the resources to deal with. Maybe it was my father. He'd never have said anything to me, even if it had been him, but I know he still had links in the region, that there would have been numbers he could have called.'

She felt that their time was almost up, tried to sneak a glance at her wristwatch. Then, a small but palpable shift in the atmosphere of the room.

'Benedict tells me that you saw your father in Palaiokastritsa. Or you thought you did.' His voice didn't change in any way that she could discern, but there was a certain coldness in it, something that set her on her guard.

'I didn't think I saw him. I know I did.'

'It would be strange, wouldn't it, for him to be here without telling you?'

'That's one word for it.'

'And Patricia Sinclair with him, the mother of our esteemed leader. Strange is, indeed, the word.'

They sat in silence for a few moments longer, then Drinkwater collected up his papers, nodded at her, and began to write something on his notepad.

VII.

THE SUMMER PASSED. Nina saw Benedict most days: after a period of slightly frantic energy in the wake of Humphrey's death, he had grown quieter and more distant. It was as if he were looking for Humphrey in dark corners at dinner or on evening walks, as if he expected to see a face over her shoulder, or high up in a window. They still swam together in the mornings. Boyd had started to swim with them and, on warmer days, Violet would come, too, executing a severe breaststroke, pushing out into the bay with her bathing cap on, her head high out of the water.

One morning at the end of July, a pod of dolphins came arrowing up the channel. Nina and Boyd were furthest out, first aware of them as flashes of silver moving beneath and around them. Then the dolphins were everywhere, leaping from the water, darting from one side to another, rippling spirits from another realm. Violet kept saying *Oh my goodness*, while Benedict just laughed and laughed, treading water and throwing his head back at the sheer, sublime beauty of these creatures. It changed the atmosphere on Spyland, that visitation; it built a bond between the four of them. Benedict seemed better, more whole, afterwards.

Nina saw more and more of Boyd. Partly, it was just that he was the only person even close to her age. She loved the older folk, but Boyd was still in touching distance of youth, mid-thirties, she reckoned, with an engaging boyishness about him, a shiny mischief in his blue eyes. He had asked to come on one of her coastal walks with her, and they'd set off early one morning, offering Angelos a packet of cigarettes to run them over to the main island before breakfast. The west coast path was the least well-maintained stretch, the rockiest and most prone to sudden, dizzying drop-offs where the land had collapsed into the sea.

They walked the west coast down from Liapades, along the cliff faces above green coves, through pine woods and olive groves, until they came to a small white monastery set on a hill above a beach. It reminded Nina of the larger complex at Palaiokastritsa, except that here there were no monks, no tourists, just a dozen or so scrawny-looking cats mewling in the shade. Boyd was only interested in the beach below, though. During his final interview with Clara Sinclair, in which the C had made it clear that he was being sent to Spyland for a period of *recuperation*, she'd passed him a slightly tatty black book: *Prospero's Cell* by Lawrence Durrell.

'She told me her mother used to hand it to people, a kind of black spot,' Boyd had said to Nina over dinner one evening. 'But Clara read it and thought it rather wonderful. She was consigning it to me not as a mark of exile, but as part of the healing process.' He'd lent the book to Nina – Clara was right, it was a thing of wonder, as if Durrell had looked into her heart and spelt out the truth of her growing love for Corfu.

Durrell described the beach here, at Mirtiotissa, as the most beautiful in the world. It was tricky to reach by car, only accessible by navigating the long, rutted track that led to the monastery. That was why the stretch of glowing golden sand, which was indeed glorious, was largely populated by locals, perhaps ten or twelve of them, their number further swollen by a group of young people – Scandinavians, Nina thought – playing a guitar at the far end where a spring broke from the rock and fell in a cataract into a small pool: a natural shower for the swimmers, the water a counter-rhythm for the guitar. Nina only noticed after looking down at the beach for a few moments that everyone on it was naked. There was something touching and ancient about the golden bodies on the golden sand, a scene from Homer.

She and Boyd made their way down stone steps between scrub oak and then out onto the beach. The sand was fine and warm, and two massive rocks stood protectively about fifteen feet offshore, causing the sea here to be very still and entirely translucent. Nearer them, under the lip of a rock – a *beetling* rock, Nina thought – was a small shack selling beer and sandwiches, overseen by a woman whose smile seemed as shining as the beach. She was dressed, but she was the only one.

Boyd was the first to strip off, sneaking a quick glance at Nina before walking down to the water, his bottom very white. There was a couple throwing a ball in the shallows – Boyd caught the ball, laughing, tossed it to the woman. He then dived in and turned back to look at Nina. She felt suddenly that everyone on the beach was waiting for her and so, before she had time to regret it, she pulled down her shorts, her pants, lifted her top over her head and stood there, feeling the breeze upon her, before walking down to the shore. Her body felt bathed in light, made of air, and it was as if the sun upon her burnt away any trace of shame or bashfulness at being so exposed. The water on her skin was like a benediction. As she immersed herself, the memory of dolphins came to her, and she felt that she and they were kin, these creatures with their glabrous beauty, their levity.

She swam out to where Boyd was treading water, then they went together past the rocks to where the sea rose and fell in deep blue swells, and they could feel the stretch of the Ionian all the way out to Sicily. Boyd saw something below, dived down, and came back up holding a shell of strange and intricate pinks and dimples. Afterwards, any shyness between them lost, they sat on the sand and ate sandwiches from the shack, drinking cans of Fix, feeling the sun on their bodies and talking about Durrell and Corfu. Boyd had his sunglasses on, and she could see herself in the mirrored lenses: her body stretched thin on the sand, the dark pile of her hair falling over her rucksack.

They were quiet for a while, looking at the shimmer of the sun on the dancing water, when Boyd spoke. 'I need you to know that it had nothing to do with me.'

'What do you mean?'

'Your father being here with Patricia.'

She felt her breath catch. 'How do you know about that?'

'Drinkwater told me. He's concerned.'

'About what?'

'You, them. There's something going on. I'm not so out of the loop that I don't pick up on these things. I thought about speaking to Clara, but seeing that Patricia is her mother, I'm not sure how . . . impartial she can be.'

Nina glanced sideways at him, but he was still staring out at the water. 'I'm lost, Boyd. Why would it have anything to do with you? I really have no idea what's going on.'

'Listen, I'm still trying to work my way through what this means.' Here he turned and looked at her. 'Your father is a ruthless man, you know that, right?'

'I . . .' She realised that she probably did know this. A memory came to her and she found, to her surprise, that she was relating it to Boyd, almost before she could stop herself. 'My father was always very kind to us when we were kids. Too kind, probably. You see through it, even very young, when we were four or five, the sense of someone trying too hard for you. He was bright and fun and always had a little present for us from some distant place, but you knew that he'd rather have been working. That he resented the wasted time. That's why he sent us away to school when we were seven.'

Boyd offered her a cigarette. She shook her head. An aeroplane, far above, dragged a streamer of vapour through the sky. Two of the Scandinavians further down the beach – boys with long limbs and pale hair – went and stood in the cataract together, pushing each other and laughing as the water fell down upon them. Nina loved that she could imagine them into antiquity, how their nakedness took away the mark of time.

Turning her mind to what had happened to her at school, she found herself hesitating. She didn't want to inflate it into something bigger than it was, something that had stained her. 'It was my sister first. Sadie. She was twelve, thirteen, the year before she went to Roedean. We were at a little prep school in Sussex. Full of the daughters of doctors and accountants. Incredibly sleepy, boring, even. But there was the English teacher, Mr Cooper. We all loved him. I'm not sure what the headmistress was thinking letting this handsome twenty-something come in and teach us *Romeo and Juliet*. Girls used to draw him in their exercise books, we used to watch from the dorm window when he went running – I can remember him outlined on the Downs.'

'You always had a good turn of phrase.' Boyd looked at her sideways. 'Hold that thought, I'll grab us another beer.' He strode down the beach, the white bottom now sandy, stopping to say something to a young Greek woman who laughed up at him. There was something tiger-like about the way he walked, the impression of a man who took pleasure in the flow of his limbs. Now he was back, opening a can of Fix and passing it to her, then cracking one for himself. 'Go on,' he said, 'tell me about Mr Cooper.'

Nina thought for a moment. 'It was worse for Sadie than for me. I don't say what he did was okay, at all. But with me it was just kissing, some touching and making me touch him. With Sadie I think it went much further. She was in love with him, of course.'

'And this Mr Cooper, was he over all the girls? Or did he just have a thing for the Woolf sisters?'

'It seems like it was only us. I mean there was an investigation when it all came out, but I don't think they ever found anyone else. Sadie didn't even know about me. She was furious when she learnt. Wouldn't speak to me for a year.'

'But you were ten years old?'

'Eleven, I think, at its height. Sadie thirteen by then, in her last term. The reason I'm telling you this, though, is that it showed a side of my father, or rather the two sides of him. Mr Cooper had written a letter to Sadie, all about how they'd stay in touch when she was at Roedean, how he loved her and wanted to marry her when she was old enough. Anyway, we were back for an exeat and my mother found this letter. My father was very calm about it, asking us both into his study to establish the facts of what had happened. Sadie cried a lot, but my father was so gentle, so careful with us both. He drove down that evening to see the headmistress.'

She remembered how hairy the back of his hands were, Mr Cooper, and how his breath always had the sour sweetness of wine, his lips a perpetual purple tinge to them. He wasn't *that* handsome really, not close up, Nina thought, but he had told her that Sadie loved him and it made her, Nina, feel sophisticated and debauched when she sneaked down to his study and let him kiss her and touch her, just as he was kissing and touching her older sister.

'Time passed. It was as if the whole thing had been forgotten. It was the summer holidays and we were about to go and see our grandmother in Croatia. Our mother never came with us on those trips – I think she and my grandmother didn't get on. It was after supper and we were in our rooms packing when my father called Sadie and me to his office. He was sitting there, his gold lamp with its green shade glowing. He had this strange expression on his face, and I looked down at the desk and saw dozens of photos. I could tell that Sadie had seen them too, because her mouth dropped open and she made this little sick noise. She ran out of the room, but I stood there, completely fascinated, looking at the mess someone had made of Mr Cooper.'

'Someone? It wasn't your dad then?'

'I'm not sure. Maybe. He was strong enough, and Mr Cooper was a bit of a weed. But I had the idea that he wanted things both ways – to be the sensible adult going through official channels to get the man sacked, but also . . . some physical revenge. Brutal. And he wanted us to see that doubleness. "Do please tell me if anyone ever touches you again."' She did a half-decent impression of her father.

Boyd finished his beer and extinguished his cigarette in the dregs. 'When I started in the Service, I reported to your father,' he said. 'He was terrifying – physically, but also this reputation for being so . . . withering. I really respected him. It's why, when he asked, I agreed to go and speak to you at Oxford, to give you the tap.'

'He requested it?'

'Take it as a compliment. He didn't ask for your sister.'

'I don't think Sadie is the type.'

'He was always so efficient, formidable, but it worries me that he's here, particularly with Patricia Sinclair. Usually he was only called in when there was dirty work to be done.'

'We never really know our parents, do we?' she said. 'Just the fictions they rehearsed for our sake – gentler, kinder, cleaner versions. We learned to lie by watching them lie.'

At this, Boyd turned onto his stomach, looking in her direction, although his eyes were hidden by the mirrored lenses. She was suddenly very still on the sand, her skin prickling under his gaze, as if her body, warm and open to the world, had become a book that he was reading. Boyd picked up a handful of sand and, very slowly, let it drop into her navel. It was like watching time, Nina thought, feeling the particular wonder of the warm sand falling upon her. When her navel was full, he moved in broad circles around it, leaving a trail of fine crystals that glimmered on her belly, that sat in the thatch of her pubic hair. He let a final trickle fall into the cleft between her legs. It was as if all her life had gathered itself on her skin. She realised that she had not been breathing, and took in a gulp of air.

Boyd turned away from her, looked down the beach, adjusted himself on his towel. Then, as if no time had passed at all, he stood and pulled on his shorts, his t-shirt. 'I had suspicions after Humphrey died, you know,' he said. 'An idea that something might be coming home to roost. Just be on your toes, lock your door at night, and tell me if you see anything else. It's not that I think your father would ever seek to harm you, but people tend to get hurt when he's around.'

Nina allowed herself to linger in the peculiar asymmetry of it: Boyd clothed, herself bare. His gaze, cool and searching, moved over her like a brushstroke, awakening a pleasant but almost forgotten sensation: the memory of inhabiting her body without hesitation, of delighting in its power, its capacity to draw a man's attention and hold it. Then she pulled on her clothes and they walked up the track to the road, where they'd catch a bus to Glyfada and then on to the Old Town. Nina felt as though she'd been granted some sort of grace: the light, the sun-drunk bodies, the sense of a place outside the currents of time. Thoughts swarmed in her head so that she hardly noticed when, once they were on the bus, Boyd reached out and took her hand in his. They stayed like that, still and silent, hot palms touching, until they pulled into the bus station and stepped out into the warm evening, when Boyd, carefully, like he was casting something precious into the breeze, let go of her hand.

VIII.

AUGUST WAS ALL aflame. It was as if they lived in the water. Salt rimed Nina's arms and belly, settled in the scar on her shoulder, on her cracked lips, under her skin even after she showered. It was too hot to walk, or even to think of going over to the main island. None of the buildings had air conditioning, but the villa had thick walls and large ceiling fans, and so they would congregate in the dining room after a day at the beach, drinking and playing cards and speaking about the heatwave. Like good English people everywhere, they loved to have weather to talk about.

'I haven't slept in weeks . . .'

'A pigeon fell down dead mid-flight . . .'

'I scalded myself on the balustrade . . .'

'Cooked and dressed before it hit the ground . . .'

'The revolution will start with fire . . .'

This last was from Hugo Poynton, who had not responded well to the heat and had begun to fly the flag of the Italian Communist Party from the window of his bedroom in the villa. Almost all of the residents of Vidos congregated in the dining room those dog day evenings. The inhabitants of the village would walk up together, Benedict and Harris in deep conversation, Violet hanging back, Deirdre and Struan silent, watchful. Nina and Boyd usually sat together, an island of youth amid the grey hair and walking sticks, the present moored in a sea of the past. She met the Pottinger brothers — both of them in their seventies, both in stiff tweed despite the heat, something military and pinched about them. Dennis Robertson was another she got to know in the heatwave: a small and good-natured Scot, perpetually beaming at the world around him. There were others — benevolent, grandmotherly types, intense-looking men in their sixties, old gents with walking frames and complicated hearing apparatuses — who were silent either out of choice or ill-health, but who nonetheless came here in the evenings to sit in the breeze that blew through the open windows of the dining room.

Nina and Boyd often played backgammon those evenings. The day on the beach together seemed to have loosened something between them. She discovered that she liked him, and could feel that he liked her. Once dinner had finished and the tables were cleared, games of cards would start up. As the sun dropped behind Corfu, lamps would be lit in the room and the air outside seemed to breathe in jasmine, tobacco flower, honeysuckle, lavender. Harris always had wine with him and would pour a glass for those that wanted it. Nina and Boyd would sit bent over their backgammon board, so close together their heads were almost touching, lost in the game. Edward Lane would often come and perch on the arm of Nina's chair, watching them play. He would sit still, his white hair tamed, his chin resting on his hand, looking intently at the board. Then, just as Nina was about to make a move, he'd give a quiet cough of protest, and she'd see the trap that Boyd had laid for her. Neither she nor Boyd — nor, indeed, Edward — acknowledged this help, but it brought some balance to their games, which were otherwise one-sided, Boyd having spent much of his time in captivity playing backgammon with his bored FARC guard.

The morning swim had become an institution and a necessity for the residents of Spyland, as much a part of the fabric of their lives as their games of bowls — more so, perhaps, after the decision had been made to stop watering the bowls green: as if in relief, the grass died almost overnight, and Nina looked from her window now onto a desert of brown and yellow. Edward Lane still occasionally went out to practise on the lawn, insisting that he wouldn't let a little heat stop him, carrying his leather bowling bag like a shield against the fury of the sun, his white legs hairlessly linking tight tennis shorts and socks pulled up very high.

Nina often saw him out on the parched lawn at night, rolling the bowls again and again, landing them in precisely the same place each time, as if aspiring to a kind of perfection here that he'd been unable to achieve in life. There was nobody to play with him, though, and so the only witnesses to his victories were Nina, silent and sleepless at her window, and the white rabbits who came out to search for any remaining nibbles of greenery in the moonlit night. He'd pack the bowls into his leather bag, give a little nod to the green, acknowledging a noble foe, then turn sharply on his heel and stride back up to the villa.

The mornings were a procession to the pontoon: all

of the inhabitants of the village came out to swim now, and many others made their way down from the villa to join them, so that Nina felt like a guide and a lifeguard at once, watching nervously as Edward Lane – in gaudy Bermuda shorts – or Dennis Robertson – in indecently skimpy Speedos – lowered themselves gingerly off the pontoon and into the water. Harris, it turned out, was a fine swimmer, while Struan and Deirdre never went in above their waists. If you had happened to be passing Vidos on a yacht that blazing August, and had looked over towards the gently curving beach that formed the island's eastern shore, you might have seen a strange flotilla moving through the sea.

At the front of them, like a figurehead on a ship, a dark-haired girl with wide eyes and a prominent nose. Behind her, a host of bobbing white heads, navigating the water with an eccentric combination of historical strokes. Benedict continued to wear his diving mask, like some spindly Cousteau ready to descend to the depths. Violet swam ramrod-straight, first one way, then another, like a periscope scanning for enemy submarines. Boyd had agreed with Nina that he should always swim at the back of the group, keeping watch for any of the older or less able swimmers wont to drift off with the current, or those who began slowly to lose momentum until they were stalled, sinking, and required towing back to land.

It was in the close heat of this August, a Sunday evening whose air lay heavy on the island, that Edward Lane went missing. Nina was the first to notice. He was not at dinner: absent from the arm of her chair, she lost badly that night. She didn't say anything: many of the residents preferred to take dinner in their rooms with the windows open, ceiling fans spilling salad leaves from their bowls. But Edward did not appear in his bright pink Bermuda shorts for the swim the next morning. Nina mentioned it to Mrs Samways when she went to collect her medication, and before long the search was on, with Costas and Angelos beating paths across the island, calling out *Mr Lane, Mr Lane*. Drinkwater ascertained that no boats had left for Corfu the previous day, while the only regular visitor – the provisions drop from the supermarket in the Old Town – wasn't scheduled until Tuesday morning.

It was a mystery, and it seemed to light a fuse in the minds of the residents, many of whom had spent their lives looking for people who did not wish to be found, or evading those who sought them. First the bullets that night on the hillside, then poor Humphrey, now Lane gone, a space between thoughts that no one wanted to fill with words.

In the dining room that evening, there was a febrile, speculative air. Costas and Angelos had gone to the Old Town to see if Edward had somehow made the crossing and resumed the search for his Cold War adversary. Inspector Metallinos had been informed, had said he would notify his officers. Now a posse surrounded Drinkwater – the Pottinger brothers shooting their cuffs and intoning darkly about *bad actors*, a white-haired lady whose name Nina had not learnt in time to be polite, suggesting that Lane had been abducted by the Sigurimi. Harris told anyone who'd listen that the *damned fool* had likely wandered off in search of *bloody Malkin*.

IX.

THE MORNING SWIM had morphed into a different thing for Nina: an act of compassion, a paying back of the kindness shown to her by the others on Spyland, by the island itself. But she no longer had her time alone in the ocean in the mornings, and she missed the cleansing solitude of those swims, the way she felt herself being rebuilt beneath the waves. So it was that she had begun coming down earlier and earlier, giving herself at first half an hour, then an hour, then sometimes two hours of swimming before she took up her role as nursemaid-cum-lifeguard. She had started leaving the villa before dawn, when the stars were still faintly visible in the sky, freckles of light on the face of the morning as it went from blue to silver to gold above her.

It was the day after Edward's disappearance. Nina had had a bad night – damp sheets, waking dreams, Edward's kindly face moving through dim subterranean light – and had come down particularly early, so that it was still quite dark when she slipped gently off the pontoon into the water. She backstroked out into the channel, looking up at Lyra and Cassiopeia, the Pleiades and Andromeda, and thinking of the countless others during older wars, bearing heavier weights, who'd drifted in this same sea, looked up at these same far-flung stars, and felt something lift in themselves.

Dawn came up over the Albanian mountains, light charging down the valleys and over the peaks and now illuminating Pantokrator on Corfu, the fortresses of the Old Town, the ruins on the heights of Vidos. On a whim, she decided to swim round the island: it was still a good few hours before anyone would appear on the pontoon, and she felt alive and buoyant. She set off with the current, heading south in the direction of Paxos, a languid front crawl, breathing every three strokes, first one side, then the other.

Boyd had come into her room last night. He had been drinking with Harris down in the village – she caught the scent of Mavromatis, the bittersweet kumquat on his breath when he sat down on her bed. She had been about to turn out her light – she was reading a novel from the bookshelf in the dining room. Mostly it was filled with Dick Francis and Wilbur Smith, but she'd come across a copy of another book by Lawrence Durrell, *Justine*, which she found enchanting and infuriating in equal measure. It was, she thought, as if her father had written a novel, the beauty at its heart concealed by a frantic need to impress.

'How are you getting on with it?' Boyd asked her, his words slurring a little. 'I read all of them when I was a teenager – the *Alexandria Quartet*. Life-changing, I think. Out of vogue now, of course, but they'll come back.'

'It's . . .' She searched for the word . . . 'Preening. He gets in the way of what I want to feel in the novel. If I compare it to, say, Penelope Lively, there's the same elegance, the same complexity, but with her it adds to what I'm feeling, with Durrell it interrupts it.'

He was silent for a while, long enough that she had begun to feel vaguely discomfited. It was still very hot, and she wore a vest and pants to sleep in. She pulled her sheet up to her chest.

'Are you all right?' she said with a half-smile.

He turned towards her, his bleak blue eyes watery in the light of her bedside lamp. 'I just feel . . . wretched,' he said, and his voice was so cracked and broken that she instinctively dropped the sheet and reached over to take his hand. Coming closer, the smell of alcohol was stronger, and she realised that he was more drunk than she'd imagined.

'What is it?' she asked. 'Come on, now, it can't be so bad.'

Another long silence. She thought about how time moves differently when you're drunk. She wondered if an alcoholic like Harris had a constantly altered perception of time, or if the strangeness of drunken time had merely come to seem like the normal flow of hours. Boyd looked at her. With the hand that wasn't holding hers, he reached out and touched the scar on her shoulder.

'I've only gone and fallen in love with you, haven't I?'

Nina laughed, because this was the only sensible thing to do, but then saw the look of hurt and humiliation on his face, the flush that came to his cheeks, and she made her face immediately serious.

'You don't love me, Boyd,' she said. 'You miss your wife, you're a red-blooded type, and I'm the only woman here under sixty. Now come on, let's get you to bed and hope that you don't remember this in the morning.'

She saw him look at her appraisingly as she stood up in her underwear and pulled on her dressing-gown. She looped his arm over her shoulder and lifted him from the bed. He was heavy. Unsteadily, they crossed to the door. Boyd's room was down the corridor and around a corner. As they turned, they almost ran into a frightened-looking Hugo Poynton. He, too, was in his bathrobe, his bald head ghostly in the dim light of the hallway.

'Have they found him yet?' he asked. 'Have they found Edward?'

Nina propped Boyd against the wall; he smiled woozily at her. 'Not yet,' she said. 'Now what are you doing about so late? Mrs Samways will have a fit if she catches you.' She took him gently by the elbow and led him back to his room. She left him sitting on his bed, looking lost and frightened, adrift in a world that no longer made sense to him. By the time she returned to Boyd, he'd slumped to the floor and was snoring and burbling drool. She nudged him with her foot, the nudge became a kick, and he woke with a grunt, looked up at her and grinned.

In his room she helped him take off his shoes, then laid him out on the bed, still fully dressed. The image of him as she'd first met him came to her mind. In the wood-panelled Oxford study of Professor Dolunc, Boyd had carried about him a whiff of danger and exoticism, but more than that, he was somehow the opposite of the cloistered, inward-turned world in which she found herself. Her friends – even Colin – were all deeply smitten with Oxford, with the idea that they looked through one rare, sharp eye. They had spent their young lives specialising and specialising until here they were: working for years, decades, some of them, potentially, on the letter 's' in Wordsworth's *The Prelude*, or the impact of humidity on the oxidation rate of tertiary amines, or how changes in horseshoe design influenced the outcomes of twelfth-century English cavalry movements. She had begun to long for the broadness of reality, for danger and dirty places. Boyd, notwithstanding the sharp suit and shined shoes, seemed to offer that.

In his bedroom, five years later, it appeared that he

was now asleep, and so she looked down at him – unchanged now he had gained back the weight lost in the course of his breakdown, his skin burnished by the summer, his hair longer than when he'd arrived. She bent to place a kiss on his freckled forehead.

'You need to be careful,' he said.

'What's that?'

He reached up now, pulled her towards him. His breath was hot in her ear. 'There are bad people at the Office. People who care more about their ambitions than about their country, than about you. I tried to protect you, Nina, I really did. If you go back, you need to be on your guard.'

'Which bad people? What are you talking about?'

'Just be careful. Don't trust anyone. Maybe not even here. I'm scared for you. I'm scared for myself.' He put his arms around her, drew her down until she was almost lying on top of him, placed a kiss on her cheek, then on her mouth. She let him, tasting his breath, which was sweet as Mr Cooper's had been sweet all those years earlier, and she thought how the men in her life were all so similar, variations on a theme, but then maybe that was just because they were men. His tongue was a slippery mollusc in her mouth, the sweet rankness of his breath overpowering. He reached a damp hand up inside her dressing-gown, fumbling a little with the muddled folds of her vest and then his hand was on her breast. She felt very distant through all of this, as if she were watching it happen from above, and when his other hand moved down inside her pants, she let it.

Her swim had now taken her to the southern tip of Vidos, near to where, only nine months ago, but seeming like a lifetime, she and Benedict had hidden in a cave from their armed pursuer – whether he was one of those Boyd had warned her about, or merely a poacher, she still wasn't sure. Now she turned towards the Old Town, very close across the water, with the Old Fort and the university, the Palace of St Michael and St George and all the ramshackle loveliness of the place lit up in the golden dawn. There were a few people already down swimming in Faliraki, the small beach beneath the town walls. They seemed close enough to touch as Nina watched them, treading water, and yet also distant, characters in a Mediterranean movie by Antonioni, the sort of thing Colin used to make her watch at the weekend, during which she'd fall asleep on the sofa.

Just then, a man with black hair and square shoulders took a running leap and dived, there below the fort, into sparkling water, and she thought again that it was her father. He swam a great distance beneath the surface, coming up by the rocks at the base of the fort, and she couldn't make out his face amid the gentle rise and fall of the water. She shook her head and swam on.

The west side of Vidos was steep and rocky, a few abandoned fishermen's huts falling quietly apart, the restaurant with its Fix beer bunting. Nina swam past, picking up her pace as the current worked against her, although the flow was softened by the curve of Corfu's coastline. She reached the northern tip of Vidos, could see the bare rock of the prison island, Lazaretto, off towards the mainland. She thought of the writer who'd said that Disneyland only existed to persuade Americans that the rest of their lives were real. Perhaps Lazaretto was there, with its memories of prisoners of war and, before that, lonely Corfiots suffering their way through leprosy or the plague, to persuade the inhabitants of Vidos that they were free.

She picked up her pace, feeling as if she were almost riding on top of the water, rather than through it, her mind emptying as she moved: no thoughts of her father, of Boyd or the past. She was only here, in the sea, coming now to where the rocks built up into a cliff and there, above her, the villa. The ivy had all died back over the summer, leaving ghostly patterns on the pale pink stucco. The window of the dining room was open and she saw, for a moment, before he drew back into the shadows, Drinkwater standing there, looking down at her.

She carried on swimming: below her were rocks jewelled with urchins, fish moving in fated little jags, swifter than her eyes were able to follow. She crested the northern corner of the island and looked down the coast towards the beach, where people gathered along the pontoon. They were waving gesturing down into the water. She heard Benedict's voice, high and desperate over the others. She lengthened her stroke. It had taken her longer than she had expected; she felt a prod of guilt and then chided herself for it, knowing they could wait for her, that her swim this morning had been an act of grace. She moved closer to the pontoon and could see that Harris and Violet were in the water, wearing goggles, looking down. She waved to them, then pulled faster, showing off a little, aware of her own elegance.

Time moved very slowly as she came towards them, the rocks shelving down and then up again, the urchins pronging towards the light. Below her, Edward was lying, as if terribly relaxed, on a slab of rock, just where the light began to dissipate and blur. There was a serene look on his face; his hair seaweeding in the currents; around his neck, his bowling bag had been tied, weighing him down. He looked so calm, so untroubled, that Nina's first impulse was to laugh. Then she looked up and saw Harris and Violet in the water, the expressions on the faces of Benedict and the others on the pontoon, which she had not been able to read at first, but which she now saw as horror.

She took a deep breath and dived down, feeling her ears pop, holding her nose and blowing out until the throbbing pressure lifted. She was next to Edward almost before she knew it, five, perhaps seven metres below the surface of the water, and she felt like staying there for a while, in the peace of the depths, before she had to face the reality of Edward, her neighbour, her friend, lying here in the murky light. She reached out and, not yet feeling the need to breathe, but rather with the calmness of one who could live down here for a lifetime given the chance, lifted the bowling bag from around his neck. It was heavy, and when she let go it fell first onto the slab of rock upon which Edward was lying, and then, as if conveyed by some invisible oceanic hand, rolled off the edge and down into the deep nothing that stretched all about them. She looked down at Edward, his head with its beetling eyebrows, his eyes wide-open and astonished. A tiny stream of bubbles emerged from his nose. She hooked her arms around him and kicked them both off, up towards the surface, towards an explanation.

PART 4

Oxford, May 1948

I.

His final year of university and Benedict was running. He had started to do this in the mornings, rising before the rest of the house was awake, stepping out into the cool light, his plimsolls loud on the gravel and then soft on the grass of the orchard as he made his way into the fields.

The atmosphere of the house was stimulating and intense, but he knew it could overwhelm him if he were not able to escape like this. He was also aware that he was heading towards a life in which he would be tested, and his body lacked the animal confidence of Humphrey and Arkady. He felt like a child next to them.

But when he was running in the rising light of morning – and now it was approaching eight months that he had been following this same route, sending himself out even if the previous night had been soaked in alcohol – he could feel himself growing. A wild joy gripped him as he crested the hill and looked down over rolling Oxfordshire, the spires of the city just visible through the mist.

He picked up his pace as he went down into the valley and felt as though he were flying, his feet scarcely touching the ground, skylarks loud in the high morning air, a bevy of grouse roused to panic when he reached the bottom of the hill and came to Youlbury Pool. Mist rose from the water, ducks muttered, a willow reached down and stirred the surface with its branches.

Benedict thought of Oxford as something half lost already, a place he'd passed through like man on a train. The months had vanished: reading in the Radcliffe Camera in shafts of golden afternoon light, magnolia petals drifting across quadrangle lawns, the hush before evensong. Long nights of argument and wine, of Communism recast as charm. He and Humphrey had slipped into each other's lives and out again, as if trialling versions of love they might one day acknowledge. There had been Venice in winter, Berlin in spring. And, once or twice, there had been Philby – smiling across a dark table at the Turf, too poised, too knowing. Even then, he had felt less like a man than a warning. Benedict's studies had been challenging, inspiring; he missed this academic version of himself even as he was still living it.

For their final year they had taken a house in Boars Hill – Patricia's find, a draughty mock-Tudor tucked behind Scots pines. Too big, too solemn, but perfectly removed. From the upper windows, Oxford looked like a place they'd already begun to leave behind: towers and spires ghostly in the mist. Patricia was the first to name the house: 'the antechamber', she called it. Not quite an ending, but not home either. A place to wait, elegantly, for the world to begin.

Benedict had had no furniture of his own, so he and Humphrey went to an antiques shop in Summertown and bought a bed and dresser, a bookshelf and bedside table, which were then loaded into a pantechnicon and driven up to Boars Hill.

Benedict's room was at the top of the house, in the eaves, a cosy, dusty place, with a rug on the floorboards and a window that looked out over the fields. Most nights, Humphrey slept up there with him.

Benedict ran on, not for escape now but for proof – that he was becoming something solid, capable. In the motion, there was a gathering – a sense of strength accruing day by day, almost unnoticed. As if, in these quiet mornings, he was at last becoming the man he had always half-imagined he would be.

II.

LUNCH AT THE Randolph on a bright early summer day. The beef Wellington disposed of, the second bottle of claret almost gone. Philby, who came to see them whenever he was back in the UK, said, as if it had only just occurred to him, that there was someone he wanted Benedict to meet.

They went through to the bar, everything a little fuzzy and lurching to Benedict, who watched Philby's consumption of alcohol with a mixture of admiration and terror, never trying to match it, but merely to follow in its wake. There was a young man in tweed sitting at the bar: blond hair falling about his face, a face that was, as he turned towards them, radiant. He was drinking water, Benedict noticed.

'This is Edward Lane,' Philby said, giving a strange little bow. 'We rather hope that he'll be joining the

Service once he's finished here. I thought, Benedict, that you might take an interest in him.'

Lane was studying history. Benedict had heard his name bandied about as one of the brightest students in the year below, that particular sheen that attached to the coming together of good breeding and academic excellence in young men and women at Oxford. Benedict knew, having one but not the other, the value of each.

Lane's father was in the House of Lords, his family line long and storied. He was also, it was impossible to ignore, very handsome. They sat there at the bar for the afternoon and into the evening, long after Philby had left to catch his train. Benedict persuaded Lane to move from water to beer, and thence to a bottle of wine. They retreated into a corner of the bar and continued their conversation.

Whether it was the alcohol or the fact of Philby having brought them together, Benedict found that he spoke to Lane with unusual ease. Lane confessed that Philby had praised Benedict extensively, had urged him to befriend the older boy.

They had not slept together that first evening, but they had gone for dinner at Christ Church, Lane's college, and then to his room. Benedict had sensed something in the air between them, a complicated stew of feelings that mixed the younger man's admiration for one only, in the grand scheme of things, marginally further along the path to a career in the Service, with Benedict's own sense that whatever he might have with Humphrey, it was messily inchoate, not something that bound him to anything chummily bourgeois.

So it was that, after a second supper in Christ Church, and several glasses of brandy, they had found themselves sitting very closely together on Edward's bed, where it had seemed the obvious thing to begin wrestling, then kissing, and then it was morning and pale light was coming in through open curtains. Benedict placed a soft kiss on Edward's cheek and slunk out through the silent quadrangle and onto a bus for Boars Hill.

When he got home, no one was awake, and so he crept carefully up the stairs to his room.

III.

THEN OXFORD WAS over and they were scattered to the winds. Benedict was the first to go. Over dinner at the Reform Club, Philby had told him he would be sent to Corfu, where he'd be tasked with helping to better the fortunes of Operation Valuable. This project to destabilise Enver Hoxha's Albania in collaboration with the newly formed CIA had already become something of a Service joke, lurching from catastrophe to catastrophe.

'Honestly,' Philby told him under his breath, 'it needs to continue that way. The key is to do just enough to make sure the operation fails, but never make it obvious that you are out to bugger it.'

Humphrey was sent to Cairo to source agents within the Free Officers movement, a group within the army whose power was growing daily under the aegis of a bright young general, Gamal Abdel Nasser.

Humphrey was ostensibly a cultural attaché in the embassy, charged with implementing a series of British Council initiatives throughout the country. His life, so he wrote to Benedict a few months later, was a dreary one, learning Arabic in the morning and then smoking in glum teahouses and gloomy salons, as first one minor officer then another complained to him about the British presence, the spendthrift fop on the throne and the increasing discontent of the *fellaheen*.

Harris was in Finland, listening to intercepted phone calls over the border, and freezing, he told Benedict in a telegram. There was ice on the inside of his windows and could Benedict please send him some decent wine? Patricia was going to Cambridge to study Russian for six months: she would then be sent to Moscow, the greatest prize for any spy. Arkady had returned to Russia where, Benedict assumed, he would wait for Patricia. They were in love, Benedict supposed, and the separation would be difficult for them.

Only Violet would stay in London, working in SIGINT, writing and decoding messages for agents in the field, arranging dead drops in the dusty corners of an Empire that was showing the first signs of crumbling, or within the increasingly muscular and self-confident Soviet Bloc, where agents who had once acted with impunity now found themselves being watched.

IV.

BENEDICT TOOK THE train across Europe to Venice again, feeling he was haunting the steps of his younger self. In Venice, he boarded a ship, watching *La Serenissima* fade into the April dusk, the snow-capped Dolomites dimly visible behind the spires and domes of the city.

He stayed on deck for a long time, looking out into

the deepening dark, the occasional glimmer of an Italian city somewhere off the starboard bow of the ferry. He went down to his cabin just after midnight and slept as the boat rolled across the Adriatic.

He stayed late in bed and the sun was high over an empty sea when he went back out on deck. He read and wrote in his journal for much of the day, feeling the pitch and roll of the ocean beneath, until, as the last rays of light stretched over the water, Corfu rose like a dream to the east.

He spent the night in a hotel overlooking the Spianada, astonished to see a cricket pitch there, as if sliced up and carried from Marlow like a Victoria sponge. He wasn't much of an athlete, in truth, but cricket always seemed to him the most noble and elegant thing, more a folk ritual than a sport. He was delighted when, on that first day in Corfu, he sat waiting for Philby in a café on the Liston and players began to congregate on the square in immaculate whites. They started play and Benedict found himself so transfixed that he didn't notice Philby sitting down opposite him.

'A taste of home,' Philby said.

Benedict came out of his reverie with a start. 'Kim! Would you like a coffee?' Philby inspected his watch. 'Something stronger. It's lunchtime, after all, and I'm celebrating.' He signalled to the waiter, who brought over a cold jug of retsina and two glasses. 'I've just heard that I'm to be heading up our Washington office. The absolute beating heart.'

'That's wonderful,' Benedict said.

'It's going to change everything. They are hopping with delight in Moscow.'

'I don't doubt it.' What Benedict found harder to understand was how Philby managed to rise through MI6 while at the same time undermining its activities and ensuring that its most significant project to date – Valuable – was a byword for failure.

'It turns out that working with the CIA has its benefits,' Philby went on. 'I'm a man who gets things done, or so they seem to believe. Allan Dulles and Frank Wisner requested me by name, would you believe it? All of this means, of course, that you arrive at the perfect moment. Oh, good shot!' A ball landed with a thunk on the cobbles not far away from them. Philby rose, picked it up and returned it fast and low to the wicketkeeper.

'When will I be going out to the island?'

'To Vidos? Tomorrow. You should be down at the port at nine sharp. Tonight, I want to introduce you to your handler here, Oleg Petrushkin. We'll take you through the dead drop procedure, show you how to get in touch with Oleg urgently, should you need to.' A sudden wistful note in Philby's voice. 'I'm going to miss it here. It's been heavenly.'

Petrushkin, it turned out, was a large and melancholy man who lived in a drab and sparsely furnished apartment on Alexandras Avenue in the new part of Corfu Town, over towards the airport.

Under an unshaded bulb, they sat and drank a glass of warm vodka with him. Other than the small table and chairs in the centre of the room, and a cranky-looking wireless transmitter in one corner, the apartment was bare.

'He'll likely not last long here,' Philby said as they made their way back towards town. 'Handlers have a relatively short shelf life. Moscow tends to get a little twitchy after someone's been in place for a year or so.'

'He'll be moved on?'

'Or recalled and sent east. Especially if there's the least suspicion he's grown accustomed to all the Western decadence, the cocktails and, you know, the peace of mind.'

Benedict said goodbye to Philby outside the Cavalieri Hotel, where the older man was staying. They stood under a streetlamp in the mild spring night, swifts shrieking in the air high above. Philby was a little drunk, as he had been, Benedict realised, for most of the time they had spent together. Philby put his hands on Benedict's shoulders.

'It gives me great comfort that you should be here to carry on my work,' he said. 'When Arkady and I thought of recruiting from Oxford, I could scarcely have hoped for such a luminous collection of young people.'

He gave Benedict's shoulders a tipsy little shove on each important word. 'Patricia is marvellous, of course, but it's you I have the greatest hope for, Benedict. You will need to make some bloody difficult decisions out here, but you'll do so knowing what a vital role you are playing in the building of a more equal world. Good luck, and when next we meet, I expect us to be much closer to a final victory.'

V.

When Benedict went back to England for his Christmas leave, he didn't see anyone save his mother: they sat in the house in Marlow in brooding silence.

Snow fell on the street outside, on the carol singers going from house to house, on the children playing with their new bicycles. It fell in flurries and gusts, sweeping along the high street, where Benedict had worked in the paper shop for a summer before Oxford. It fell on the red brick and flint of Sir William Borlase, the grammar school he'd attended, and on the fast-flowing waters of the Thames where he'd rowed and fished with his father.

Snow fell on Violet, too, who had gone to Finland to spend Christmas with Harris. She had flown into Helsinki and he'd met her at the airport. She'd brought a case of wine with her, which they began to drink on the train that took them north and eastwards, through snowfields, small towns, distant hills, all silver and black in the Arctic moonlight.

They finished their second bottle on the bus from the station to Kemijärvi, the town by a lake where Harris lived. His house was low and wooden, hidden away in a thicket of trees by the frozen lake. The roof was covered in a layer of peat, the rooms low and cosy.

Violet didn't notice the radio mast in the garden, the bank of equipment on one side of the drawing room. She only saw the fire that Harris's housekeeper had lit in the grate, the little woodburning stove in the bedroom, and the bed, into which she dragged Harris by his tie, and from which neither of them emerged until late the next morning.

Snow fell outside the window of the Radcliffe Infirmary, coming down in heavy flurries on the abandoned observatory, above which a little of the day's weak light still lingered. Patricia stood at the window and watched the snow, dreaming ahead to a time in which this chapter of her life was over.

No one was with her. She had no time for kind midwives or the conversation of the other mothers on the ward. She was glad to be having the child, but only because of Arkady, who had sent her a card showing a robust-looking young woman standing proudly by a sheaf of wheat. Вместе к победе, it said on the front – 'Together to Victory' – while on the inside, it read Плоды труда принадлежат нам всем – 'The fruits of labour belong to us all'.

Patricia was deeply frustrated by the delay to her plans. She had kept the pregnancy from everyone in Cambridge, then feigned illness just before she was due to leave for Moscow and went back to the house in Boars Hill. She telephoned her mother in Venice a week before the baby was due, outlined the situation in clipped, unsentimental terms, told her that she would be bringing the child out to the Palazzo as soon as she was on her feet. Her mother would look after it until it could be sent to school. Patricia would come to Venice and get it settled. Then she had work to do.

She peered down at the baby – a girl, it transpired, whom she had named Clara after Clara Zetkin, whose approach to Marxism she much admired. Rather sweet, if you liked that kind of thing. The Cause was calling, though, and she looked forward to leaving Clara with her mother in the same way that, as a child, she had looked forward to the end of the holidays and the beginning of the new school term. The sense of putting foolish things behind her, of getting on with the job in hand.

Only Humphrey didn't have snow. He had ash instead, falling like snow through the smudged Cairo air. They were burning rubbish in the Coptic Quarter to the west and the wind, coming from that direction, blew clouds of smoke and ash over Zamalek, where he now sat at a wrought-iron table, smoking in the sun.

He was on his third Bloody Mary, and when one of the white-suited waiters passed by, he ordered another.

He was at the home of Osborne Phipps, the MI5 man in Cairo, who out of Christian spirit rather than friendship had invited Humphrey to spend Christmas at his villa. There were an indefinite number of children – Humphrey thought perhaps four – that appeared to belong to Phipps. They were being chased around the garden by Mrs Phipps, a flushed, hectic-looking woman who reminded Humphrey of his own mother, and a number of other assorted staff – ayahs and houseboys and the like. Phipps had gone inside some time ago, complaining of a headache. It was not yet lunchtime.

You wouldn't know it to look at him, but Humphrey was basking in a rare moment of professional success. He had befriended an enigmatic figure at the Greek Club in Alexandria, a man who called himself Prince Mehmed and wore the *qeleshe* hat of an Albanian. The Prince was the aide-de-camp of King Zog of Albania, who was living in exile in the court of his friend Farouk, the louche and ineffective King of Egypt.

The Prince, who was a few years older than Humphrey, had been unusually forthcoming about Farouk's increasingly tenuous position on the throne. King Zog had spies within the Free Officers who brought information of an imminent move to foment a revolution. Humphrey had reported this back to London, where the news was received with a deal of excitement and interest. He had, of course, then reported at greater length and in more specific detail to Moscow.

Now, though, Humphrey lifted both of his glasses as a small boy came careening into the table, pursued by a larger boy waving a cork-rifle and making peow-peow noises. The ash continued to fall. Humphrey drained one drink and started on another. The children, tireless, ran on.

VI.

BENEDICT TRIED AT first to think of the Pixies as names on pieces of paper.

There seemed to be a near-endless stream of young and idealistic Albanians willing to leave their exile in Greece or Italy. They volunteered by the dozen to come and be thrown to the wolves of Hoxha's Sigurimi. And no matter how badly the missions went, the horror stories of torture and summary execution, of terrible retributions on the Pixies' families, they kept coming.

It was Willard Bunce, the CIA man on Vidos, who'd christened them Pixies, Benedict presumed for the same reason that he focused on their names. It was a way of caring less when they died. The Albanians were small, certainly, but they looked more like the dwarves – the *zwergs* – from Wagner: sturdy, ruggedly handsome, ingenious folk. There was no questioning their bravery, but every time a group of them was dropped into the hills of their homeland, or ferried across the channel to Sarandë – so close here they could practically swim – they were swiftly rounded up and killed by the Sigurimi.

This, of course, was because Philby, via a dead drop in the Old Fort, had conveyed the details of every mission to Petrushkin, who made sure that the secret police knew when and where the Pixies would land. It had led to the Sigurimi developing a reputation far beyond their skills or numbers.

'I've met them,' Philby had told Benedict. 'You couldn't imagine a less impressive collection of brutes and drunkards. Vicious, though – I'll give them that.' Now Benedict was the traitor, and no matter how many times he told himself that his actions were all in the service of Marxism, for the children and grandchildren he couldn't quite yet imagine, he felt a kind of taint in the air around him, the sense that he had taken a terrible wrong turn in life.

It was now September and Bunce was under pressure from Washington to get results. There had been six missions since Benedict had arrived on the island, all of them failures. The Pixies would come and stay at the villa for the week beforehand: it was Benedict's job to make sure they understood how to work their wireless transmitters, how to fire their pistols and, in the event of capture, the correct way to bite down on the cyanide capsules with which they were all provided.

Benedict did not know what it was to die of cyanide poisoning, but he liked to imagine that it was swift and painless, like falling asleep after one drink too many.

'Dulles says we're to go up with them this time,' Bunce told him over breakfast. They ate in the entrance hall of the villa, where five rusting wrought-iron tables had been dragged in from the terrace outside. 'He wants to make sure the pilots aren't fucking with us. Thinks they could be in the pay of the Sigurimi, dropping the Pixies into their laps.'

VII.

THE NEXT NIGHT, Benedict found himself sitting with Bunce and the Pixies in the rattling hull of a Dakota, idling on the tarmac at Corfu airport. He'd taken a particular shine to this group of Pixies – they were very young, younger than him, and full of idealism and braggadocio. One of them, Besian, was a priest, the leader of a Christian cult in the Accursed Mountains, in Albania's rugged north. He was tall and wiry and had a small blue cross tattooed beneath his right eye.

Benedict had had a drink with them the night before, and Besian, forgoing the beer and sipping his water daintily, had told him about the Sigurimi raid on the chapel in which his congregation practised. He described the shadowy figures arriving during the saying of Midnight Mass, the broken windows, screams, the men placed in shackles, the women horribly misused. Several of his flock had been shot dead. He had watched them torch the chapel. All his books, his memories. He, Besian, had finally escaped, leaping into a river from a moving train. Now he wanted only revenge: his dark eyes burned with it.

Another Pixie, Dritan, from Korçë, was a musician. He had brought his guitar and, just before they turned in for the night, he played it slowly. The other Pixies all seemed to know the song, and they took it in turn to sing sad verses, first Dritan, then Besian, then a student named Arjan and a former soldier called Llesh. They had joined together for the chorus, which Benedict was able to follow, more or less, save the odd word of dialect.

It spoke of longing for the homeland, for the high

mountain passes, for the clear waters of the Vjosa. For the love that waits for them at home in the hills. They finished the song and raised their glasses to Benedict. In the silence that followed their cheers, Benedict fancied that he could hear their hearts beating.

Then, just before he left, Besian asked if he could take a picture of them all together. 'I will develop it when we return,' he said, arranging his Kodak Brownie on the mantelpiece and fixing a cable release mechanism to it, so that he was able to appear in the shot himself. 'You will keep the camera for me, Lieutenant Pierce, for when we meet again.'

'Yes, yes, of course,' Benedict said, attempting a smile.

'I feel that we will meet again, you know,' the priest said, those dark eyes very wide, very trusting.

Benedict couldn't sleep that night: in his mind was the dark shape of the dead drop box in the wall by the Old Fort, the knowledge that his actions would lead directly to the deaths of these men. They would be terrified, they would cry out for their mothers, or some would feign courage, and this was worse. Besian would call on his vengeful God, would offer prayers for the souls of his fellow Pixies. He would be noble, whatever indignities he was subjected to.

They were better men now than he would ever be, Benedict knew this, and he felt judged and wretched, conscious of how far he'd strayed from the image of the man he'd aspired to be. He often pictured his father at times like this, the quaint certainty of his patriotism, the clarity with which he'd gone to die.

Now the engines of the Dakota rose in pitch and the aeroplane began to move forward across the tarmac. He saw the four young men, who were lined up across from him and Bunce. Besian had swapped his priest's robes for khakis. They looked like children dressing up as soldiers, their parachutes strapped to their backs, their field jackets slightly too big for them, guns like toys. He caught Besian's dark eyes, saw the cross on his face twitching slightly, and forced himself to smile.

Then, with a roar and a lurch, the plane was airborne, and Benedict looked down through the porthole to see the lights of the Old Town and the dim shape of Vidos, and then darkness. There was turbulence over the channel and he felt his stomach turn over, a jag of fear as the plane bounced first one way, then another.

He went up to the cockpit, where the pilot, another Albanian, was peering down through the windscreen. 'That's Sarandë,' he said, 'and up there Gjirokastër.' Benedict could make out a scattering of lights in the dark hills ahead. 'We follow the mountains; the drop site is just south of Elbasan.'

It seemed only a matter of minutes before they were preparing to open the jump door at the rear of the plane. Benedict and Bunce strapped themselves into their seats. The Pixies checked their gear, shouting over the engines, slapping each other on the back. Bunce yelled forward to the pilot and, with a clang, the hatch swung open. Then, like leaves in a gale, the boys drifted out into the night, passing one by one through the jump door and tumbling into the ravening darkness.

Besian was the last to go, his eyes meeting Benedict's before he jumped, and Benedict couldn't help but read something: accusation, acceptance, even forgiveness, in those large, dark eyes, tear-filled in the rushing of the wind.

Then they were gone, and Bunce and Benedict were very silent on the way back. That silence pursued them over the coming days: there was no contact from the Pixies, they did not respond to coded attempts to contact them. The MI6 agent in Tirana with whom they were due to rendezvous on the Friday night reported that they had not appeared. He tried three more times to make contact with them, then, fearing that his own position might be compromised, he headed back into the safety of Tirana's endless slums.

A week later, Benedict did something he had never done before: he left a note in the dead drop box asking for information on what had happened to the last Operation Valuable mission.

Petrushkin's response was brief and unsentimental: *Intercepted immediately. Questioned. Terminated.*

Benedict took the film to be developed in a pharmacy in the Old Town. He kept that picture with him for many years: five young men, one of them Judas. It was Besian who stayed with him: the eyes, the tattooed cross, the sense of a vast and all-encompassing love that emanated from him as he threw himself into the air.

PART 5

Corfu, September 1996

I.

IT WAS ALL anyone could talk about: Clara Sinclair was coming to the island. Even Nina felt a jolt of excitement when she heard that the C herself would be visiting. The whole idea of Spyland was that people were sent here to be forgotten, to be expunged from record. It had taken the death of not one but two once-lauded agents to bring the place onto the agenda of the most important figure in the Office. Even Inspector Metallinos was excited. He'd been on Vidos most days since they'd found the body. It seemed that Lane had been badly beaten prior to drowning: his ribs were broken and his skull shattered.

'It was a vicious attack,' Metallinos had told Nina. 'The work of someone who didn't just want to kill him, they wanted to punish him, too.' The thought that Lane had suffered before he died made her heart ache.

'If you think Humphrey was murdered, does this make it – what? – a serial killer? Should we be scared?' They were sitting in the dining room again. Someone had procured Metallinos an ashtray.

'It's possible,' he said, shrugging his shoulders. 'Quite possible. I certainly wouldn't be sleeping soundly, were I here.'

'Are you not here?' Benedict said.

'Only for the present moment,' the inspector replied.

'Well, I haven't slept soundly for as long as I can remember,' Nina said, tapping one of his cigarettes from its soft packet. 'I'm not sure many here are good sleepers. Harris, perhaps, but then he has a deal of help.'

Metallinos leant across to light her cigarette. 'It seems the British government is concerned,' he said. 'In Athens, they speak of your Chief a great deal. Some say good things, some not so good, but they talk about her. She will be your next foreign secretary, I hear, or maybe the prime minister.'

'She's an impressive woman.'

'She is coming here to reassure you?'

'Or to make sure that the story doesn't get any further.'

'You British love your secrets.'

A few days later, Nina and Benedict were having a post-swim cup of tea with Violet. Harris was still in bed, his snores occasionally audible from the back of the cottage. There was a jangling in the air, even here, because it was the day before the C arrived. Vidos felt, Nina imagined, as Caribbean islands must have felt before a visit from the Queen.

'One thing I don't understand,' Nina said, dipping a biscuit in her tea, 'is how come she's Clara Sinclair? Patricia Sinclair didn't marry, right? You couldn't be in the Service if you had a husband.' She saw a look pass between Benedict and Violet, of warning or worry, she couldn't tell. 'So do people know who Clara's father is? And if they don't, isn't that something they'd want to know of a C? Something pretty important from a national security perspective.'

Violet looked meaningfully again at Benedict, who began to speak through a little cough. 'There is a degree of mystery when it comes to Clara. She is . . . an enigma.'

'I would imagine,' Violet picked up the thread now, 'that Patricia herself knows, although, honestly, it's quite possible that she does not.'

'I believe that those at the top do know,' Benedict said, 'and of course Patricia herself was fairly near the summit for long enough that she may have found some form of accommodation with the top brass.'

They heard Harris stirring in the room at the back, the clearing of his throat, a groan.

'I worked for Clara for almost a year,' Nina said. 'She was amazing. Maybe all your bosses are at that age, but she had this astonishing way of making you feel like your career was the only thing that mattered to her. I'm not sure that I had a real sense of duty until then. I would have died for her, quite literally.' She felt the truth of this once she said it, aware suddenly of the role her loyalty to Clara had played in the risks she had taken, the various missions whose unravelling had led to her being marooned here with the Office's failed and forgotten.

II.

NINA FELT THE atmosphere change when Clara Sinclair stepped into the dining room. Almost everyone was here: the inhabitants of the village, the villa, the assorted staff.

Mrs Samways looking avid, Drinkwater looking nervous. Even Metallinos was there, standing with Angelos at the back of the room. He looked like a crow, Nina thought, in his black suit, dark hair swept back, winging slightly above his ears. Then Nina, like the other residents, turned to look towards the woman herself. Sinclair had aged – even she. It had been two years since Nina had last seen her, five since she'd worked for her directly. She was, Nina reckoned, not yet fifty, but there were elegant streaks of grey in her hair. She wore a navy trouser suit and high heels. She looked like she had just stepped from a meeting in Whitehall.

Clara Sinclair had arrived with her own security detail: two slightly bored-looking men, clearly ex-services, who now stood in one corner of the dining room, patches of sweat darkening their shirts. Nina couldn't imagine Clara sweating. Drinkwater stood beside her, looking uncharacteristically anxious. He kept smoothing his moustache with his thumb and forefinger. He cleared his throat and the room was silent.

'Ah,' he said, 'Our Chief, Clara Sinclair. Some of you will have worked with her, some of you will have worked with her mother.' Here he let out a nervous little laugh. 'Many of you will know why she is here. To – ah – answer questions and hopefully to quell any rumours that might be going round after the . . . the tragedies we have suffered these past months.'

Clara went to stand with her back to the windows, framed behind by the sea and the mountains. Nina couldn't help but think of the woman who, until recently, had been prime minister. Even though that role was now filled by someone else, someone greyer and kinder, Clara had begun to dress like the prime minister: the square shoulders, the wide lapels of her jacket, the brooch. She was almost unrecognisable as the woman Nina had worked for, her eyes harder, her lipsticked mouth set firm, everything about her radiating power. Nina caught her eyes for a moment, expecting some spark of recognition, a smile, even. But Clara moved past Nina, her gaze resting instead on Benedict for a moment, before she began to speak.

'I thought it was important for me to come here *personally*,' she said, and even her voice had changed, Nina thought, the accentuation of certain words seeming to address Parliament, rather than the dining room of a home for the elderly and unhinged. 'I was so *very* sorry to hear of the deaths of two of our most celebrated colleagues. I can only imagine how *difficult* this period has been for you all. I remember the very sad series of deaths here following the Fall. We have always wanted this to be a place where you might feel safe, you who have given so *much* to our great nation. But we also want you to be *free*, and with that freedom comes some degree of risk.' She gestured to one of the security officers. He ran up and handed her a bottle of water from which she sipped, delicately.

'Excuse me,' she said, with a little smile. 'I want you to know that we have liaised at *length* with Inspector Metallinos and his colleagues.' She gestured towards him; he raised a shy hand in acknowledgement. 'We have agreed that there is almost certainly no link between the two deaths, just as there was no link between the deaths that occurred here two or three years ago. There is no evidence that either Humphrey Musgrave or Edward

Lane was murdered. There should be no reason for *any* of you to lose any sleep over this.' Here she swept those hard grey eyes across the audience. There were perhaps thirty residents present, all of Spyland save one or two of the incurables in the san, whose existence was only ever revealed by the yelps and squeals that came sometimes, late at night, from one wing of the building.

'What about the bag?' Nina was surprised to see that it was Boyd asking the question. She hadn't avoided him, exactly, since the night they'd spent together but something in her recoiled from him. Since they'd made – what? – whatever it was, it wasn't love – she'd felt altered, as if something had shifted just beneath her skin. 'I heard that a bag was tied around Lane's neck. And that there were marks on his body consistent with a struggle.'

'Ah, Boyd.' Clara's smile didn't rise to her eyes. 'It's good to see you up and about.' She paused for a moment. 'It is our firm belief that Edward Lane very sadly took his *own* life. His behaviour had been increasingly erratic, as I'm sure you know. We think that Mr Lane used the bag as a way of drowning himself. And that the marks to his body were as a result of coming into contact with rocks on his way to the seabed. I have spoken at length to the inspector . . .' Here she wafted a hand towards him again. 'He entirely agrees with our conclusions.' Nina looked sharply at Metallinos, whose face betrayed nothing of his thoughts.

Clara attempted another smile. 'I know that all of this must be *terribly* distressing for you, but I hope also, that, on reflection, you'll recognise that this remains the very best place that you could possibly be. I have asked Mr Drinkwater to be *particularly* vigilant in the coming weeks, and he assures me that he is on hand should any of you wish to discuss these tragic events any further.' With that, she gave a curt nod to Drinkwater and, flanked by her bodyguards, left the room.

Nina walked with Benedict down to his cottage afterwards. The light outside was beautiful, the wistful late summer light of a September evening. They made tea in his kitchen and then went together to sit on the balcony to drink it. One by one, the stars came out over the Albanian mountains.

III.

NINA AND VIOLET walked down through the woods to the shore. It was a cool morning, October now, a week after the visit of Clara Sinclair. The weather had turned like it does in Corfu: a summer that seems to last forever, reaching into the autumn until suddenly, one day: tank-grey skies, a thin mizzle falling, Albania vanished. Nina was under-dressed for the chill: she had come up to the san first thing, as soon as she heard about Harris. Violet was wrapped in a shawl, blue shadows under her eyes. She told Nina how, the night before, Harris had woken as if from a nightmare, clutching his chest and cursing furiously. She'd run through the rain to fetch Mrs Samways. Now Harris was in a medicated sleep, a monitor bleeping his heartbeat, his face placid, pallid, still.

When they got back to the cottage, Nina made them tea, then switched on the heating. It was gloomy and she went around the drawing room, turning on lights and picking up evidence of the previous night's drama:

a photo frame on the floor, its glass cracked, the crack beheading a young woman with a hesitant smile in graduation robes. A scatter of pill packets, a bottle of wine – empty – that had rolled under the small table at which Harris and Violet took their meals. Violet sat in an armchair, her hands folded in her lap. She hadn't touched her tea. Nina could see a single tear making its way down her cheek.

She sat down on the sofa. The mizzle had steadied itself into rain. It was loud on the roof of the cottage, visible in squalls and flurries on the surface of the water outside.

'We met at Bletchley Park,' Violet said. She was looking off into the rain, her hands still folded in her lap, her tea undrunk. 'It was 1942 and we'd started at university. I was at Cambridge, he was at Oxford. Both of us doing maths. A chap from the Ministry of Defence came and spoke to my tutor. He put me forward with a group of others – the only girl, of course. I was selected. Harris was already there – the chap had been to Oxford first, it seemed. I had always rather preferred numbers to boys, but Harris was different. Honestly, I know you can't see it now – that's what a life does to you – but he was so terribly handsome. It hurt me to look at him for too long. We fell in love. It was really as simple as that.

'When the war was over, I applied to transfer to Lady Margaret Hall, so I could be closer to him. It was all a bit of a bazaar in those days, and everyone was terribly aware of how much we codebreakers had done for the war effort, so it was waved through without too much trouble. It all seemed preordained somehow. We would marry once university was over, I'd have children with brains the size of planets, we'd live in a beautiful house in Cotswold stone and fill our house with babies, friends and flowers.' She now seemed to realise that there was a cup of tea beside her. She reached down and took a sip.

'Then Philby appeared. We were both hugely impressed by him. Particularly when he revealed that he was a very senior member of MI6. We'd been playing at politics. Met Arkady and Patricia, read Marx and Rosa Luxemburg and Gramsci. Philby painted a picture of the good we could do in the world, the role we could play in building things back after the Holocaust, the Blitz, Dresden. We were both very idealistic, Harris perhaps too much. There was one catch, though – women in the Service couldn't marry. So Harris and I were together but had to book hotels under pseudonyms, couldn't celebrate the fact of our love with our families. It was cruel, really.'

Nina saw that Violet was crying more forcefully now. She searched through her pockets for a tissue, found one, inspected it, and handed it over.

'I do think of all the time we wasted,' Violet went on. 'Our lives on hold. We cannoned around the world on one pointless project, then the next. It seemed thrilling at first. I remember going to see Harris in Finland. He was stationed there just after the war. It was the most beautiful week, Russia a snowball's throw away, extraordinary light and the darkest dark.

'The problem was that Harris had such enormous ambitions. He'd always liked a drink – we all did in that generation – but he found his idealism crashing against the rocks of realpolitik. His ideas ignored or passed over, his vision for a fair world swept aside by all that capitalism. Well, he began to drink in a manner that was rather less . . . convivial. I mean, you've seen him, my dear, you know what I'm talking about. But every time I see him reach for a bottle, I remind myself that life has not been fair to him, not fair at all. He has always held himself to such high standards. The world, too. And year by year he berates himself and the world for not living up to them.'

'When did you get married?' Nina asked.

'The Sixties. I had to leave the Service for a while for it to happen. I hope in some small way that losing me might have played a part in persuading Esmond Harrington to change the rules.'

'He was the C at the time?'

'And I was rehired in 1973, although rather sub-rosa. It wasn't officially permitted to be married in service until we had a woman prime minister. I feel like that might have been the real agent of change. In the meanwhile I'd had Katherine. We always said only the one, and she was a dear little thing. She and her father don't talk now, but that's because he says things when he's in his cups that he really doesn't mean, not at all.'

'Was it the drink or the Communism that sent him out here?'

'I suppose a little of both. He'd been sidelined, rather. Made a mess of an operation in the Belgian Congo. Patricia Sinclair was in charge. There was a local plot to unseat Mobutu and somehow the details leaked out and a number of young men were killed. One of them turned out to be high-ranking CIA. Anyway, it seems it was Harris's fault that the whole plot unravelled. Patricia came away from it all mysteriously unscathed, of course, but she always did.'

'She was a friend of yours, Patricia?'

'We were close. Have you met her? She's still formidable, I believe.'

'Other than seeing her with my father that time. Which, by the way, still baffles me. No. I worked for Clara, of course.'

'Ah, the coming Clara. I have heard it said that Patricia now channels her enormous reserves of ambition into her daughter's career. It was strange, Clara being out here last week. No sign of her after the deaths a few years ago. The Christmas Massacre lot. It did appear that they were suicides of one kind or another, I suppose. I do call it suicide, still, when a person drinks themselves to death. I often wonder if Harris would be happier dead.'

There was a pause here, the sound of rain drumming on the roof. Nina found her mind drifting up to Harris lying in medicated sleep in the san, then outwards. She thought of the long tether of marriage – her parents, the what-might-have-been of Colin. How could anyone make their wedding vows without laughing, knowing how the self shifts with time, with grief, with love? And yet here, on Vidos, she had seen it: fidelity, not to sameness but to the act of staying. Perhaps that was the greatest hope that anyone could have – that two people might alter in ways that were still recognisable, and that something essential might endure, a flicker of the original light, carried gently forward. She saw that Violet had fallen asleep. She reached over and carefully took the cup of tea from her hands, placing it on the table between them.

'Some suicides take twenty or thirty years to complete, that's all,' Violet said, rousing herself for a moment and making Nina jump. Then she closed her eyes again and slept on. Nina sat there, thinking, looking out on the dim world, the furrowed sea, as the rain continued to fall.

IV.

NOW, TWO DAYS later, in the early afternoon, they were sitting in the cool green light of the san. Harris was on the mend, sitting up, looking blearily at them. His eyes were very red, his face pale.

'I must have given you a shock.'

'You did, my love.' Violet was holding his hand.

'The old ticker . . .'

'That's right. You need to be more careful.'

'The doctor who came to see me yesterday, Greek chap over from the mainland, spoke the most remarkably good English. Told me I needed to cut down on the booze.'

'Yes . . . But we knew that, didn't we, dear?'

Nina stood, put a hand on Violet's shoulder and walked out, feeling that this was not a conversation that needed an audience. She went down the corridor, remembering her own time in the san, when her mind was a wildfire, a gnawing, feral thing that consumed and charred everything it touched. She remembered scratching through the skin of her arm until she could see the glossy whiteness of tendons beneath. She remembered the gloves they taped to her wrists, the feeling of trappedness, with nowhere to look but inwards.

She took a right-hand turn down another corridor – she was never quite sure of the layout of the san: it seemed unnecessarily convoluted, arranged to appeal to the mad. Following the corridor to the end, she turned the corner and found in front of her another row of doors. One of these was open and she went inside, first sitting on the bed and then lying down.

It was very much like the room in which she'd spent her first weeks on Spyland: the same pale green walls, the institutional smell, the wash basin in the corner. The same silence, although, she realised, tuning her ears to it, that there was a soft sound coming to her through the afternoon air. She got up, walked further down the hallway. She came to a door that was shut. From behind it, the sound of a woman crying. Nina thought for a moment, then knocked. The crying stopped, then started again. Nina tried the handle of the door: it was locked. Nina thought about saying something, then remembered her own state of mind when she first came to the san, and backed off.

There were more noises further along the row of doors. Coughs and groans, more crying, although next it was a man's voice. Nina realised she must be in the southern wing of the san, where they housed the incurables, those who'd lost themselves entirely. It was a job that did that to you, one way or another – they were all incurables in the Office, even the ones who felt themselves invincible in the wood-panelled boardrooms of VX.

She went back to the empty room and sat down on the bed again. She could hear the crying more clearly now: not changing in pitch or intensity, but utterly distraught, unhinged, familiar. She recognised it as the sort of crying she had done, not only when she was in the san, but at other times – after Colin, after Beirut, Doha, in particular. She thought of Doha almost never now. Partly because it was the first of her several calamities, partly it was the memory of Tamim, looking at her imploringly, almost disappointed.

She had been well-briefed before the operation in Doha. MI6 had been made aware that a young sheikh from a prominent family, Prince Tamim bin Abdullah Al Zaman, had been financing a new network of jihadist organisations. There had been attacks in Dar es Salaam and Manila, a hijacking in Spain. It was thought that, as well as providing his own family's money to the terrorists, he was also raising funds from like-minded Saudis and Emiratis. Nina's mission had been to pose as a high-class Eastern European call girl, to get close to the sheikh, to learn as much as she could from him.

She had spent a week in the Brecon Beacons with a red-faced former SAS staff sergeant who trained her in close combat and self-defence. Her lessons in psychological resilience involved having the staff sergeant bellow at her in a small, cell-like room. Her impulse throughout was to laugh. She was given maps of Doha, detailed explanations of escape routes and signals. She was twenty-two, she was excited, thrilled at the vision of herself as she boarded the plane to Prague, where she'd stay for a week fleshing out her cover story, before flying to Doha. Colin had come to see her off at the airport. She had never felt so distant from him, from the smallness of Oxford.

In Prague she had lounged in a red negligée on velvet sofas in the brothel, chatting to the other girls in English or in German. There was one girl from Belgrade there, Daša, who was very beautiful and very sad and whom

Nina spoke to in Serbian, hoping to make friends, but who was already lost, had long ago beaten a retreat inside. Occasionally, a punter would gesture towards Nina and be told by the buttery brothel owner, Mr Šmicer, that she was not working that day. Nina was surprised when this happened, feeling that – small, wiry, with her nose – she was at a marked disadvantage to the tall, icy blondes who surrounded her.

Then she was landing in Doha, felt the blast of the desert heat hit her as she walked down the steps of the aeroplane. She was met by a driver who would be taking her to her room at the Sheraton. She found out on the way that he was Nepali, that he had worked for the Al Zaman family for three years, that he picked up a girl like her every few weeks. There was an edge in his voice and she wondered if he looked down on her. She asked about his family, who were back in Kathmandu. When he dropped her at the hotel, he turned to her, something chiding in his voice. 'Be careful,' he said. 'These are not good people.'

After checking in at the Sheraton – a massive white building overlooking the harbour – she went for a walk along the Corniche. There were dhows coming in from the Gulf, black kites drifting in the sky, heat and dust in the wind. Everything about the place was exotic and vividly alive: she was here on a secret mission, in the service of her country, on the side of the light. She had been told that the sheikh would call on her in the evening, either that night or the following one, and so she headed back. She ate dinner in her room – a small bowl of salad, her stomach wouldn't take much more than that – and waited.

He didn't come that night. She turned out her light just after midnight, unable to sleep and with the sounds of the Corniche coming up to her, the engines of cars and the occasional ship's horn. She went to her window and looked down over the harbour, the lights of the city, then the waters of the Gulf rolling away in the darkness to Iran. When she woke in the morning, there was a note pushed under her door. *Prince Tamim apologises for his absence last night. He looks forward to seeing you this evening at 9 p.m.* It was written on an ivory card in a feminine hand, the Al Zaman crest at the top. Nina spent the day lying by the pool, soaking in a sun of almost unbearable heat, thinking ahead to the night.

When Boyd had given her her final briefing, sitting in one of the meeting rooms at VX, the blinds drawn, the smell of the previous occupants' lunch in the air, there had been no mention of how, precisely, she was to get close to Prince Tamim. In the Brecon Beacons she had been shown how to kill herself with a shoelace or a shard of glass from the window, should she be captured. But she hadn't been told about seduction, about what she was expected to do during the time the sheikh was with her, what she might be asked to give up for the sake of her country. She had asked Boyd outright.

'Am I going to have to have sex with him? Is that the expectation here?'

She was pleased to see him blush, stutter, rock back in his chair a little. 'No, gosh, no. I mean . . . Listen, Nina, like with anything, you need to steer a line between what the situation demands and what your conscience will allow. You're a resourceful girl, a woman, I should say. I wouldn't be sending you out there if you weren't. Every operation entails a degree of risk and there's clearly a risk here. You might, perhaps, indicate that you're suffering your monthly visitation. I believe it's quite taboo there, although it has never bothered me.'

She squirmed a little inside when he said this, but then it was how he tended to talk to the women in the office, the young ones at least, as if they would, inevitably, be a little bit in love with him. He wasn't Nina's type at all – too sure of himself, too polished, too easily imagined as the captain of school.

When nine o'clock came, she was sitting on the end of her bed in a very short dress and high heels, no knickers. She hadn't been able to eat even a salad this evening. Then she'd been worried that he'd see the tray – only the bread roll even nibbled – outside her door, so she went and placed it outside a door on the floor below. There was a man in the lift as she made her way back up, an American, who said, 'Good evening,' and then looked at her wolfishly. Her dress *was* very short. She took it by the hem and wriggled it down a little. The American grinned at her.

She went back into her room and looked at the clock: half past nine. She wondered what she would do if he didn't come, whether she should use the dead drop they'd established in Souq Waqif to get a message to whomever it was that MI6 had on the ground there. She'd been given a number to ring in case of an emergency. What constituted an emergency, in a life like hers? Then there was a knock on the door.

Prince Tamim was smaller than she had imagined, although it may have been that the two bodyguards who flanked him were so huge. The sheikh's face fell when he saw her. He came bustling into the room.

'Šmicer sent you, right?' He had an American accent. He had studied at Brown, International Relations, although, from the files she'd read, his time at university was spent driving fast cars to New York, where he'd park in front of nightclubs in Chelsea – the Limelight, the Tunnel, the Roxy – making the most of his diplomatic plates. Accusations swirled around him – rape, assault, even murder. He had a thing for very young girls, apparently, liked rough sex and sometimes skipped the sex and went straight to the beating. No charges were ever brought, a network of bodyguards and diplomats helping to smooth over any unpleasantness. Now he looked at Nina with barely disguised scorn. 'You are not at all what I go for, not at all. You look, I don't know, Jewish or something.'

She had spent weeks preparing for this moment, but she felt suddenly tongue-tied, panic rising in her chest now that this man was here before her. He was short and narrow-faced and had a scraggly moustache, hair shiny with wax. He wore a suit over a polo shirt, expensive-looking trainers and a great deal of aftershave.

'Mr Šmicer sends his regards,' Nina said, her accent that of one who had learnt English through sitcoms and the cinema, slightly husky, all of her intricate backstory packed into the careful modulation of her voice. 'He says that he thinks you will not be disappointed. Maybe I pour you a drink?'

Tamim looked at one of the bodyguards with a shrug, then back to Nina. 'Fine. Make me a gin and tonic. One for yourself, too.' He waved the bodyguards away.

They left. Nina listened out for, and heard, the ping of the lift as they descended.

'Come and sit beside me,' she said. She placed the drinks on a coffee table and patted the sofa. 'I want to know all about you. Mr Šmicer says you have more power than anyone else in the Gulf. He says that I must make sure that you are very happy.'

Tamim came and sat with a sigh, taking off his jacket and tossing it over the back of the sofa. 'Šmicer doesn't know what the fuck he's talking about,' he said. 'He's got no idea what I do here. No one does.'

'You're a man of secrets.'

'I'm a man who understands that the world is changing. And that if we don't stand up for ourselves we are going to lose everything. People here live as if there's no future.'

'But you don't?'

'I have studied history, I have read more books than you can even imagine. I know what's coming.'

There was a long silence, during which he stared at her unblinkingly, sipping his drink. She did her best to look demure, meeting his eyes and then glancing swiftly downwards.

'Let me get you another.' She went to the minibar, mixed a stronger G&T, brought it back to him. Sitting down, she turned a little towards him, allowing her skirt to ride up. 'Your family, do they share your vision? Your father, he is very important, that is what Mr Šmicer says to me.'

'My father is as bad as the rest of them. Leading us down a path of servitude and ruin. There are people who understand, though. More people than my father and his *murtaddīn* allies imagine, even in their nightmares.'

'And these people, some of them are powerful like

you?' She felt like a hunter closing in on her prey, her footsteps becoming stealthier as she drew nearer.

'Some,' he said. 'Some are very powerful indeed. I do not share their superstitions . . . but I understand their rage.' She saw his eyes move down her body to her skirt. He reached a slow hand across the sofa and pushed the skirt up higher. She lifted herself for a moment and felt him fold the skirt up on itself so that she was naked from the waist down. He leant towards her. 'I don't like it when the girls have hair down there. I told Šmicer this. I will make an exception for you, though. I like you. You are different.'

She stood up. 'Maybe we should go over to the bed,' she said.

He grabbed her arm and pulled her back down. 'We go where I say.' Sudden anger in his voice. Then he was on top of her and taking off his polo shirt. There was a large mirror on the wall beside them and she could see that he was looking at himself, caught for a moment in the sight of his chest, his stomach. He began to kiss her, his mouth very wet, his moustache tickling her nose. She was surprised at how calm she felt, now this was happening. She realised, and she remembered the force of this realisation years later, thinking back to it on the bed in the san: that she had somehow accepted this as a price for her career, for her place among the men of MI6. And she was willing to make a sacrifice, her body an offering. So it was that, when Prince Tamim stood up and took down his trousers, grasping her hair and pulling her face towards his groin, she went about pleasuring him with only a hint of distaste. She pushed her mind away to a walk she and Colin had taken a few weeks back out to the Trout on Port Meadow. She remembered the sun on her skin, Colin's happy prattling about his teaching, swallows lacing through the air. When Tamim forced her head back with a sharp yank and sent her sprawling onto the sofa, she managed to look like she was enjoying herself.

Much later, back in England, she had to describe in front of a panel of senior officers what had happened. She still found it hard to piece together the events of that night. She remembered his hand about her throat. His nails were long and she could feel them breaking her skin. She managed to roll away from under him and there was an absurd period that must have been only a minute or two, but seemed like much longer, when he chased her around the room like something from *The Benny Hill Show* – she could almost hear the music.

Then, when he finally caught her, he punched her twice, hard in the mouth, so that she felt the imprint of her teeth on the inside of her lips, tasted blood. She fell back on the bed and he put his hand to her throat again, although this time he didn't seem to want to have sex with her, just to hurt her. While the one hand held her down, the other punched her in the ribs, the breasts, the face. She was good with discomfort, usually: as a child it had been a kind of party trick of hers, at prep school, to leap into the swimming pool even when the surface bore a crust of ice, or to hold her finger over a flame until the flesh bubbled. Tamim was versed in pain, though, hitting her in the same areas, again and again, burrowing his way through until he found places where there was no resistance, and it felt like he was punching her in the soul. Finally, she blacked out.

When she came to, he was still straddling her, naked, grinning. Into her mind just then came the faces of the other girls in the brothel in Prague, the ones she'd met and the others who'd been sent here before her to be hurt by Tamim. She took a painful breath, formed her hand into a fist and hit him as hard as she could, just as the staff sergeant had shown her, in the declivity below his Adam's apple, a place of unguarded softness. He'd reared back, grasping at his throat, and Nina, triumphant, had forced herself up, batted his arm aside and punched him again. It was this second blow that killed him, or that's what they said afterwards, the team who came to clear up. In the moment, though, Nina stood over Tamim as he writhed on the floor feeling as if flames were coming off her, and it wasn't until he stopped moving, and his lips had turned a pale shade of blue, that she stopped burning.

It took just fifteen minutes from her telephone call – she remembered to use the agreed code, felt at once ridiculous and childishly anxious, as if she had been summoned before the headmistress at school – for the extraction team to arrive. What happened to the bodyguards, she never found out, nor was she made aware of what political wranglings occurred to smooth it all over. Boyd intimated that the Qatari Emir was not entirely disappointed to have this unpredictable firebrand off his hands. Nina was interviewed by a number of different agencies, then finally by a panel on which – it came back to her now – Patricia Sinclair had sat, a strangely familiar figure, the aged shadow of her daughter.

Nina shook her head, clearing the memories, the image of her sitting on the Hercules as it bounced through the sky back to London and crying, endlessly, hopelessly, just as a young woman was crying on the other side of the wall now, here on Vidos, where agents came to die. She walked out into the labyrinth of corridors of the san, finding her way finally back to the room in which Harris was now sitting up in bed, a cup held carefully to his chin.

Violet turned as she entered. 'Ah, we were wondering if you'd lost yourself in this warren, weren't we, dear?' She looked encouragingly towards Harris, who gave a pinched smile over his cup of tea.

V.

A WEEK PASSED. A late afternoon. The doctor over from the Old Town, leaving, told Violet and Nina that Harris would be on his feet before long, but must stay off alcohol for at least a month. Nina watched Harris force a look of, if not happiness, then acceptance, onto his face as Violet took his hand and squeezed it. They had brought up books and a newspaper – a few days out of date, but it didn't feel like it mattered. Harris's voice had become higher and more fragile since his attack. He seemed to Nina to have aged a decade in the space of a few days. Death was close enough for most of the inhabitants of Spyland, Nina supposed, that the falls and turns and attacks that they suffered must have felt like rehearsals for the inevitable encounter ahead, the one from which they would not recover. Nina wondered if a life of danger made this process easier, or if living in a world in which people dropped dead merely served to foster a sense of your own invincibility. They left Harris, the paper open but unread on his blanket, his eyes staring into the distance.

As they walked down from the san through the darkening air, Nina could see banks of cloud building over the Albanian mountains, lightning flashing in the distance. 'Is that coming our way, do you think?'

Violet licked a finger and held it to the wind. 'I rather think so. It has that dead feel you get before a storm, don't you think?'

'I like storms,' Nina said.

'Listen, my love,' Violet said, 'I wanted to do something to say thank you for your support lately. I've been so worried that I've scarcely had time to acknowledge what a brick you've been. Anyway, it was the market in the Old Town today and I asked Angelos to get me some lamb chops and a box of that wonderful *bougatsa*. I thought we might ask Benedict and Boyd over, make a little party of it.'

Nina glanced at Violet for a moment, wondering if the older woman knew that there was a new source of complexity in her relationship with her former boss. But Violet's face revealed nothing but the pleasant expectation of a night amongst friends. They continued their walk down the hill, thunder rolling distantly, the wind picking up and lifting white crests on the waves in the channel. Nina went up to the villa for her medication, promising to come and help Violet in the kitchen as soon as she was done.

In the villa, all was quiet. Nina was late and Mrs Samways was not at the dispensing window. She made her way up the wide wooden staircase, looking at the wan portraits of jaded British diplomats on the walls. She wondered how many of them had suffered as she had suffered, how many had dark and secret lives hidden under the respectable veneer that was captured here, in flaking oil paints, bleached by the sun and yet still gloomy, all tweed, stern gazes and shadows of Empire.

She reached the top of the stairs and heard voices coming from Drinkwater's study. Obeying an impulse that, if she was being honest with herself, had been active long before she joined the Office, she ducked into a doorway and listened. It was Drinkwater speaking, Mrs Samways' voice barely audible.

'I let him into the san because those were the orders I received,' Drinkwater was saying. 'He's my superior and he's acting directly on the orders of the C. He said he only wanted a conversation, to make clear that this whole thing needs putting to bed.'

Mrs Samways responded, but her voice was soft and Nina wasn't close enough to hear her. She looked for another place to hide and, finding none – the door to Drinkwater's study was open, the lights on, his shadow visible in the hallway – she stayed put.

'We are here to look after these people but we are also here to serve our country. Sometimes the best kind of service lies in not asking questions.'

More muffled sounds from Mrs Samways, then footsteps. Nina hurried out onto the landing, feigning breathlessness, as if she had just run up the stairs. 'I'm so sorry, Mrs Samways,' she said. 'Oh, hello, Mr Drinkwater. I was just up at the san with Harris.' She looked at him carefully when she said this, then to Mrs Samways. 'I missed my meds. May I get them now?'

VI.

IT WAS JUST beginning to drizzle as Nina made her way down to the village in the half-light of evening, her mind full of what she had just heard, or half-heard. It turned out that she wasn't much needed in the kitchen, Violet being a quick and expansive cook. Instead, she laid the table in the drawing room: smaller than the one upon which Benedict and Humphrey had entertained, but made of the same polished olive wood. After this, she stood on the veranda, a shawl of Violet's wrapped around her shoulders, and watched the storm coming in. She turned Drinkwater's words over in her mind. The problem with understanding anything on Vidos, she realised, was that there were so many layers of history to peel back, so much that could be understood only in the light of a different time, with different loyalties.

The rain was now coming down hard, rattling on the roof of the cottage, falling loudly on the water. Every so often, there was a flash of lightning over the channel, illuminating the wildness of the waves, which were slopping over the pontoon, crashing onto the beach, booming against the cliff below the villa. Nina felt something lift inside her at the roar of the wind, the flash, the pause and then the clatter of the thunder, which told her that the storm was still far off, over Albania.

Benedict arrived first, fighting with his umbrella. He embraced her and Violet, asked after Harris, fixed them all a gin and tonic. Nina lit a fire in the brick fireplace that was rarely used but which seemed made for a moment like this. Benedict came and gave her advice on getting it to take, holding a sheet of newspaper over the face of it until the roar of the fire almost drained out the storm. Boyd came in soaked, bedraggled, a hangdog air about him, his red hair plastered to his head. He approached Nina, made as if to hug her, then realised how wet he was and changed his mind.

Over dinner, candlelit and cosy, Nina considered whether she ought to tell the others about Drinkwater and Mrs Samways. She half-wanted to wait until she was alone with Benedict, but then, during a pause in the conversation, the words just tumbled out. 'I heard something,' she said, and then described the snatches of information. Violet pushed her plate away and looked narrowly at Nina.

Boyd, who had done his best to dry himself with a tea towel, waited until she was finished and then spoke. 'Should we go up there? To the san? It's Harris they were talking about, right? If the bad actors get to him . . .'

'The bad actors? What do you mean?' Nina looked at him sharply.

'I mean that there are dark forces in the Office now. I was sent out here because I was a mess, that's true enough, but also because I'd started asking questions about precisely why we were turning a blind eye to the movement of arms in ex-Soviet states, the activities of criminal gangs in Russia.'

Benedict was leaning forward in his chair, very alert. Nina noticed that he had hardly touched his plate. It felt as if everything was primed, poised, coming to a dangerous head. Then the lights went out.

'Golly,' said Violet, although, in truth, only a table lamp in the corner of the room had been lit. The candles moved light across their faces, the fire flickered their shadows on the walls.

'I'll stick my head out and see if the villa has lost power,' Boyd said. He turned the handle and the strength of the wind wrenched the door from his grasp. The candles on the table were blown out and the lamp fell from the table with a crash. Boyd wrestled the door back shut and then leant against it. 'Jesus,' he said.

Benedict bent to relight the candles from the fire. Nina began to pick up the shards of the lamp, carrying them through to the darkened kitchen. Violet sat very still at the table, her face set hard. Boyd was still standing by the front window, looking out. The wind was very loud now and Nina felt suddenly the precariousness of the cottage, heard the oleanders thrashing against the wooden walls outside, the groaning of the timbers.

She called over to Boyd. 'I remember you telling me, a few weeks back, that there was something wrong at the Office, that there were people there I needed to be scared of. I thought you were just drunk.'

'Not so drunk,' Boyd said, coming to sit beside her. 'There are strange things going on at VX.'

'Surely there always are,' Nina said, then she let out a little shriek. Over Violet's shoulder, outside, she saw, for the briefest moment, a masked face.

'What is it?' Benedict said, but Nina was already rushing to the window, pressing her nose against the glass. It was very dark outside, the rain falling in sheets, the bushes near-flattened by the wind.

'Blow out the candles,' she said. Boyd was still smiling, uncertain, but Benedict and Violet caught the edge of panic in her voice. Benedict blew out the candles and then ushered Violet towards the darkest corner of the room, away from the fire, which was sputtering out.

'What did you see?' Benedict asked.

'A face at the window. Only for an instant, but I'm certain.'

Now Boyd bent low and made his way to the front of the cottage. Nina went to her jacket, hanging on the back of her chair, and from the pocket she drew the pen that Humphrey had given her. With a flick of her thumb, the blade shot out. 'Is there a back door?' she asked.

'Yes,' said Violet. 'Through the kitchen.'

Boyd cupped his hands against the picture window at the front of the cottage, then came to join Nina in the kitchen. They went through in the darkness to a small room that smelt of Violet: washing powder, freesias, freshness. Boyd reached for the door handle. 'I'll open it. You duck out. Keep down. I'll be right after you.'

Then the door was open and the wind howling and Nina was drenched by the rain. She felt disoriented for a moment, looked wildly around, and then Boyd's hand was on her shoulder and they moved low to the corner of the cottage. Nina gripped the knife, aware that it was better than nothing, but only just. No one there. Boyd pointed at the front of the cottage and they crept through the oleanders, heading for the beach.

Nina found herself wondering, in a trailing part of her mind, if it might be her father who was here, coming after them. It appeared to be his role in the Office now: a fixer of unpleasant problems, a hitman, or so they said. Maybe he had been instructed to wipe them all out, one by one. She wondered whether he would be able to kill her, his daughter. She realised, again, with only half her mind trained upon this, that she was preparing herself for what might be ahead, for the fact that she might have to use the blade – small, but very sharp – on her father. She found, slightly to her surprise, that she thought she probably could. Then, all of a sudden, Boyd moved swiftly forward, and Nina followed him. There was the sound, audible even over the wind, of a gun firing twice. A body came tumbling down the steps of the cottage and landed at their feet.

Boyd reached down to pull back the balaclava just as Violet and Benedict emerged onto the veranda above. Nina noticed that Violet was holding a revolver. It was darker than ever, but there was no doubting the face of the man who lay there on the shingle, the life draining out of him through a hole in his chest and another in his stomach. It was Harris.

Violet came down the steps, the revolver in her hand. A Model 36, Nina noticed, still smoking. Violet fell to her knees, dropped the gun on the ground and took Harris's head in her lap. The rain fell down on them and the sea roared and all the world spun about that still point, a husband and wife in the darkness: one dead, one his killer.

PART 6

Ajaltoun, near Beirut, September 1957

I.

THEY WERE ALL aware of it: that this was the first time they had all been together since the house at Boars Hill. Nine years. Today was Benedict's thirty-first birthday, although no one had remembered and he worried that it might be conceited to bring it up. Not a meaningful birthday, anyway, he thought. His most meaningless so far.

A butler brought mint tea in a silver teapot. It looked like something you might rub to summon a genie, Benedict thought. In the distance, the call to prayer.

'Mr Philby will be with you imminently,' the butler said, speaking the last word carefully, as if he had only just learnt it.

They sat in couples on the benches in the courtyard: Harris and Violet, Benedict and Humphrey, Patricia and Arkady. They all knew that Patricia had had a child. Benedict had taken the boat from Corfu for the christening in Venice. It was at Santa Maria dei Miracoli – fitting, Benedict thought, for what appeared an immaculate conception. He assumed – they all did – that Arkady was the father, although the subject was never directly addressed and Benedict was surprised to discover that Patricia had inscribed his own name on the birth certificate.

'It'll keep things simple,' she'd said. 'I hope you won't be a beast about it.'

Benedict was rather proud, if anything, and although he did not meet the girl until many years later, he liked the idea that she should grow up with his name filling the space of father in her mind.

The child's name was Clara, and now, Patricia told them, she was at boarding school in Kent. According to Patricia's mother, who kept up with these things, she was a gifted student and played the viola beautifully. Benedict pictured a slim, serious girl, a kind of shadow of her mother when first he met her, the viola clamped tightly beneath a pointed chin.

After the birth, Patricia had spent three weeks with the child in Venice, her parents scarcely concealing their delight at this new project – a baby! – before heading to Moscow to begin life as a spy.

They had seen each other individually and in different combinations: in the early Fifties, Harris arranged it that he, Humphrey and Violet might be posted to Corfu to help with Operation Valuable, which on Benedict's watch had gone from disastrous to irretrievable.

They had spent two happy years in the old villa on Vidos, Benedict capering around them like a faithful dog, joyful to be amongst friends again, to have someone to whom he might confess his guilt and sorrow at the young lives he was sending to their bloody ends. Sometimes not so young: there was a priest whom they hauled off the side of the fishing caïque, a government minister who believed that he was defecting to the West, but found that the spies he thought would help him were in league with those he fled, and had put a bullet in the back of his head.

When Valuable was finally shut down, Benedict was posted to Berlin, Harris to Vienna, Violet to Karachi, Humphrey sent reluctantly back to Cairo. They all remembered it happily, that time together. Happier somehow without Patricia and Arkady there.

Benedict had gone out to see Humphrey in Egypt a year after the coup d'état. He was not thriving. He had been tasked by MI6 to do everything in his power to protect the regime of the dilettantish King Farouk, while his MGB handlers insisted he support Nasser and the Free Officers. Within weeks of his return to Cairo, the King was deposed, the Egyptians in charge. Humphrey began drinking heavily, pretending to MI6 that he was getting close to Nasser in order to learn of his plans while, in fact, informing Nasser of the many and Byzantine British schemes that sought to ensure that the new regime failed.

Humphrey had swiftly become overweight, florid, something drooping about the edges of him. The time on Vidos together, Benedict came to acknowledge, had been the end of something.

'Some men are made to live trapped in the jaws of a dilemma,' Humphrey had told Benedict, 'and some are not.'

They had toured the pyramids together, taken a boat on the Nile, hiked into the desert and waited until the sun set and the stars were a milky sweep above them. They made love and promises to one another, finding in this intimacy after so long apart some memory of their very earliest days together, although Benedict realised that much of this was, perhaps inevitably, tied up with the wish to make contact with the young men they had been, but were no longer.

Over the week they were together, Humphrey's moroseness, his drinking, began to weigh on Benedict.

The night before he was due to return to Berlin, they'd sat on the roof of Humphrey's building, an old and elegant apartment block on Sharia Talaat Harb, and looked over the rooftops, the minarets, the smoke rising from ten thousand fires.

'I don't know what I'm doing,' Humphrey said. 'Do you? Do you feel like you're bringing us closer to a just world?'

Benedict was thinking about Besian. He thought about Besian a great deal: the young priest had become the epitome of Benedict's many betrayals, a stand-in for all the other lives lost. He saw the dark eyes, the tattooed cross, in his dreams.

He patted Humphrey on the hand and said something comforting. Life was an adventure, he thought, and he had arranged his own to be as adventurous as possible. Berlin was very different to Corfu, different to Oxford: a place of danger and intrigue, shadows and assignations. He felt like a proper spy there. His secretive missions and meetings, his rendezvous with his Russian and Stasi handlers – it all gave his life electricity, and that electricity lit up an underground world, one whose clocks and cleverness defined and directed the world above, the ordinary, oblivious people.

Patricia had made a great success of her time in Moscow, compensating for the delay entailed by the birth of her child by applying herself with ferocious vigour to both sides of her secret life. Arkady, who was now Deputy Director of Foreign Intelligence within the MGB, fed her a steady stream of incidental or semi-fictional material, which she sent to London via dead drops in Gorky Park.

All the while she was briefing the MGB on the war in Korea, on Egypt, on the location of British nuclear research facilities. Patricia was a star at 54 Broadway, MI6 headquarters, and she was equally lauded in the Lubyanka. She was having several affairs at once, alongside Arkady and with his apparent support: with the Deputy Minister for Foreign Affairs, responsible for Soviet engagement with Albania and Yugoslavia, with General Ivan Sergeyevich Kuznetsov, Chief of Staff of the Soviet Air Forces, with Elena Mikhailovna Vasilieva, a senior editor at *Pravda*.

Now, meeting up at Philby's place in Beirut, it was clear that a kind of hierarchy had been imposed upon them by time and events. Harris and Benedict jostled for last place, with Humphrey perched precariously above them. Violet was next on the ladder, coolly detached, even austere. Patricia radiated something optimistic and self-possessed that the others did not, not even Arkady, gaunt and shadowed, worked to the bone.

She took a sip of mint tea as Philby walked into the courtyard.

II.

'IT'S MY FATHER's house,' Philby said, gesturing at the sandstone walls and arched windows. 'He's in Saudi Arabia at the moment. I've rather shacked up with him here. Lovely place to be, up in the hills.' He looked at his watch. 'I think it's probably not too early for a snifter. You'll join me, won't you, Harris? Arkady? Anyone else?'

'Don't mind if I do,' said Humphrey, who was the reason they were here. He had been made Station Chief in Beirut, rather to his surprise but almost certainly thanks to his father, who had been someone important in the era of pith helmets and viceroys. He was wearing a blue linen suit and a white shirt open at the collar and looked louche and tanned, happier than when Benedict had left him in Cairo four years earlier. Benedict wondered if his time in Berlin had aged him; it felt as though he'd lived a dozen lives in the smoky backrooms of the Schwarzes Café, amid its velvet gloom and whispers.

Now, on the pretext of visiting Humphrey, they had all come, to Philby.

'Karim, could we have four pink gins?' The butler appeared for an instant, inclined his head, retreated. Benedict noticed that Philby's stutter was worse when he spoke to Karim than when he was talking to them. 'I won't waste your time,' Philby began, lighting a cigarette. 'This is, I suppose, a passing of the torch. You'll have seen the newspapers, the speculation, my very public shaming and then the half-hearted exoneration. Since Donald and Guy defected, I've been living on borrowed time.'

Karim arrived with the drinks in heavy crystal tumblers.

'Thank you,' Harris said, taking a long gulp. Benedict saw that Philby had a drinker's strawberry nose, broken red filaments under the skin of his cheeks, perpetually bloodshot eyes. He wondered if, for Philby, the drinking had come first, then the lying, or if he drank to ease the passage of the lies. Philby was like a warning shot, a picture of what they would all look like if they continued on this path.

'You've done a marvellous job, all of you,' Philby went on. 'I have to say that when Arkady and I selected you — and you may have believed that you had agency back then, but do believe me, you *were* selected — we couldn't have hoped for a more committed, intelligent and resourceful bunch. And while our group from Cambridge has, in one way or another, been compromised, either by luck or judgement, you Oxford lot have held yourselves above suspicion. I still have sufficient clout to know who's in and who's out, and all five of you are spoken about in the most radiant terms.'

'Despite,' Patricia interjected, 'the fact that every project in which we involve ourselves is a failure — never our fault, of course.'

'An example of both the stupidity of those in charge and their blinding snobbishness. You are from good stock, Oxbridge types. You have read Shakespeare and Virgil, you listen to Bach and Britten. You understand what an LBW is, you know in which direction to pass the port. One day, I fervently believe, we will recognise the meaninglessness of such distinctions, that much deeper and more powerful bonds tie us to all other men, no matter their background, their race, their reading habits. You have been welcomed into the Service for the same reason that I have managed to keep up my deception for so long: the idea of you playing for the other team simply doesn't occur to them. And, as you've seen in my own case, even when the evidence begins to stack up against you, they will do everything they can to find ways of believing you.'

'But you feel that your time is running out, don't you, Kim?' There was something very warm in Patricia's voice. Benedict found himself wondering if they had ever been lovers. He knew that Philby's wife was in a sanatorium somewhere, driven to the edge and then over it by her husband's lying, his drinking and infidelity. He was still, though, very charming.

'I am no longer a betting man, but if I were, I'd wager a decent sum on my being in Moscow by this time next year. If not then, soon after. I feel very calm about the whole thing. I hear from Donald and Guy that they are well looked-after. I have given my life to the service of the motherland, I may as well live out my days there.'

They said their farewells at the entrance to the courtyard: the six friends had booked two taxis to take them back to Beirut. As they left, Philby embraced them one by one. He gave Benedict his service revolver. 'I have a dozen pistols of one sort or another here,' he said, 'but none has served me half as well as this one. I hope you never have to use it, Benedict, but if you do, know that she fires straight and true.' To Humphrey, he gave a fountain pen from whose lid emerged a vicious blade. Violet was given Philby's cipher wheel, which was beautiful and ornate. He handed Harris a miniature camera, a Leica. Arkady was given a microdot viewer to interpret the messages that Philby would send to him in the coming months, in preparation for the defection. Finally, he put his arms around Patricia. They stayed there for some time, very still, until Philby drew back, pulled a ring from his finger and gave it to her. 'You may return it in Moscow,' he said. 'It was my mother's.'

The taxis took them through the hazy heat of the

afternoon, down through forests of cedar, into the bustle and hum of Beirut. They were staying at the Excelsior on Phoenicia Street, which was very grand and to whose nightclub, the Caves du Roy, they now repaired, a little giddy at being together once again.

The maître d' led them to a table near the dance floor. The music was heady and otherworldly, a shimmering mix of sitars and balalaikas that seemed to ripple in the air. Arkady ordered drinks, and soon champagne flutes were being raised in unspoken toasts. They danced beneath the chandeliers, laughing too loudly, their reflections flickering in the mirrors like ghosts. Their conversations turned to Philby's legacy — his work, their work — and the beautiful, elusive future.

By the time midnight struck, they had already begun their goodbyes, though no one quite said it. Arkady and Patricia were bound for Moscow at dawn, Harris to Vienna by way of Rome. Violet's route would take her through Muscat. Their plans diverged like fracturing lines on a map, the dance floor a crossroads where, just for a moment, they could imagine their younger selves dancing beside them.

Harris and Violet were the first to leave. There was much embracing and shaking of hands. Violet cried a little, and then Benedict watched Harris take her by the elbow through the crowd of dancers, saw the solicitude with which he stood aside to let her pass up the stairs and away. Arkady and Patricia left next, promising Benedict that they would find a pretext to come and visit him in Berlin. Then he and Humphrey were alone at the table, an empty bottle of champagne between them. They went up to bed together, although whether this was for company or for something more, Benedict would have been hard-pressed to say. Already half of him was back in Berlin, helping to secure the defection of a scientist. He and Humphrey spent a few drunken hours fumbling with one another in the darkness, then it was suddenly dawn. Benedict rose very softly, packed his bags, and left.

III.

FIVE YEARS PASSED. Philby would not have won his bet – the esteem with which he was held by his colleagues, and particularly by Nicholas Elliott, the Head of Mission in Beirut, meant that his fall from grace was more protracted than anyone might have predicted.

His wife, in and out of nursing homes for several years, had now died, and he had married again: to Eleanor Brewer, the wife of a *New York Times* journalist who had left her husband for Philby. Benedict was always impressed that Philby had managed to get so much done: the journalism, the spying – for both sides – that went on right until his defection, when his private life was such a terrible smash. Eleanor was his third wife; there were five children living orphaned lives in British boarding schools, or in the homes of relatives.

And with the amount he drank on top of this, it was a wonder that his defection, when it came, was effected with such smoothness. Benedict detected the hand of Patricia Sinclair in the operation. Philby was now living in Moscow, a hero there.

Benedict was back in London, working on the Russian desk at 54 Broadway. He was heartbroken, but not unpleasantly so. Indeed, he was almost luxuriating in the melancholy of having ended things with a young MI6 recruit named Lucan Woolf, whom he'd tapped up at Oxford and with whom he'd launched into an affair of operatic intensity. The first time he'd stood on his tiptoes to kiss Lucan, the younger man had been scandalised.

'That's really not my kind of thing at all,' he had told Benedict. 'What's more, it's illegal, you know.' He was tall and absurdly, cinematically handsome, dark hair swept back over a smooth, sensitive forehead, large eyes, very wide apart, lips as full and red as a woman's. He had a nose from a Canova sculpture.

Over the months, Benedict had persuaded Lucan not only to fall in love with him, but also with Communism. It was a great success, at least this was how Patricia saw it, but she insisted that Lucan be sent out to help her at the Moscow station. She needed another person she could trust, someone to help her manage the complexity of the double life she was living there. So they were to part, Benedict and Lucan, now when they were so happy.

He had driven Lucan to the airport, both of them crying. Lucan was almost ten years younger than him, only twenty-seven, still a boy, really, and Moscow seemed so far away, so deep within enemy territory. He was, Benedict realised, terrified.

'I will come and see you,' Benedict said, grasping his hand, then letting go to change gear. 'You must know that you'll be doing the most terribly important things for the cause. Far more than I'll be able to do here. I'm jealous of you, really. To be there, at the nerve centre. And with Patricia and Arkady, too. You'll adore them. And they, you.'

A long silence. West London passing greyly by outside. Lucan spoke in a soft voice, almost inaudible. 'I don't know if I can do it without you. It was all for you in the first place, not for the global proletariat or the international workers. But you.'

'I know, I know, and you've done so well already. Just think of what's to come, of all the years we'll have together.'

They had arrived at the airport. On a grey day, Heathrow was the greyest place on Earth. They sat in the car for a few minutes in silence, composing themselves. Then Benedict went and retrieved Lucan's suitcase from the boot.

It was, Benedict noted, a child's suitcase, the sort of thing with which a young man might be packed off to university and discard the first chance he got. They stood on the pavement outside the terminal building. He didn't embrace Lucan, but shook him very firmly by the hand.

'Good luck,' he said, and then he got back in the car and drove. Lucan just stood there, a diminishing figure in the rear-view mirror looking on, a picture of loneliness.

IV.

IT WAS NOT, to Benedict, at least, a surprise that Lucan failed to flourish in Moscow. Benedict had helped him with his Russian but it was, in the end, only passable. The first notes of concern came after just a few months. A message from Patricia, encrypted, asking quite *what* Benedict had sent her.

Lucan, it seemed, had not come out of his apartment

for the first week he was in Moscow, claiming he had a cold. Then, when he arrived at the embassy, where he would ostensibly be working as a clerk in the consular section, he behaved in a fashion that Patricia described as 'profoundly erratic, maybe lunatic'.

Lucan, it seemed, had rather enjoyed the image of himself as a double agent. He spent his time creeping around the embassy, surprising consular staff as they emerged from the lavatory, standing on the corner outside smoking endless cigarettes and looking up knowingly from beneath his fedora.

He was twice caught carrying classified papers as he left the building. He became swiftly drunk at an embassy party, telling the ambassador's wife he was in Moscow on business so secret that if he told her, he'd have to kill her.

On one occasion, he followed a GRU officer to the home of his mistress and then tried to film them through the window from the fire escape. He slipped, fell, dropped his camera and was on crutches for a month.

Now, it seemed, he had disappeared. With Lucan absent from the embassy for three days, Patricia was sent to visit his apartment. The door was open, papers and clothes strewn all over the place, his passport and wallet still in a drawer by his bed. He was finally discovered passed out under a table at the Kraken, a notoriously suspect bar in Zamoskvorechye.

Benedict heard of Lucan's misadventures from Patricia, then from others on the Russia desk, then from Kenneth Snow, Director of Counter Espionage, himself. He was called into a meeting room at 54 Broadway, where Snow sat, regal and straight-backed, at one end of a long walnut table.

He was as cold and pale as his name, with hair so blond it was almost white, his eyes a limpid grey. There was a square-shaped, frowning man on one side of him – Benedict faintly recognised him – and a woman taking notes.

'This . . . unpleasantness has come at a difficult time,' Snow said. 'You will be aware that Operation Frostbite is nearing its most critical stage. Information is on a need-to-know basis, but you will have gleaned I'm sure that we are attempting to accomplish the defection of a general in the KGB. This defection is of vital importance not only because it would be the highest-ranking *Cheka* officer to have come over to our side, nor simply because we know that he is currently one of the key players in a vast operation to infiltrate Western embassies in Eastern Europe.

'The reason we cannot – please, Miss Neill, stop transcribing for a moment – fuck this up, is because this is a joint op with the CIA and we have fucked up so royally and repeatedly in the eyes of our American friends that we are on the very last dregs of our last drink at the last-chance saloon. Philby has made us look like – excuse me, Miss Neill – fuckwits of the highest order and he has also made the CIA look like, well, precisely. They are out of patience with us and if we make the traditional dog's breakfast of this operation, right when we're in a position to bring him over . . . Well, it doesn't bear thinking about.'

Only the scratch of Miss Neill's pen broke the silence. Benedict met Snow's eyes. 'How, precisely, can I help?'

'You can start' – the merest hint of anger here from Snow – 'by explaining how it is that this absolute fucking shambles of a young man was sent to such a sensitive location.'

'I was asked to assess the quality of his Russian phrasing, his cultural and operational readiness for deployment. I did not see anything that suggested to me that he would be a liability.'

'And yet liability he is, I'm afraid. It will be up to you, Mr Pierce, to clean up this mess, and sharpish. I have booked you on the 10 a.m. flight to Sheremetyevo tomorrow morning. You're to get this silly oik home, one way or another. I simply will not have him ruin the most important operation we've mounted for a decade. I'm worried that if we just order him back, he'll kick up a fuss. And Miss Sinclair is too busy to chaperone him. You'll have to do the shepherding. A good lesson for you, to think rather more carefully about your recommendations.'

Benedict recognised that this was an order, rather than a request, and so he stood to leave.

'You might just go and spend an hour with Mr Smith, here,' Snow said, gesturing to the large man beside him. 'Mr Smith is in charge of Special Operations. He'll get you kitted out ready for your journey.'

What this kitting out involved, Benedict discovered, was a trip down into the basement of 54 Broadway, where, behind a heavy door, there was an armoury and research centre.

Mr Smith was a man of few words, it seemed. He disappeared into an alcove at the back of the large, low-ceilinged room, in which small groups of scientific types in white coats gathered around workbenches. He returned with an attaché case, which he opened on the table in front of Benedict. It contained a series of vials and syringes.

'You'll have a document to get this through customs at Sheremetyevo,' Smith said in a scratchy voice. 'Very fine needles. He'll think he felt a tickle when you inject him. I've put plenty in there, so you can have a practice beforehand. Vials on the left are incapacitants, vials on the right are Mickey Finns. So depends if you want him conscious or not. First one helps if you want to take the lad back on the plane in a wheelchair. He'll be eyes open but won't speak or move.'

Now Smith pulled out a single vial with a milky substance in it. He held it up to the bare electric bulb hanging above them. 'This is ricin,' he said. 'In case you need to take him out permanently. What's nice about ricin,' he said, a previously absent warmth entering his voice, 'is that it's slow-acting. Thirty-six, maybe forty-eight hours before you see any symptoms, and even then, he'll be on the khazi for an hour or two before he realises something's up. You can be well clear by then.'

He closed the case and reached into his pocket for an envelope. 'This is the note for customs. You're a salesman of veterinary goods. Also in here is a map of the Service dead drop in Gorky Park. You'll find a revolver in there and some roubles. Try not to spend them if you don't have to. Easy place to get over-excited, Moscow. Some beautiful women.' He gave Benedict a conspiratorial leer. 'Miss Sinclair will have more information for you out there.'

Smith walked Benedict to the door. He opened it and then leant forward, his voice so low and gravelly that Benedict had to incline his head to catch it.

'If I might say one thing, Mr Pierce.' Benedict could feel his breath in his ear, could smell his breakfast. 'If they ask me to put ricin in the case, it's the ricin they want you to use. Do you follow me?' Benedict nodded his head and, the case suddenly much heavier in his hand, took the elevator up to his desk.

V.

THE DRIVE FROM the airport into the city centre reminded Benedict of some of the unlovelier suburbs of Berlin. He passed row after row of monstrous high-rise housing. Long blocks of utilitarian buildings, no grass or greenery, the few trees leafless and spindly.

It was March and snow still lay in dirty heaps on the ground. He had breezed through customs, the official not bothering to inspect his case and looking with only faint interest at his passport.

Benedict had never been to Moscow before. He felt a shiver when the Moskva came into sight, the glittering onion domes of the city's cathedrals, churches and the grand geometrical towers of the various ministries.

He was at once in enemy territory and coming home, but it was more that he had lived so long in this place in his mind, in Dostoevsky and Chekhov, in the poems of Anna Akhmatova and Osip Mandelstam. It was both utterly foreign and intimately familiar, this birthplace of the doctrine of friendship and equality which had for so long coloured his world.

He was booked in at a down-at-heel hotel near the Sanduny bathhouse, the proprietor sitting in a yellow cloud of cigarette smoke at the reception, muttering inaudible threats at Benedict as he walked up the creaking stairs.

He left his bags in the poky room with its sagging bed, wrapped a scarf around his neck and set out into the bustling streets.

It was, he found, hard to think of the people here as his brothers and sisters. They were not the square-jawed and admirable Soviets of his imagination. There was a threadbare, grasping feel to the city. Faces were sallow and hollow-eyed. Dirty children, under-dressed for the weather, begged at the entrances to the metro stations, huddling over the vents for hot air. There were queues outside the bakeries and grocery stores, the drab Muscovites shuffling forward, looking like they'd long ago given up whatever spirit saw them through the war. Fur-capped babushkas sold chestnuts on the corners of Kuznetsky Most, clapping their arms and squawking at one another like crows.

Benedict bought himself a cone and ate the steaming chestnuts as he made his way through Red Square and down to the river.

He was aware, almost from the moment he left his hotel, that he was being followed. His tail was a bushy-haired man in his fifties – camel coat, stooped against the wind once they got onto the bridge, a slight limp.

Benedict thought he would be able to lose him easily enough. The KGB, he knew from Philby, had green-lit his arrival in the country, so this would be some low-ranking Militsiya officer, notified by the landlord of his hotel that a foreigner speaking over-precise Russian had just checked in.

He walked slowly over the bridge, taking his time to look down at the murky water, across at the golden domes of the Cathedral of Christ the Saviour, wondering if, perhaps, Dostoevsky had stood here, or Tolstoy, or Lermontov, feeling the ghostly footsteps of men he'd admired since he could read: men whose work came before the political movement that was changing the world, but who fertilised the soil in which it had grown with such vigour.

He was certain that, had it not been for his love of Russian novels, he would not have fallen with such swift certainty for Communism.

He dawdled on, using a pocket mirror to take the occasional glance at his tail. On the far side of the bridge, spying a group of teenagers surrounding a busker at the entrance to the park, he hurried into the crowd. He stooped to tie his shoelace, looking through a jostle of knees to see the legs of his pursuer moving with sudden haste past the group and along the railings that separated the park from the road.

He stayed down a little longer, drew a cloth cap from his bag and placed it firmly on his head, then went back in the direction from which he'd come.

He scurried into the entrance to the park, found a kiosk from which he purchased a copy of *Pravda*, then sat on a bench, his hat pulled low over his eyes, his mirror positioned so that he could see the man pass by once, then again. He watched him leave, puffing loudly, then went to the dead drop – a hollow tree at the far end of the park, underneath the gloomy bulk of the hospital.

The revolver was a Makarov PM. Benedict had used

one like it in Berlin, never in anger, but as a way of feeling more confident when he went to meet agents in the east of the city, or disaffected KGB men in the shadows of Potsdam apartment blocks.

VI.

BENEDICT ARRANGED TO meet Lucan for dinner the next night at Café Pushkin on Tverskoy Boulevard – Patricia had recommended it as one of the few places he could get a decent glass of wine to fortify him for what lay ahead.

He spent the day with Patricia, wandering from one museum to the next, alternately planning Lucan's assassination and trying not to think about it. He would be thirty-seven on his next birthday. His father had been dead by this age.

He and Patricia had lunch with Philby at a restaurant by the river. She was bright, her voice loud, her manner brusque and brassy. Philby was drunk, quiet, drooping morosely over the borscht, which he left untouched. Benedict pushed his food from one side of his plate to another as the traffic crept along the Sofiyskaya Embankment towards Balchug Street. He was beginning to know Moscow. He found himself wondering idly if the next time he'd be back here would be as an exile, living like Philby in a city-shaped cage. There were worse places to be, he supposed. But surely not very many.

Philby embraced him hard when they said goodbye.

There was a fine painting in the State Tretyakov Gallery by Pavel Korin. It showed a woman looking serenely back at the viewer, something melancholy yet challenging in her eyes. She reminded Benedict of his mother, whom he had not seen for several years.

He stood in front of the painting for a long time, wondering what she would make of the man he had become. He had spent Christmases with her until, one year, he was obliged to remain in Berlin: he was in charge of a surveillance operation on a French diplomat who was said to be leaking vital information about NATO intelligence operations in Eastern Europe to the Stasi via his East German mistress.

The lovers were due to meet on Christmas Eve and Benedict phoned his mother to say he would not be coming home. The resignation in her voice almost floored him. After this, it just became easier for him not to see her, to fabricate excuses and obligations that meant she was left in the little house in Marlow, alone with her memories. He hated himself for having abandoned her, but she made him hate himself when he was with her: the smallness of her ambitions, the pettiness of her grudges and jealousies, the remorseless persistence of the love he felt for her. Now here he was in Moscow, and there was bitterness in his heart.

It was time to dress for dinner. Patricia came with him to his hotel room, watching him change as she lay back on the bed, blowing smoke up towards the ceiling.

'I'll be thinking of you, darling. I'd do it myself if I could, but I do think it's important for you to be the prime mover here. To clear up your own mess. I'll stay as close to you as I can, all evening. Now, come, let's get it over with. Do you have the vial, the syringe? Your revolver for emergencies?'

He patted his breast pocket, then his hip, and she rose, looked at him appraisingly, straightened his tie.

'You've hardly aged a day since I first met you, do you know that, Ben? Shocking how youthful you look. No wonder these young men keep throwing themselves at you.'

They made their way down the staircase into the lobby, where Patricia kissed him quickly. 'We should go our separate ways here, but I'll be right behind you, darling.'

VII.

THE PUSHKIN LOOKED like a French brasserie, all gilt mirrors and white tablecloths. Lucan was there already, waiting at a table near the back of the room. He stood up when Benedict entered, waving eagerly.

Benedict made his way through the tables, stepping aside as a waiter came past with a tray bearing three steaming plates of goulash.

Lucan crossed the last few yards to Benedict, taking him in his arms.

'Let's sit down, shall we?' Benedict said. Patricia had given him a packet of cigarettes and he drew one.

'You smoke now?' Lucan said with a laugh. 'I thought you couldn't bear them. And there was I trying to hide the fact that I was smoking again. May I cadge one?'

It was one of the most draining, miserable hours of Benedict's life. Lucan was frenetic, self-deprecating, apologetic.

'I really do feel like I've ballsed things up rather here. But, honestly, I had the very best intentions. I wanted to make you proud, I still do. But it just seemed as if everything I tried went wrong. I ended up feeling such a terrible impostor. And I know she's an old pal of yours, but I do feel that Patricia didn't make things easy for me. I thought she was supposed to be one of us, a Communist . . .' He said the word in a scandalised whisper, then looked about him. 'But whenever I tried to speak to her about it, or to confide in her, she'd give me the most awful glares.' Benedict found that he could imagine it. 'I would have thought she'd be keen to take care of someone so close to one of her pals.'

'She's busy,' Benedict said. 'But you've nothing to worry about now. The Service understands that sometimes things just don't work out. You did your best. We'll find something else for you. Please, Lucan, you mustn't blame yourself.'

They finished a bottle of wine, then moved on to vodka. The food was almost edible. Benedict found himself hoping, somehow, that they could pause time, could continue eating the dishes brought out by the handsome waiters, who moved between the tables like dancers, could continue drinking the good, cold vodka, raising their glasses to each other, to Moscow, to Comrade Krushchev.

But then, all of a sudden, it was over, and they were standing outside. Snow was falling thinly. Lucan wore an absurd white *ushanka* – Arctic hare, he told Benedict – a long leather jacket, black and white fur boots. He looked like a character from Pasternak: romantic, remote, already fading.

They were both drunk, Benedict realised. Lucan staggered into him when they set off, then turned to face him with a wide grin.

'Is that a gun in your pocket?' he asked with a laugh. It was. 'Are we going back to mine?' His voice was high and hectic. 'I think we probably should. Worth checking that we're not being followed, though. Can't be too careful.' He made a performance of looking first one way, then the other, a child's idea of spycraft.

Lucan, Benedict knew, lived on the other side of Kitay-gorod, down towards Zaryadye Park. They walked through the snowy evening, stepping from one pool of light to the next beneath the street lamps, and Benedict felt the vial of poison in his breast pocket like a sliver of ice.

He tried to imagine himself in a quite different reality, walking through a strange and beautiful city in the snow with his young lover, but he kept running up against the grim inevitability of what was to come.

They walked through Red Square like tourists, the guards standing impassively at the gates of Lenin's tomb, disregarding the snow falling harder now, blowing about them in billows. The domes of St Basil's looked exotic lit from beneath, as if they were drifting through a blizzard, unmoored from the earth.

Lucan led them up one of the streets off the square, pointing out the language school where he took Russian.

'It turns out that I'm hopeless,' he said. 'You were such a good teacher back in London, but it goes in one ear and out the other.' He gave a shrill laugh.

They passed a grand apartment building, large and square-fronted, the sort of place that would have been called a *hôtel particulier* in Paris. There was scaffolding up the front of it, a huge crane rising into the snowy darkness above. The entrance was a porte-cochère, made for carriages. Set within the black doors, though, was a wicket gate, and Benedict noticed it was open.

'Let's go in,' he said, and before Lucan could answer, he'd made his way through the gate and into the courtyard of the building. It was dark and empty, stacks of bricks and tiles in one corner. Ahead of them, there was a large doorway.

'It'll be closed, I imagine,' Lucan said, but it wasn't – Benedict tried the handle and it creaked open, leading through an entrance porch to a hall with stone stairs disappearing into darkness. 'This is magical.'

Lucan took off his hat and made his way up in the half-light. Here and there a window let in the ambient glow of the city, spotlights on the sights of Red Square. Soon they were walking through empty salons and dining rooms, their footsteps echoing under the high ceilings. They went up another floor and it grew lighter still – French windows gave onto balconies with even more Moscow. 'Imagine living here,' Lucan said. 'Perhaps we will someday, once all the work is over.'

There was scaffolding at one end of the room they were in. They went to sit down on the boards of it. Lucan swung his legs up and lay back, fashioning a pillow from his *ushanka*.

'What do you think will happen to me, when I get back, I mean? Will they make me do something frightful and dull?'

Benedict lay down next to him, looking up at the jagged shadows on the ceiling.

'At least you'll be there,' Lucan went on. 'I think, maybe, I made such a balls-up here so that I'd get back to you sooner. I really do love you, you know.'

Benedict felt the ice in his heart expanding. He turned and kissed Lucan on the mouth. They kissed for a while, then Benedict took off his jacket, folding it carefully on the floor beside them. They had both warmed up a little and now Benedict helped Lucan to slip out of his trousers, then his pants. He took Lucan in his mouth.

'Wait,' Lucan said. 'There's something I need to tell you.' Benedict looked up. Lucan's face was half in shadow. 'I . . . I have been meaning to tell you all night, but there just wasn't the time. And I've been so terribly nervous. I need to tell you that I've met someone, I've met a girl. And while she doesn't mean to me what you mean to me, I have been seeing her rather a lot.'

'What's her name?' Benedict said. 'Is she a local?'

'No, not at all. She's from Shoreham-by-Sea. She works in the Embassy, speaks wonderful Russian. She's been helping me with the language. Her name is Nelly.'

'Nelly. Lovely. It doesn't matter, it doesn't matter at all.' Benedict felt hopeless, picturing the young woman, enchanted by the tall, dashing spy, with his Roman nose and dreaming eyes.

'Listen, I don't know about these things, about the practicalities of it all, but I wondered if you might arrange for her to come back to England with me, when I go. She's awfully bright and very beautiful. I really think you'd get on. And of course it won't change a thing between us.'

'Yes, yes, that all sounds perfect. I'll speak to Patricia. I'll clear it. Of course.'

Lucan smiled down at Benedict, then lay back and gave himself up to the pleasure of the warm mouth.

With his left hand, Benedict stroked Lucan's thighs, his balls, moving his head slowly back and forward as he did so, flicking his tongue across Lucan's pulsing cock. Lucan groaned in pleasure, his eyes tightly closed.

With his right hand, Benedict reached for the vial, which he then gripped between his legs. He drew out the syringe. It required enormous concentration, half-drunk as he was, to break the seal on top of the vial and slide the needle in, one-handed and still moving his tongue.

He realised he'd been caressing the same perineal patch for a minute or so, and moved quickly to stroke the balls, which he felt gathering themselves, ready to empty.

It all happened like a chain. Benedict reached round and jabbed the needle into the flesh of Lucan's bum. 'Ow,' Lucan said, and then, 'Unngh,' as he came in three warm streaks into Benedict's mouth. Then another noise, and they both turned to see, coming through the doorway with a flashlight, the Militsiya officer who'd been following them, a fedora thick with bushy hair.

'Ah,' he said, then, 'Ah,' again. *'Golubye!'* He stood, shining his torch accusingly, looking at once triumphant and unsure of his next move.

Benedict, swallowing, reached down again into his coat, drew out the Makarov PM and shot the man through the chest.

'Crikey,' Lucan said, pulling up his pants.

VIII.

THEY DRAGGED THE body over to a cupboard in the corner and, with a degree of difficulty, shut the door.

The gun had seemed extraordinarily loud in the echoing room, and Benedict was keen to leave swiftly.

They went down the stairs two at a time, a feeling of sudden release, of lightness, all about them. There was, in Benedict, a sense that he had done something irrevocable, but that at least it was done, and quickly. Macbeth and Duncan, he thought. But no, Macbeth and Banquo. At least he'd had the guts to do this himself.

'I think I've got a splinter,' Lucan said, rubbing his bottom as they passed through the wicket gate and into the snowblind street. 'It hurts something awful.'

They rushed, almost running, but the snow was all about them and they met no one. When they had walked for ten minutes and were sure they weren't being followed, they stopped. They were on Revolution Square – Benedict could see the Bolshoi peering out through the trees.

'Listen,' he said. 'I'm not so far from my hotel here.'

'Oh, well, let's go there.'

Benedict took a deep breath. He knew he had time, that the poison in Lucan's body had a long fuse. But he wanted to be alone, wanted to mourn the loss of his lover, not witness it.

'Do you mind if we don't?' he said. 'We can have supper again tomorrow. Can plan properly for the future, for our life together in London. I want to meet Nelly, too. But I'm so tired and I've just killed a man and I don't think I'll be much company.'

'Of course, of course. But, wait, come here.'

Looking about and sure that there was nobody around, Lucan leant forward and kissed Benedict, and it was as if they were in a private chamber of snow, the wind singing all about them, their arms around each other, and anyone seeing would have said that this was love, the deepest kind, and yet even then, as Benedict gently bit Lucan's full lips, the poison was spreading through his body, the fuse burning down.

As they said goodbye, Lucan took his ridiculous *ushanka* from his head and handed it to Benedict. 'It will keep you warm while you're here,' he said, and then turned and was swallowed by the snow. Benedict stood for a long time, letting the snow settle on his eyelashes, on his cheeks, on the *ushanka*, knowing that even after all the betrayals and double-crossings, after Besian and the other Pixies sent to die, this, tonight, was the worst thing he'd ever done.

Full of self-reproach and regret, he walked through the streets in which his future might lie, certain that whatever happened here in the years to come, Moscow would always be the city of Lucan.

IX.

THE CALL CAME on a secure line a month later. Benedict was in Century House, writing up notes on the relationship between Tito and Zhukov. He didn't speak Serbo-Croat, and there were a large number of files in that language, and so he was forced to leave his seat every so often to ask someone on the Balkan desk to translate for him.

He felt neutered when he didn't know a language and made up his mind that, by his death bed, he'd be conversationally fluent in every major tongue. It was a secretary who came to fetch him, one of the blonde girls with crystalline accents with which George Verney – the C – insisted on surrounding himself.

'Mr Pierce, a call for you on the line from Moscow Station. Will you come up to take it?'

He followed her to the phone booth in a room on the fifth floor overlooking St George's Circus. He nodded at the girl, picked up the receiver and heard Patricia's voice.

'Bad news, Ben,' she said. 'Your beloved Lucan is still alive.'

In a strange way, Benedict already knew this. Lucan had been visiting him in his dreams, a silent, judgemental presence, busy with shopping or talking, breaking to look at Benedict with disappointment in those wide, dark eyes.

'It was ricin: there's simply no way he could have survived. You must not have injected him properly. Or at all.'

'I did, of course I did.'

'Well, then, how do you explain him turning up here with his girlfriend? She's a piece of work, I'll tell you that.'

Benedict felt suddenly very tired. 'What can we do?'

'We can do very little. The girlfriend, Nelly, informed me that Lucan had told her in great detail about the compromised positions of Benedict Pierce and Humphrey Musgrave, of Violet Chisholm and Harris Davenport. And apparently he showed her some compelling evidence regarding my own links to the Soviet regime. What's more, she said, and I have to say I rather liked her by the end of it – spunky little thing – that she had written up this information and sent it by telegram to Lucan's mother in Yugoslavia and her own father in London.

Her father is a QC. He won't, apparently, release the information as long as Lucan and Nelly are permitted to leave Moscow and are allocated other roles within MI6.'

'Is he all right, Lucan?'

'As much as he ever was.'

'So what will happen to them?'

'Arkady is already speaking to people in Yugoslavia. I've cleared things with Verney. They will go back to London for a bit, then they'll be sent out to the Belgrade station. His mother lives on an island somewhere between Split and Dubrovnik. They'll be fine there for a while. When the time comes, we can have them neutralised. We've more than enough people on the ground to make that happen.'

PART 7

Corfu, October 1996

I.

THEY CARRIED HARRIS into the cottage. Boyd took him under the arms, and Nina and Benedict held a foot each. He was heavy, as if life still weighed upon him. Violet walked beside them. They processed up the steps and into the darkness of the drawing room, where they laid him out on the sofa. Violet took his head in her lap again. No one had spoken since the shots were fired and the silence had grown so large and dense that Nina wondered if anyone would ever speak again.

She got up, stoked the fire, relit the candles and brought them over to the seating area near the entrance to the cottage. There was something hieratical about the flickering lights on the dead man's body. If she believed in a God, she would have said His name then, would have asked for whatever mercy that God might offer them. Instead, it was Violet who spoke first, addressing herself not to those who sat in the chairs on either side of the sofa, or to Nina cross-legged on the floor, but to Harris.

'I knew they'd get to you, my love. I knew in the end they would. You always were one to act rather than think. I'm sorry that I made you poorly. I thought it might keep you out of their grasp. But, still, it would only have been a matter of time.'

More silence. The wind outside had finally begun to die down. It was, Nina thought, well past midnight. It was still raining, but the rain was softer now, pattering its fingers against the windows at the side of the house, no longer so loud on the roof above them.

'Who is "*they*", Violet?' Boyd's voice was low and confiding. 'Who got to Harris?' Nina saw that he was holding Violet by the hand. Benedict, in the other armchair, was sitting straight, his face unreadable, his hands knitted in his lap.

'You don't know?' Violet said. 'I thought everyone knew. I thought everyone was in their pocket. Why, Patricia and Arkady of course. Their great power grab. Ably helped by their henchmen: Lucan Woolf, Snow and Smith.'

Nina looked up at the mention of her father's name. Violet caught her eye. 'We have – all of us – tried to keep it from you, my dear. There was a hope, I think, that it wouldn't be so bad. That Patricia would leave us to rot out our final years here in peace. I understand that a journalist was digging for information, though. That's right, isn't it, Benedict?'

'I believe so.' His words very flat. He didn't look at any of them.

'I'm sure of it,' Violet went on. 'Benedict, you see, thought he'd play the hero. Spoke to friends from the old days about Patricia's past. Wrote letters to such and such at *The Times* and the *Guardian*. Why he couldn't just leave things be, I don't know. But then he's suffered, too.'

Benedict took off his glasses, polished them with his

handkerchief, then put them back on. 'I did what I thought was best. I couldn't let her and Arkady get away with it. Desecrating everything we'd built together. Exchanging the purity of that vision for mud. Murdering my dear Humphrey.'

Boyd was sitting back, smoking, his face in shadows. 'You're speaking about Arkady Malkin,' he said. 'I've read about him. He's one of the SVR, right? The ex-KGB lot busy slicing up Russia between them. But how is he linked to Patricia Sinclair? And how does that bring us to Harris?'

Nina gestured at Boyd, who threw her a pack of cigarettes. She lit one from a candle. 'Shouldn't we go and get Drinkwater? We need to inform the police, to get this dealt with properly, professionally.'

'I wouldn't be so sure that Drinkwater isn't one of them,' Benedict said. 'At least, I think he understands it's within his interests to turn a blind eye to what they're doing. That's what he did with the post-Christmas Massacre crowd, but then someone like Lucy Fellowes was more obviously a risk to Patricia and Arkady. That period just after the Fall was terribly difficult for Patricia. All of these files suddenly available with her name circled in red ink while she sat right at the heart of MI6. And now with her daughter as the C. They nixed six or seven of them in all. Suicides, drink, old age stumbles. Tried to bump off Edward Lane more times than I could count. With Lucy Fellowes it was supposed to be drowning, even though she was the most wonderful swimmer, as good as Nina.'

'I suppose the ease with which they disposed of the SovBloc gang gave them confidence with us.' Violet picked up the thread. 'When you have a group of people who've lived their lives at the very edge, a little nudge into the void is a simple business. I am furious with you, Ben, for writing to those journalists. But I think they would probably have come after us in the end.'

II.

NINA NOTICED THAT Violet was shivering. She found a blanket and draped it over her shoulders. Violet looked up with a smile, her face all light and shadows in the flicker of the candles.

'Patricia and Arkady met a very long time ago, in a far brighter and more optimistic world. We were all of us Communists of one shade or another. Benedict was a fervent Marxist, weren't you, my love? We had this very stern conviction that we were the agents of history. Arkady recruited Patricia during the war, then she recruited us. And we spied for the enemy for the best part of thirty years. Some of us more energetically than others.'

'Double agents.' Nina had thought of her friends — if she thought of their Communism at all, which seemed so anchored in another world — as quaint, weathered idealists. The sort who might once have stood with copies of the *Socialist Worker* outside Boswell's on a grey Oxford afternoon, half earnest, half performative. This was something else though — and she felt her mind slowly readjust to the reality. Betrayal. Not just ideas over drinks but dark acts in silence.

'Yes.' Violet's eyes were very red, her voice very low.

'There was such a stink over Philby and Blunt, and then Cairncross's name came out. The Office simply couldn't face another raft of headlines. We were sent out here to be forgotten, although you'll notice that Patricia never quite made it out with us.'

'You weren't forgotten enough.'

Here Benedict held up a finger. 'If I could just take a moment to explain myself,' he said. When they were silent, he seemed to be suddenly lost for words. 'I . . . I . . . remember how bewitched I was by the grace and the glamour of the future. We were doing something that would endure, that would make life better not just for ourselves and our children, but for millions.'

'You always were a terrible romantic.' Violet smiled at him.

'We all were, I think. We weren't individuals, we were joined by our love – for each other, for everyone. And then the moment the Soviet project collapsed, Patricia and Arkady leapt from Marxism to the most feverish sort of capitalist excess. I couldn't let it stand. I won't let it stand.'

Nina realised that she had grown quite accustomed to the fact that there was a dead man listening. She wondered if perhaps they should lay him out on the bed at the back of the house. But Violet looked so comfortable with him there in her lap, as if he were merely snoozing and she were singing him to sleep.

'How is Clara implicated in all this?' Nina asked.

Benedict thought for a moment. 'Plausible deniability, I think, would have been her approach. Patricia, you see, didn't make C because a female C simply wouldn't have been contemplated at the time. She was always terribly ambitious for her daughter, though. So Clara rose and rose, her mother's hand firmly in the small of her back. The youngest ever C. The first woman in the role. The idea initially, I imagine, was for Moscow to have someone installed at the very pinnacle of the Service. Then the Wall fell, and what had been a political ambition turned into a plan about wealth and power.

'Arkady has been hoovering up the former Soviet monopolies. The KGB had the networks of connections, they had the money. Arkady seized control of Sovetskoy Narodny Bank in 1991, used the assets to buy half of Siberia. And he looked at his daughter, Clara, and saw the opportunity to put this new wealth to use. She was brilliant, lauded and yet, to him at least, entirely malleable. His money, her power. Patricia sitting like a spider behind them both.'

There was a clicking sound and the lights came back on, surprising them all. Some burbling at the back of the house as a boiler sprang back to life.

'So Humphrey and Edward – their deaths were linked to this, too?' Nina said, looking from Violet to Benedict. There was a long pause.

'We felt terribly lucky, really,' Benedict said, 'to have had all this time together. On the outside, I wasn't the most faithful of . . . well, whatever I was to Humphrey. No question of us getting married, not at that time and certainly not here in Greece. I'm not sure what it would have meant, anyway. Posted to different corners of the world, our hours and days together snatched and always insufficient. Then, to end up here, in each other's pockets, to have twenty years of happiness landed upon us by mere circumstance. We were thankful for every day of it. I had imagined our old age apart, in exile, or in prison. This was heaven, it really was.'

Nina saw that there were tears in Benedict's eyes.

'They got hold of us one day in town, Snow and Smith, your father, Nina. Tried to persuade us to do the decent thing and top ourselves. Save them the bother. They explained it very clearly: it was simply too much of a risk to have us go on living. Malkin was about to make the final move to secure his political position in Russia, Clara and Patricia were putting in place the first steps of their own complex game.'

'And you were the last link to history,' Nina said.

'An inconvenient history, precisely. Humphrey and me, Harris and Violet. They needed us all to exit stage left.'

'That evening, in the woods. They were trying to assassinate you?'

'It was their second, rather less elegant approach. One of Arkady's goons with a hunting rifle. Make it look like an accident. Your father was horrified that you'd been caught up in it. He was the most reasonable of them all, your father. Hated me, of course, for what had happened between us . . .'

'What was that?'

'Ah, that's for another day, my dear. But you must understand that I feel very keenly my share of the guilt for everything that happened. After all that time, your father, Malkin and Patricia, the reappearance of a whole world I thought we'd left behind, it was as if someone had stirred the murky pond of my past, all these dark and forgotten objects rising to the surface. We knew our time was up. Humphrey and I discussed it like the adults we'd become. A good innings, batting longer into the evening than most. Had the best time, now time to go.'

'What happened with Humphrey?' Nina felt things slowly clicking into place, a world which had seemed befuddling in its lurches from one tragedy to the next now emerging into focus.

'It was Edward, of course it was bloody Edward. They played on his vanity. Told him he'd been sent out here to complete this final mission. Edward knew that Humphrey had been a Communist. From then it was simple: a stroll down to the harbour, a small injection of something – sodium thiopental, maybe – just to make sure he slept until the water took him, then heaving him off the side of the dock. Humphrey was a lovely man, you all know that, don't you? The loveliest of men.' A long silence. The rain fell, pattering on the roof, on the windows.

'I had to get my revenge. Of course I did. That's how we work. Lane was in the bowls hut one evening. I confronted him. A cosh to the head. Then, that night, dragging him down to the water. I tied the bowls bag around his neck and down he went. I think their plan was for me to be persuaded to kill the others, too.'

'Not quite, Ben.' Violet's voice was suddenly sharp. 'You don't imagine that you and Humphrey were the only ones they contacted? They came to me first. I think they realised that Harris would make a pig's ear of it. And I – like you, Ben – had long had the sense that we'd stolen this time from the world, that we were terribly lucky to have survived this far. I just tried to spin it out for a wee bit longer. Thought we might manage another year, even two. But then when Humphrey went, and then Lane, I knew they had got to someone.

I wondered if it was you, Boyd, actually. If you had been sent out here to accelerate things.'

Violet now looked at Nina, something kind in her pale eyes. 'Then your father turned up here the other night. He's staying in an apartment on Alexandras Avenue, down in the New Town. Harris was already asleep. We sat in these very chairs and had a conversation about it all, your dad and I. Malkin plans to run for president in the spring; he wants all this out of the way before he does so. And he wants to ensure nothing stands in Clara's way when she makes her play for the top job – PM, or foreign secretary – whatever he decides will be most useful to him.'

Boyd was scrabbling in his pockets. Nina picked up the cigarettes and tossed them to him. He smiled and lit one, then let out a breath of smoke.

'Oh, go on then,' Violet said. 'For old times' sake.' Boyd passed her a cigarette and lit it for her. She exhaled, coughed a little. 'It was the one thing I realised, very early. That when it came to Patricia and Arkady, what drove them was the route that Communism gave them to power, rather than the change it would make to the world. They wanted to control people, wanted to shape millions of lives. Whether it was Marxism or capitalism or fascism that got them there – I think that mattered very little to them. I had a sense of it even at the very beginning, back at Oxford. Anyway, knowing that the end was near, I gave Harris a triple dose of his heart medication. I thought if I could get him out of the way for a while then Benedict and I might be able to put up some sort of resistance. But, as I say, it was only delaying the inevitable.'

'So what do we do now?' Nina asked.

'We wait for them to come,' said Violet simply. 'It will be hard for them to do away with all of us at once. They're in a hurry, but I'm not sure even they'd be that bold, even with the sway they have. That nice Inspector Metallinos will ask questions, I'm sure. But they'll be several steps ahead. Arkady always was.'

Their cigarettes burnt down, the rain fell on, the odd flash of lightning far in the distance, too far for the sound of the thunder to reach them. Hours passed, the still, unminuted hours of the deep night. Finally, footsteps coming up the steps outside, a sharp knock on the door.

III.

EVEN AFTER ALL she had heard, it was still a shock to Nina that her father was there, his bushy black hair plastered to his head by the rain, his jacket hanging damply from those broad shoulders. Behind him, stood a thin, pale older man with white hair. Lucan Woolf spent the briefest moment taking in the scene. 'Hello, Nina,' he said, and, unthinkingly, she rose to hug him.

'Hello, Dad,' she said.

'Do you remember Mr Snow?' He nodded at the man who was now bending to inspect Harris with a kind of academic interest. 'You'll have met him when you were a child. Now listen, darling, why don't you run up to bed at the villa? You and I can chat about all this later. I'm sure your head's full of the most astonishing nonsense at the moment, but I'll set you straight, I promise. I didn't want them to send you out here. I should have pushed back harder against it . . .'

'I want to stay, Dad. Please.'

Lucan looked at Snow, who shook his head. 'Take her up, will you, Boyd?'

Boyd gave a helpless shrug and stood, reaching down to take Nina by the arm. 'Come on. This isn't our battle,' he said.

'He's right,' Violet said. 'All this should have been ironed out years ago. You go on up, dear. We'll be along just after. Or we'll see you for your morning swim.'

'No!' Nina was crying now, straining against Boyd, who had both of his arms around her and was pulling her towards the door. She met Benedict's eyes just before she was dragged out into the night. He was smiling and gave her the smallest nod, and she sent to him, in that moment, all the love and strength she could muster.

IV.

AT THE FRONT of the villa a large, bald man stood in the rain, a shotgun slung across his chest. He frowned at Boyd and Nina as they emerged into the small cone of wet light above the entrance.

'Boyd,' he said. 'Everything cushty?' His voice was a growl. 'You'll stay with her until Snow and Woolf are back?'

Boyd just nodded and the man stood aside to let them through. The villa was quiet, only the sound of waves on the rocks below, the occasional rattle of a window or creak of an upstairs floorboard.

Boyd held her on the bed as she sobbed, comfort and constraint in the pressure of his arms. It was not sorrow, not yet, but instead the frustrated rage of a child that made her pound her fists and shriek into her pillow. She should have stayed with them, should have fought with every last shred of spirit to remain in that room, to protect Benedict and Violet. She had not stayed with little Amar and Samija, whom she had sworn to protect in Sarajevo, and was yet to forgive herself. Now she'd left two more people she loved. She wondered, even there, in the midst of her fury, if this was what life was, a series of losses and betrayals, the full chambers of her heart slowly emptying.

'I'm sorry,' Boyd said. 'I'm so sorry.'

They were both still in their sodden clothes, their hair damp.

Nina shuddered, tried to shrug out of Boyd's embrace. 'You were one of them all along. A snake. I trusted you. Back when I worked for you, I trusted you, and I trusted you here. I was an idiot, twice over.'

Boyd drew back now, sitting up on the bed, his hands held out towards her. 'Hold on. You have to understand – they were traitors. I don't know anything about this great plot, about Arkady Malkin. It sounds pretty far-fetched to me, although I wouldn't put anything past Clara Sinclair. But Benedict and the others – people died because of them. I'm not saying they deserve to die for it, but they have to face justice of one kind or another.'

'So you were sent out here to make that happen?'

'I honestly had nothing to do with it. I was sent out here because I lost my mind. They let me know that some of the residents were posing problems, trying to dredge up the past. I was told I might be asked to finesse the situation, and that if I made a decent fist of it, it would increase my chances of a swift return. Isn't that what you want, too, Nina?'

'What I want is for you to get out of here. To fuck off and leave me alone.'

'I can't do that,' Boyd said quietly. 'But I promise that nothing will happen to you. Nothing bad, I mean.'

She stared at him furiously for a moment, riffling through her options in her head, forcing clarity into her thoughts. 'At least let me change. I'm soaked to the skin. You can wait outside for a minute.'

Boyd looked at her briefly, then shrugged. 'Give me a shout when you're done,' he said. She noticed that he didn't quite close the door when he went out. She shut it firmly, then turned to face the room.

V.

SHE NEEDED TO tell Metallinos: the thought came to her like a revelation. It was the work of a moment to open the window and drop into the flowerbed outside. It was still raining hard, but there was a soft light coming down through the clouds as Nina ran across the bowling green: morning. She knew she didn't have much of a start, knew also that Boyd would be faster than her on foot. She forced herself to pick up her pace as she passed the long white block of the san, then the ruined church. From there, she could just make out the contours of the shore ahead of her. Across the channel, Corfu itself was hidden by the curtain of rain. She slipped, regained her balance, went hurtling forward down the slope towards the dim shape of the abandoned restaurant, at whose dock the boats were moored. Except – and this she realised with a familiar panic, the panic of nightmares – they were gone. The dock itself had been damaged in the storm, one side of it listing dangerously, planks and debris scattered around the small inlet, the waves crashing around and all over it.

Nina looked desperately up and down the shore but the rain was falling harder than ever, needling off the surface of the sea until it seethed and, with the louder detonations of the waves, sending up a spray that the wind caught and flung back at her. She looked up the hill and saw the shadowy figure of Boyd and, beside him, the square shape of the man with the shotgun – Smith, she assumed. She started running again, although this time it was with less of a plan, more as a way of buying herself time. It was difficult to run down here by the shore, though, where the sand was damp and claggy, stretches of beach inter-rupted by sharp black extrusions of rock. She stumbled over one, pitching forward, the jagged edge raking her knee. For a moment, she stayed there, the pain hot and precise, before rising again, the torn denim around her knee soaked through, the blood blooming darkly.

She ran further, to where a fallen pine tree lay across the beach, its branches trapped in the surging water, its roots zagging from the soil from which it was just wrenched. She vaulted the trunk and then crouched down on its far side, catching her breath for a moment. She could see Boyd and Smith standing down by the restaurant, looking towards her, talking. She stood, turned towards the sea and, before she could subject the idea to scrutiny, threw herself into the waves.

VI.

SHE INHALED A mouthful of water almost immediately, the weight of her clothes catching her off-guard. Her jumper was like a straitjacket, her shoes absurdly heavy on her feet, her jeans shackling her legs. She felt herself pulled downwards, then a surge of water picked her up and flung her into the branches of the pine tree, knocking whatever breath she had left from her chest.

She grabbed a branch, hauled herself up and threw a leg over the trunk. She kicked her shoes off, tore off her socks, pulled her jumper over her head and cast it aside, then she struggled out of her jeans. Her mind went — as minds do — to the beach on the other side of Corfu, to the sight of Boyd walking naked towards the sea. She remembered the freedom she'd felt there, unencumbered by her clothes and her cares. It seemed so distant in both time and space.

Boyd and Smith were on the beach now. Smith had his shotgun raised and Boyd was shouting at her, gesticulating. Nina slipped into the water again, moving more easily, powering with her arms, breathing in the troughs between waves, looking up once to check her bearings, then realising how pointless this was. Black water, only water. She would have to rely on her sense of the one island behind her, the other in front.

She thought of the number of times she had made this crossing, a boat ride that was hardly worth the name. Now, whether because of the conditions, or because she wasn't entirely clear on which way was ahead, it seemed as if she might swim like this for the rest of her life, tossed by the towering waves, which lifted her up and slammed her down like a toy in the hands of a cruel child. And always, the rain. She stopped for a moment, gasping and treading water, and realised she could see no trace of land in either direction. She felt a sudden wash of despair, imagining everyone who had drowned in these waters, a seabed committee of Icarus, Ajax and Hylas, and all the other dead heroes, sighing and waiting to welcome her.

Then, quite close, the sound of a boat's engine.

She couldn't see it at first, was only aware of the vibration in the air as she rose and fell with the waves. She wasn't cold, but she shuddered. She wondered which of them had been sent to bring her back. She began to swim with renewed energy, pulling herself through the water until now, with a glance forward between strokes, she saw looming dimly in the distance the shape of the Venetian fort. She had been carried too far north by the current, she realised. She adjusted her bearing a little and risked a glance behind her. There it was, the fishing caïque, struggling through the pitching waves. She couldn't see who was in it, only that it was heading straight for her.

She thought she was perhaps a hundred yards from the long arm of the harbour pontoon. There was no way she could reach it before the boat caught up with her. She screamed into the storm, the fury spilling out of her, not just at the fact that she had so nearly made her escape, but at the whole sorry mess of her life. She tried for one final burst of speed, swimming not so much up and over the waves as through them, throwing her arms forward and grasping at the water as if she were climbing a ladder. Very soon, though, she felt the presence of the boat, the closeness of its wooden hull, and her father's voice.

'Nina!' She remembered how loud he could be, the violence of his rages when, as a child, she had disturbed him or said something foolish. She had, even at the time, made her peace with this side of him, reading it as the necessary counterpoint to his boisterous amiability when he was playing with her: the intensity of a man who felt everything just a little too keenly. Now, with the boat almost on top of her, he spoke more softly, hardly audible over the waves and the wind, his voice kind, wheedling, even. 'Darling, come back. Let us talk it all through. All of this can be smoothed over.'

She trod water again, looking up at the boat. Her father was kneeling on the prow, his hair matted against his head. He had not, it seemed, had time to put on a raincoat. His suit was soaked, his tie loose at his neck. Angelos was at the wheel, nervously keeping the boat in position. Behind her father, hanging on grimly to a rail, was Smith, clearly suffering from the pitching of the boat on the water. He held his gun by its barrel, leaning on the stock, his face twisted into a bilious leer. Nina met her father's eyes for a moment, remembered Benedict the night before, took a deep breath and dived beneath the waves.

A sudden calmness down there, the feeling of having entered some gentler, more forgiving world. She could see the shadow of the boat's hull above her and swam hard towards where, in her mind, the Old Town lay. She concentrated on gliding forward, shooting the arrow of her body fast from the bow of her kick. Her lungs began to ache, but she knew that this was just the pressure of the water. She could hold her breath for three, maybe four minutes on land; that would buy her perhaps half the distance to shore if she could manage it now. The boat, though, was moving above her. Its shadow passed over once, then again. She forced herself forward: five more strokes. Her chest was burning, her mind fighting every urge to rise.

She broke the surface, drawing in great gulps of air, feeling as if she would never be able to take sufficient breaths to quell the panic in her chest. She could see the boat idling between her and the harbour. They hadn't spotted her yet, but it wouldn't be long. She drew herself down into the water until only her face was above the surface. Then she dived down again and swam hard, not towards the shore, but parallel to it, aiming for the Old Fort, keeping the brooding crenellations as a lodestar in her mind. She surfaced again in the trough of a wave, breathed deeply, dived once more.

She had almost reached the beach they called Faliraki, just below the Palace of St Michael and St George, when they spotted her. She heard her father shout, heard the engine roar into life. She gave up her attempts at stealth and swam hard for the dock beside the taverna, all of it shut up for winter, battered by the waves that crashed up and over the stone wharf. The beach was still some distance to her left. She came in very fast, pushed by waves that seemed to gather themselves for their assault on the land. She turned and saw the boat behind her, Angelos taking it as close to the shore as he dared. Then she was picked up in a roil of white foam and tossed towards the dock, with its vicious encrustation of barnacles and mussels. She braced herself for impact, drew in a deep breath and, at the last moment, caught sight of a rusty iron mooring ring a few feet down from the edge of the dock, frayed blue rope twisted around it. She shot out a hand and gripped it just as the wave dumped her against the sea wall.

The pain, when it came, was excruciating. The wave flipped her over and dragged her against the barnacles, keel-hauling her, raking down her back, her thighs, her calves. She thought for a moment that she was going to lose consciousness, bit down hard on the inside of her cheek to prevent it. Then the wave drew back and she had to concentrate everything on the iron ring, both hands looped through it, the retreating wave sucking her hungrily. Then, a brief moment hanging, the next wave gathering itself to break, a few seconds' grace. She pulled herself up as far as she could, and with a final burst of effort, hooked a leg over the edge of the dock and rolled herself onto the wharf.

The wave did wash over her, but this time it felt like approval, the lick of a giant dog. She was exhausted, half-naked, bleeding from her back and her legs, a gash above her eye. She looked out to sea, and there, the caïque, unable to land on the wharf, was making its way to the sheltered harbour by the Venetian fort. She rose unsteadily to her feet and began to run.

VII.

THERE WAS A path that led under the town walls, up a steep incline and out onto the main coast road. She ran up it, pumping her arms hard, breathing deeply, then turned to pass through the arch by the Palace of St Michael and St George. She was aware she must look like a madwoman: a fury tearing through the town in search of vengeance in her underwear and tattered t-shirt, her back bright with blood. There was blood on her face and streaming down her legs. She ran, though, as if she were chasing something, rather than being chased. The Spianada was empty as she ran across the cricket pitch, feeling the wet grass beneath her feet, remembering this feeling from her childhood: barefoot on the lawn.

It was now, she reckoned, nine or nine-thirty in the morning, still raining, but the clouds were lifting, a watery sunlight coming through. She ran through the municipal gardens, scandalising a group of old ladies who were sitting in the shade of the bandstand, sheltering from the rain. She ran past the doorman at the Cavalieri, who looked startled and raised his hat. She turned right at the Ionian University, ran up Aspioti Street, then down the hill and into Saroko Square.

It was busier here than anywhere else she'd been, locals shopping, a few tourists queuing at the pharmacy, some young men loitering under the clementine trees in the centre of the square. One of them whistled as she went past. She turned to him, incandescent, feeling as if there were snakes in her hair. He held his hands up, stumbling backwards into his friends, who all stood there, as if turned to stone, but she was already gone, hurtling to the far corner of the square where, she knew, the police station stood. She'd seen the elegant terracotta building on a previous trip to the town, the police vans parked outside, the sense of an operation more slick and sophisticated than could surely be required on a sleepy tourist island like this. The corners of Empire, she supposed.

There was no sign that she had been followed, no sense that her father or Smith would come after her. A benefit of the Old Town: largely pedestrianised, with an arcane and incomprehensible series of one-way systems where cars was permitted, and these, as a result, forever snarled with traffic, furious drivers leaning on their horns. Smith must be seventy, she reckoned, while her father had a gammy knee and was carrying more weight than he ought to. Angelos might have had a go at keeping up, but then she'd seen how much he smoked. No, they would have had to find a taxi, would still be crawling their way towards her now. It all, then, depended on Metallinos – if he was here, whether he would help her, or if he, too, had been compromised. She would know soon enough. As she rang the buzzer and was let into the station courtyard, he was standing there, at the door, looking down at her.

VIII.

NINA HADN'T REALISED how much she had been holding inside until he said her name in his deep, melancholy voice, and she stumbled forward as he held out his arms to her. 'There you are,' she said, in a laugh which became a sob as he led her inside, through a bright reception area and down a corridor to his office, which was dim and warm, with frosted windows and the smell of books and cigarettes. He helped her onto a dark leather sofa, then stood back to look at her.

'I will find a lady officer. She will help clean you up and bring you some clothes. Then we can talk.'

'No,' she said, aware that she was almost shouting, but feeling as if she had only the most tentative grip on the thread of her mind. 'You must get out there. They're in danger. Please, hurry, before it's too late.'

He made a pacifying movement with his hands. 'I have heard from your Mr Boyd and Mr Drinkwater. They called me a few hours ago. A bad line – I suppose the storm – but they got through at seven, maybe just before. My wife, she was still asleep.'

'And will you go out there? Why are you not there already?'

Again he pushed his hands down as if to quieten her, and Nina felt a terrible fear creep from the floor to her chest. She imagined the line that Boyd would take – Nina was ill, raving about a conspiracy, would he be good enough to take care of her until they came and collected her? She looked up at Metallinos, at his spindly form, his kindly dark eyes, his widow's peak. 'Are you with them, inspector? Are you going to betray me, too?' She felt a twitch on her left forearm, an almost overwhelming urge to scratch. Now she bent her head, exhaustion settling over her like a shroud.

Metallinos picked up his chair from behind the desk and brought it so that he was sitting at her level. 'I spoke to them,' he said, his voice gentle. 'They were very clear about the seriousness of what had happened. One important lesson in life is to acknowledge when events have moved out of your sphere of expertise. And to whom you must turn for help when this happens. Immediately I had finished speaking to Mr Boyd, I telephoned to

Alexandros Papadopoulos. He and I were at high school together in Athens.' Here he gave a regretful little chuckle that contained within it no particular disappointment with his own lot. 'He runs the National Intelligence Service. Apparently he has been interested in this so-called island of spies for some time. A team was dispatched from Athens several hours ago. They should be landing at the airport any minute now. We will go with them, Nina, once you are cared for a little, no?' That wise, kindly smile and in Nina a surge of gratitude and relief so profound that she took his hands in hers and kissed them, leaving bloody fingerprints on his wrists.

IX.

NINA SAT AT the back of the second of the two boats with Inspector Metallinos and Mr Papadopoulos, who was short and jolly and grey-haired. On the bench in front sat the female officer who'd cleaned and fed her, then provided her with a tracksuit with αστυνομια written across the chest. The officer had washed and dressed the wounds on Nina's back, knitted together the gash above her eye with strips, all the while murmuring soothingly in Greek to her. On the boat, Nina resolved to learn the language, remembering the way that people would soften when Benedict spoke to them in their own tongue. The thought of Benedict brought a sudden and sharp pain to her, and she looked ahead, towards Vidos, which was appearing out of the low cloud ahead of them. It had stopped raining and a cool wind was blowing up the channel. Gulls drifted above. Everything in her strained against the feeling, deep and certain, that Benedict was dead.

The men on the boats were large and heavily armed, machine guns across their chests, grenades at their waists. Only their eyes were visible, eyes that revealed a dreadful seriousness, a willingness to take whatever steps were necessary. They pulled up on the beach beside the fallen pine tree, the dinghies squeaking as they hit the stones.

They all disembarked and stood on the pebbles. 'I think we wait here,' Metallinos said. Mr Papadopoulos said a few words in Greek and then gestured to his men. The soldiers moved up the slope in formation, from tree to tree, then they were in the cover of the church at the island's peak, and then they were gone. Nina wondered if her father had returned here, if he and Smith and Snow had recognised that all was lost and made a run for it, or if they would try to stage some final great gesture. It was not her father's way to acknowledge defeat, she thought. But then it was absurd, three old men against these formidable soldiers bristling with weaponry. Nina heard a sound behind her and turned again. There was a boat coming towards them across the channel.

'I imagine that is Mrs Sinclair,' Papadopoulos said, his voice more heavily accented than that of Metallinos. 'I felt it was . . . politic to inform her that we'd be staging a raid on her facility. I reached her early this morning. It was lucky that she was in fact in Venice, close by. She said she would fly straight out. She was good to her word, I think.'

Nina felt a hollowness open inside her. She had been waiting for the moment of betrayal, and here it was. Clara Sinclair, whom she knew to be one of those responsible for everything that had happened here, irretrievably compromised, would come and scatter the special magic of the Office over the place, making up down and wrong right.

It was a fishing boat, Costas at the wheel, and it docked at the rickety pontoon beside the abandoned restaurant. Costas sprang up to help his passengers navigate the pier, which was slowly sinking into the sea, its boards broken or missing. First came Clara Sinclair, then another, older woman, whom Nina knew at once to be Clara's mother, Patricia – it was unsettling, the resemblance, as if thirty years had passed in the space of a few moments. Costas went back to the boat and brought out several large suitcases, which he carried a little further up the hillside.

Clara and Patricia walked towards them down the beach. Papadopoulos embraced Clara, bowing and shaking hands with Patricia. He brought them over to where Nina and Metallinos stood.

'I was just saying,' Papadopoulos's voice was warm and confiding, as if they were all having drinks at the Embassy, 'how fortunate it was that you were in Venice. And that we hope very much that this unpleasantness can be resolved both swiftly and with minimal disruption.'

Clara stepped forwards and took Nina firmly in her arms. Her back stung under bony fingers. 'Nina, my darling,' Clara said. 'You've had a frightful time of it, I hear. I am so terribly sorry. I don't believe you know my mother, Patricia, do you? She will be calling Spyland home for a little while. I was actually just bringing her out here, stopping at our place in Venice en route to collect some things.'

The older woman looked wretchedly from Nina to

Metallinos, shrugged her shoulders and then fumbled in her bag for a cigarette. Metallinos leant forward and lit it for her. They stood there, the breeze ruffling their hair, Patricia blowing planks of smoke up into the air. A pair of white rabbits came snuffling into view from a clump of oleander. All the while, on the other side of the island, events were coming to their final, inevitable, conclusion.

PART 8

London, March 1974

I.

BENEDICT THOUGHT BACK to the moment when Lucan had reappeared. He'd turned up without warning one July evening. It was 1969, after the Stonewall Riots but before the moon landing. It was strange, but he hadn't recognised him at first. Patricia had assured him that she would take care of the whole affair. Benedict hadn't wanted to know the details, but he imagined a botched operation, a poison-tipped umbrella, an apparent break-in and the valiant MI6 agent killed while trying to protect his family. But here he was. Nelly had had a daughter in Yugoslavia, Benedict knew this. He felt Lucan's presence always, even with the distance that separated them, as a stain on his soul, a kind of taint emanating from the Balkans and whipped on the wind towards him, where he sat, late into the night, translating documents in his office in Broadway.

After his time in Moscow, he told Patricia he no longer wished to work for the Russians. He realised that whatever it was that had sustained his hope in the bright future promised by Communism had died in the weeks following his failed attempt to murder Lucan. Now he retreated from the world, immersing himself in the small tasks of his increasingly meaningless role at the Office: compiling a lexicon of Soviet euphemisms, translating the debriefs of a series of rambling and low-level defectors, creating a vast index of ciphers.

After work, he took the rattling Tube back to his flat in Bayswater, fed his cat, then fell asleep in front of the television. Dreams in which Besian appeared, his face full of love and forgiveness, and from which Benedict woke with his insides twisting, his chest heaving. He always read the letters he received from Humphrey, from Harris, from Violet, but he never responded to them. His life was too grey and predictable to warrant narration. He re-read the books of his youth – Dostoevsky, Turgenev, Austen – but with little pleasure, trying, rather, to remember the first time, as a young man, when he encountered these books with such urgency, such joy in the world and its words.

He realised that life for him was smaller now, lived in the shadow of himself, an unseen mouse in a London eave. This seemed to him an essential truth of life, but also one of its most painful chimeras: the old lived in the aftermath of the errors and misapprehensions of their younger selves, revelations arriving too late to be useful. He had been foolish at eighteen, he knew this, and yet he had been happy. Now, at forty-seven, he was still foolish, but he was melancholy, lost, envious of the certain young man he had been. Certainty dates you terribly, he thought, especially if you're wrong.

The months passed as, on a train, tower blocks will pass, each one different but the same as the last. Benedict's life ticked past forty-eight and one cool September evening he was standing in the cemetery in Marlow, the only mourner at his mother's funeral, aware of how small a mark a life can leave on the world. He remembered as a child the way she would play with him on the lawn of their home as his father looked on, amused, puffing on his pipe. It seemed like no time at all had passed, but that time had swallowed first his father, then his mother's happiness, then his mother herself. He stood for hours in the gloaming, long after the priest had gone, imagining his own death, his place beside her, the shrinkage of his own life to a few letters carved on a stone, recognition of the very little that he had, in the end, achieved.

It was the following Monday that he saw Lucan coming up the stairs at Century House. The office was still, after a decade, new territory to Benedict, who felt the Lambeth address as a slight after the elegant clubbiness of Broadway. He pressed himself against the wallpaper as Lucan passed, all the breath forced out of him. This was not the boy he'd tried to kill in Moscow. Rather, this Lucan was large and powerful and, frankly, slightly terrifying: his shoulders square, his jaw set, his eyes fierce, that nose going ahead of him like a tugboat before a warship.

Lucan only noticed Benedict after he had passed him. He turned, slowly, like that warship, and fixed Benedict with dark eyes. His voice, when it came, was very quiet. 'You made a terrible mistake. Several, in fact. Everything in your life, from now, will be lived in the reflection of those mistakes.' He turned and continued up the stairs, following his nose towards the future: a man in a hurry, making up for lost time.

Benedict saw him on several occasions over the subsequent days, always in the company of Patricia Sinclair, who had returned from Moscow to head up the SovBloc desk. He felt fear, certainly, but also a kind of equanimity, because he knew that he had earned what was coming to him. The punishment would also offer release.

It would somehow have been easier if they'd come for him then, but Benedict still had supporters within the organisation, was seen as the man to go to for a particular kind of old-school analysis, for a deep understanding of the warped dynamics of Italian Communism, or Greek Socialism, or the place of literature in Soviet self-conception. With every day that passed, though, days of loneliness and solitary drinking and nostalgia, Benedict felt himself growing closer to the edge. He realised that Lucan must somehow know this: that waiting was the cruellest cut of all. That the anticipation – this slow, exquisite attrition – was a far more potent revenge than any blunt act of violence.

Benedict saw it in the way Lucan watched him from across the room at briefings, his gaze cool, dispassionate, as though evaluating a patient who was in the early stages of a fatal decline. He felt it in the silence that surrounded him, the conversations that fell away as he entered a room, the quiet bureaucratic erosion of his influence. No overt moves, no sudden retributions – just a long, deliberate squeezing of the walls around him. Benedict had betrayed him in Moscow, and now Lucan had returned the favour. He had left him to die – just not all at once.

So it was that, in the late spring of 1975, when Benedict was going through a period of alcoholism that was new and somehow fascinating to him – so this is how you do it, he thought, consigning more and more of each day to sozzled oblivion – Snow and Smith finally turned up at his flat, and Benedict felt almost joyful to see them.

It was still light at eight-thirty in the evening. He had the windows open – his flat was at the top of a 1930s building – and birdsong drifted in from the park. He'd never learnt to distinguish between the different birds. Perhaps one day he would.

As he poured himself his second pink gin of the evening – his fifth of the day – he thought how nice it would be to be able to say with certainty, a blackbird, a skylark, a robin, just as he could hear a voice and say, Czech, Gujarati, Tagalog. Then the buzzer downstairs.

He looked from his window to see them: Snow's white hair, Smith in a flat cap. He let them in, feeling relief flood through him: something, at last, was happening.

II.

HUMPHREY WAS SITTING in a bar in Gaborone, waiting for a rendezvous with his Soviet handler. He was slimmer and more sharply dressed than at any time since Oxford. He'd found new energy here in southern Africa, a sense of purpose that had been missing in Cairo. Even though it was evening, the bar was only half full. A group of young men sat around a transistor radio at a table near the door, listening to a football match. He was the only one at the bar, nursing a Castle, indulging every so often in conversation with the barman. It was warm and mosquitoes moved in giddy zags in the lamplight. He looked at his watch again and wondered if, perhaps, Alexei wouldn't come after all.

Humphrey was living a secret within a secret, ostensibly a consultant for Anglo-African agricultural development, MI6 had placed him in Botswana to manage the fallout from the Portuguese Colonial Wars. With Angola and Mozambique now run by Marxist-Leninist parties, and with both the Soviet Union and Cuba extending their influence in Africa, the British were keen to establish bastions of capitalist democracy. Part of this, Humphrey was told, would involve supporting the corrupt apartheid systems in South Africa and, more immediately, Rhodesia. In the final Russian doll within his nest of identities, he was working diligently to undermine Ian Smith and his fanatical white supremacists, channelling Soviet money towards ZANU and ZAPU, ZANLA and ZIPRA, and anyone who might destabilise this antiquated and sclerotic regime. He felt, finally, as if his actions matched his dreams. Life had begun in Africa and humanity would be reborn there. He had always been an optimist, but now he had real, hard evidence for that optimism.

Two white men came into the bar. Humphrey looked at them briefly, returned to his beer, his mind racing, dread billowing in his stomach. So his time had come, he thought. He tried not to betray anything as the heavy-set man in the Panama hat sat down on one side of him; the man with white hair, his linen suit pale and crisp, took up a stool on the other. Humphrey had a gun in a holster under his arm. He slowly slid his hand inside his jacket, wanting at least to have the option of force.

'I wouldn't, old chum,' Snow said. 'Likely to get terribly messy if you do.'

Humphrey looked around, suddenly desperate. Smith

had drawn his own revolver and laid it on his lap under the bar, pointing at Humphrey.

'I suggest we all have a beer together and walk out of here like pals. We've got a plane waiting at Tsholofelo. We can swing by your place first. No sense in making this more difficult than it needs to be, eh?' Snow signalled to the barman, who brought another round of Castles. A cheer went up from the table by the window: somebody had just scored a goal. Humphrey sipped his beer and wondered, trying to fashion himself a silver lining, if Benedict might lie at the end of this journey.

III.

HARRIS WAS DRUNK. This was not unusual, but it was problematic, in that Violet was in D.C. with Patricia, and it was time to collect Katherine from school. He had begun the day full of buoyant good intentions, waking up early to cook his daughter breakfast, singing as he fried eggs and squeezed oranges. He'd been first at the gates of the primary school just off the North End Road: chatting breezily with Katherine's teacher, remembering the names of the mothers, he'd generally given the impression of a father who was happy to be doing his bit. There had been a nanny, but she had left under something of a cloud and Violet didn't seem keen to hire another. Difficult to live under the same roof as a young woman, particularly with Violet away so much.

Patricia had rather taken Violet under her wing – this was how Harris thought about it. And while his own career was – charitably – stalled, his wife was one of those tasked with reporting back to MI6 on the progress of the Strategic Arms Limitation Talks. She and Patricia travelled under the guise of secretaries to Sir William Campbell, the Foreign Office envoy to the talks. They dressed in the dowdiest of clothes, wore their hair in severe buns, sported antiquated spectacles and never smiled. All the while they conveyed information, first to MI6, then, via a dead drop in Rock Creek Park, to the Soviets. It had always been Harris's problem, the double life. He liked to think of himself as a simple man with an uncomplicated approach. While, in theory, he approved of the aims of Communism, and certainly it had seemed thrilling when he was a student, his idealism had withered rather under the pressure of events. It was so hard to do one job well, let alone two. It ended up that both London and Moscow seemed to think him a duffer.

Harris had meant to travel into Century House that morning, to waft himself in front of Esmond Harrington, the C, who he knew was particularly down on him after a balls-up in the Congo last year. He'd been drunk for much of that month in Africa with Patricia. He'd missed Violet, missed Katherine, felt himself horribly conflicted, unable to see how anything good could come of their mission. The plan had been hatched by a young CIA operative, Jack Laing, who'd found a raddled former general to lead a coup against Mobutu. It had gone badly from the start – Harris and the general had popped into a bar at the Hotel Memling in Kinshasa, where they served impeccable martinis. They'd missed their rendezvous with the driver who was meant to take them up-country. Laing had come and dragged them from the bar and out into the street where, in a blur, they'd found themselves surrounded by a unit of the Division Spéciale Présidentielle, all tawny uniforms and leopard print. They were beaten quite badly. Harris was dumped in an alley in the Quartier Matonge. The bodies of Laing and the general were found several weeks later, floating in the river off Kinkole.

After dropping off his daughter, Harris bought himself a paper – the *Mail* at a time like this, when Violet wasn't around, *The Times* when she was – and sat on the bus, feeling chipper, reading the football results and wondering whether to have a flutter on the 3.15 at Haydock Park. He got as far as Waterloo, where, it being past eleven o'clock, he ducked his head into the Railway Tavern for a swift pint. It was his bad luck to run into Roger Highsmith, one of the SovBloc lot, who always came here for a sharpener in the mornings and wanted to bend Harris's ear about his messy divorce.

Now, at twenty past four, Harris found himself somewhere near St Stephen's Hospital, recognising that he was not really in any state to collect his daughter from school, but more pressingly aware that he was lost – the roads here looked confusingly alike with their serene stucco frontages, their box hedges and gabled roofs. He desperately needed to empty his bladder. He found what looked like a likely spot on Hollywood Road – the overgrown garden of a house with drawn blinds. The relief was extraordinary. He let out a long sigh and began to whistle. Things were looking up.

He'd be a little late collecting Katherine, but that was fine, they'd understand that he was a busy man, with the concerns of the State pressing upon him. He shook himself dry, zipped his fly. He knew that if he headed back down to the Fulham Road, he'd soon light upon the left-hand turn that would, he thought, take him to her school. He wondered if her teacher – a Mrs Staplecross, Staplehurst, Stapleford, something like that – was married. He turned and was surprised to see, blocking the gate, Smith, from the Office. Behind him stood the austere figure of Snow.

Harris felt a horrid, familiar churn. It was school again, caught out of bounds, or doing something beastly with another boy in the dorm. He wondered if there was a meeting he had forgotten, or a new mission for him, some excitement. Violet couldn't have all the fun.

'Hello, chaps,' he said, and the words came out rather more slurred than he'd expected. 'What brings you to these parts? Must collect little Katherine. Awfully late, unforgivable really.' He attempted a smile. Neither Smith nor Snow moved, nor did they smile back.

'We've arranged for someone to take care of Katherine,' Snow said. 'You'll be coming with us.'

'Oh, I say,' Harris said.

IV.

SMITH AND SNOW didn't come for Violet. It was Patricia who spoke to her, outside the loos at the back of the plane on the way back from D.C. There was a choice to be made, she said. Between her husband, who was a drunk, a busted flush, and the Cause. It was clear, Patricia said, her voice very low, that the marriage was going nowhere, clear also that Violet had talents that went far beyond those of the lurching and chaotic Harris Davenport. Violet didn't know whether this was in reference to her skills as a cryptographer, or a nod to the fact that she and Patricia had become lovers. Perhaps both. She didn't care to examine her relationship with Patricia too closely, having seen the way she had used and manipulated her friends and bedfellows over the years. It suited Violet just now to have the confidence of Patricia Sinclair. She had also been very lonely, finding motherhood rather more of a grind than she had expected, while her husband, it was true, had been a broad disappointment.

They went back to their seats and Patricia leant in very close, her breath warm, her scent Guerlain. Harris, Benedict and Humphrey were being sent into exile, she said. They were liabilities – Harris and Benedict because of the drink, Humphrey because of his new-found idealism, which he had been unable to conceal from the Office. They were all *fatally* compromised. She stressed that penultimate word hard. Now Arkady was chairman of the KGB, and she, Patricia, within touching distance of C, once that fop Esmond Harrington was out of the way. It was vital that there should be no loose ends. Vidos was being reanimated, a place to park those spies who were no longer useful and whose indiscretion might threaten the aims of a project that was growing more clearly defined and ambitious with every passing day.

Talking to Patricia made Violet tired. That even now, in their early middle age, there should be such conniving, so much intrigue. Harris was exasperating, it was true, but she missed him when she was away. Or perhaps she missed what they had had when they were young, the years of long separations followed by frantic, euphoric reunions. So much of her life now seemed bound up with the young woman she had been, like some existential delay, the past cannoning into the future. That she had a family often came as a surprise to her. She'd look up from her plate at supper to see Harris and Katherine at the table, her husband smiling gooily at their daughter, evening light slanting into the kitchen, and she'd feel that this was what was supposed to come next. It was, though, an inferior kind of joy.

Her mother was looking after Katherine when she walked into the house on Burnthwaite Road the next morning, a Saturday. It had not been convenient to come down from the country, her mother said. She had been contacted by somebody at the Foreign Office. It was presented as a matter of national security, her patriotic duty. The opportunity to decline was not offered. She was off before Violet could ask any more questions. Katherine looked up at Violet with wide, vacant eyes, and she wondered how, so suddenly, life had collapsed in on itself. Of Harris, Violet heard nothing, not for weeks. She asked Patricia, who looked at her darkly over her spectacles; she asked Harris's colleagues, who spoke vaguely of an overseas mission. She could see the thought passing from one man to the next: *this is why we don't marry each other.*

Years passed. Katherine grew into a distant, mistrustful child. Violet kept her head down. She wrote to Harris in Vidos every week, sending her letters c/o the British Vice Consulate on Mantzapoy Street. He never wrote back, but then the letters never reached him. She still worked closely with Patricia, and they still went to bed together every now and again. Katherine won a scholarship to Bedales and Patricia drove them down to drop her off. Patricia's own daughter, Clara, also a Bedalian, had by this time started to make a name for herself in the Office. Violet felt as if she was walking around with a wound, something internal that wouldn't heal, but only ached and throbbed as she went about her business. Katherine wrote to Violet saying that she would be going to stay with a friend for her first Christmas at boarding school. Violet didn't blame her, but the solitary Christmas lunch – the turkey dinner for one, the party hat, the half-bottle of sherry – was a low point. When the Easter holidays arrived and, again, Katherine wrote to say that she would not be coming home, had been invited to ski in Val d'Isère, Violet felt as if a decision had been made for her.

When she stepped onto the warm tarmac at Ioannis Kapodistrias and looked up at the long window of the terminal building, there was Harris, grinning like a schoolboy, waving madly.

EPILOGUE

Corfu, May 1997

IT WAS STRANGE, for Nina, to be living in the cottage that she still thought of as belonging to Humphrey and Benedict. Her father had the big room at the back, she was in what used to be Humphrey's study, her bed against the window, her nights loud with the sea. Smith and Snow had a similar arrangement in the cottage next door. She could see them now, standing on the veranda, looking out to the channel, to Albania. She scratched at the patch on her arm. They'd had to up her meds, but then they'd upped everyone's meds after what happened. The higher dosage turned her pee green.

Nina, coming down from the villa with Inspector Metallinos and Mr Papadopoulos that November morning, had found Benedict and Violet, sitting side by side on the sofa, her hand clasped in his, Harris outstretched on the floor at their feet. They were all dead, although Benedict and Violet had their eyes open to the beauty of the sea and the water, the endless sky and the distant mountains.

Massive doses of cyanide, it was later found, although the tests were merely for form, the whole affair handled by agreement with MI6. Papadopoulos and Metallinos treated Spyland and the events that transpired there as characteristic but forgivable British eccentricities.

There had been no more bloodshed that day. The Greek special forces descended on the villa in a dark wave, finding Snow, Smith and Lucan Woolf sitting together at the dining-room table, each of them with a mug of tea. Snow had caught a cold, and he sneezed every so often as they waited: two old men, one on the cusp of old age, who had closed this particular chapter of their lives. They'd succumbed willingly to the handcuffs. Snow asked if he might blow his nose before his hands were tied, bringing out a large white hanky.

Then Clara had arrived, and the negotiations over quite how this whole sorry affair might be covered up were begun. Clara would be tarnished by it, no doubting that. There would be favours called in, threats deployed; she had offered up her mother in the process. In the end, Clara remained — albeit with her power much reduced — as the C. The press never got wind of it all, and the deaths of Benedict, Violet and Harris were leaked out over the course of the subsequent months. They were old and old people die, in the end. Benedict's obituary concluded with the fact that he was survived by his daughter, the current Chief of MI6, Clara Sinclair.

Nina's old room in the villa was now inhabited by Patricia Sinclair, who had spent her first few months on Spyland in the san, her screams of rage and frustration audible, it was said, in the Old Town. Boyd was Patricia's neighbour in the villa; he had been given the chance to return to VX – they were in a room together for several hours, deep in discussion, Boyd and Clara – but in the end he had turned it down. He did not feel nearly ready to go, he said. What struck Nina most about these new circumstances wasn't the difficulty of adjusting, but the ease. How quickly she had absorbed the fact that the ones she loved were gone – and that those who had helped destroy them moved now through the same rooms, poured from the same teapots. Perhaps it was something in her blood, this capacity for silence, for staying. The spy's daughter learns early not to flinch.

Arkady had spent that dramatic October morning in a café on Cofinetta Square, not far from where, two years earlier, Edward Lane had first spotted him, subsequently following him to the airport, bellowing threats of revenge. He smiled at the memory of Lane's face, the bafflement that might have characterised not just that strange, final encounter, but all their exchanges over the long march of years.

He watched the rain clear, saw a young, blood-streaked woman in a t-shirt flying through the morning as if pursued by the Furies. He saw the police vans with their blacked-out windows roaring towards the harbour. He sipped his coffee, thumbed through a three-day-old copy of *The New York Times*.

He had been here a week, an absence that was problematic, given the state of his activities in Russia, but somehow necessary. He was a member of the Duma now, his presidential ambitions almost realised, his business interests buying him more power and influence by the day. They had already named a town after him in Siberia, an early attempt to curry favour. It worked: he planned to build several factories there, an opera house, perhaps. But he needed to be here, in Corfu, to see the end of this thing that he had set in train some fifty years earlier.

He was an old man, past seventy, but there was still so much ahead. He felt as if, in bringing this period of his life to an end, he was ready to begin the next. And while Clara's political ambitions might, for the moment at least, have stalled, his own were so close to realisation that he could almost picture himself in the Hall of St Andrew, all the bells of the Kremlin ringing about him, the solemnity and beauty – and length – of the address he would give to his people.

He remembered then, as if only a few weeks had passed, the black shape of his uncle in the doorway of his bedroom. It was very late, but he was still awake, because his parents had not come home and he was scared. His uncle was there to tell him that he wouldn't see his parents again, that it would be him, his uncle Vasiliy, a big man in the Politburo, with bigger things to come, who would be looking after him from now on.

He'd not cried then, nor ever, but remembered fondly his earnest, bookish father, his brilliant mother. They'd been purged along with many at Moscow State University in the days of the Great Terror, accused of bourgeois nationalism and indulging alien elements. In his father's case, this involved his love of Charles Dickens.

He looked over in the direction of Spyland, hidden

out of sight behind the Palace of St Michael and St George, and wondered if his plans had come together. Not perfectly, of course, but close enough that his past was being put mercifully to sleep. He thought of Benedict as he had first seen him – so young – coming into the King's Arms with Patricia. He remembered Humphrey and Harris, Violet and Edward.

All dead now, he hoped, just as the foppish and suggestible Arkady of his Oxford days was dead. Patricia had been sacrificed – not killed, but given to the opposition in order to satisfy some ancient requirement for justice. Clara had accepted her mother's exile with almost indecent haste.

Arkady finished his coffee and looked down at his pager. A message from Clara, his daughter. She was on the island now. Everything had been arranged. He paid and walked out into the rising light. A young couple pushed their baby across the Spianada in a pram. The last swifts came out to fatten themselves for their trip to Africa. Arkady made his way to the taxi rank and took a final look at the Old Town. It was time to step into his own bright future.

Now six months have passed and it's a glowing May evening. Spyland is polished by the sun, scoured by salt. Nina walks up from the village to the villa. Everyone is out on the bowling green. Someone – Snow, Nina reckons – has brought out a few bottles of Theotoky and they're drinking it from mugs. It's her father's turn to launch his bowl and he does it expertly, using the camber of the crown to send Deirdre, his opponent, rolling into the bushes.

Mrs Samways, sitting with a group of the incurables to one side of the green, lets out a cheer, her folding chair diving left as she does so. Even Drinkwater has a mug of wine, handed to him by one of the Pottinger brothers. He's talking to Boyd and Patricia, who are standing very close to one another.

It's a gentle scene, on an island with a history of violence. Nina helps herself to some wine, sits on the steps of the villa and looks out across the water, iridescent in the low sun. She misses Benedict, misses Violet and Harris and Humphrey, but she knows they're here, that this island has shaped itself around them. This, for Nina, is reason enough to stay.

Her father, too, is here, and while she cannot forgive him for what he has done, there is something ineluctable about family. They swim together, she and her father, most mornings, and in the evening he tells her about his life, about the times he nearly died, and how Nelly, her mother, saved him. He tells her about his plan to escape from Spyland, and how he'll take her with him. But that story is for another time.

For now, the game of bowls is nearing its end. The water of the channel is very flat, stretched like a bedsheet under the heavy golden light. The bells ring in the Old Town, carried across the water in the stillness. Someone is getting married, Nina thinks. As she sits there, she sees a figure on the hillside high above, looking down. She shields her eyes, trying to make out who is up there in the ruins above the san, watching them. Her father calls her over, though. He wants her to witness his victory.

The man in the ruins turns away, strides through the long shadows and into the woods on the south of the island, towards the cave he calls home. Under his right eye there is a tattoo, faded by the years. A small blue cross.

When the game is finished, Nina walks with her father down to the village. Behind them, Boyd and Patricia linger, talking of Larry Durrell – they call him that, Larry, as if he's a pal – their voices dissolving into the dusk. The sun has slipped behind Corfu, leaving the sky a huge, breathing blue, the stars flaring to life above the Albanian mountains. Her father takes her hand, and for a moment, she is small again, a child moving through a world that will always be vastly unknowable. Ahead, the cottages quiver with warm light, spilling gold onto the beach in long bars. A plane ghosts above them, moving between silences. The world turns.

At the house, her father pours them all a drink. They sit on the veranda, watching the dark and ancient sea slip forward, recede, return. Moths spiral in the lamplight on futile wings. Below, the waves – scarcely more than sighs – rise and fall, fall and rise, as if the sea itself were dreaming.

ACKNOWLEDGEMENTS

I spoke to many within the secret and security services for this book. They were generous with their time, smart and sensitive with their advice. I cannot mention them by name, but they know who they are and I thank them.

Several books helped greatly with my research, including MI6 by Gordon Corera, *MI6: The History of the Secret Intelligence Service* by Keith Jeffery, *Defence of the Realm* by Christopher Andrew, *MI6* by Stephen Dorril, *Queen of Spies* by Paddy Hayes, *A Spy Among Friends* by Ben Macintyre (actually pretty much everything by Ben Macintyre).

Nikos Louvros shaped the way I see Corfu. His wild and brilliant life makes me want to be wilder and more brilliant. We all miss him greatly. Annabelle and I have tried to keep Nikos's spirit alive through the Corfu Literary Festival, whose continuing success is all her doing (and, I suspect, the work of Nikos, looking on benevolently from above). I owe great thanks to so many in Corfu, but particularly to Annabelle and Philip Louvros, to Dmitris Metallinos, to Gerry Tranakas and Babbis Voulgaris and all at the Kontokali, to Lesley, Emma and Dominic and all at Ionian Estates.

Thanks to Steven Desmyter for keeping me busy between books . . .

Canongate have been characteristically brilliant as this book took shape. Leah Woodburn is an editor of rare talent and insight. Anna Frame is heaven. Alice Shortland has magical powers. Thanks to all the team. I love working with these people and it makes the whole process of turning these muddled words and images in my head into a book such a joy – and so much less lonely, in that I know they are there at the end of the writing.

Karolina Sutton and I first had breakfast at the Wolseley in February 2006. That this is almost twenty years ago seems improbable. She is the best agent anyone could possibly have. Thanks, Karolina.

Finally, as ever, love and thanks to Ary, Al and Ray. Life with the three of you is full of joy, laughter and adventure. I feel ridiculously lucky to have you.